# Kind
# Hearts
# &
# Coriander

**APRIL HARDY**

# ACKNOWLEDGEMENTS

I'm sure authors aren't supposed to have a favourite amongst their books, but I'll always have a soft spot for Kind Hearts and am so grateful to all those who helped it on its way.

Huge thanks to Emirates Airline Festival of Literature. It was for a session at the 2014 festival that I wrote the opening chapter of Kind Hearts. It was my first foray into romantic comedy and I just wanted to know if it was worth carrying on with! The encouragement I received (and still do) from EAFoL and Dubai International Writers' Centre, whilst completing the manuscript, led to me being signed by my agent, Alison Bonomi of LBA Books. I'd like to thank Yvette Judge, everyone behind the scenes, and visiting tutors Jo Wroe and Sherry Ashworth for their kind advice and feedback.

One of the best things I ever did was join the Romantic Novelists' Association – a wonderfully supportive organisation. I'd like to thank the readers on their New Writers' Scheme. The manuscript of Kind Hearts went through the scheme, which I'd thoroughly recommend to anyone starting out as a writer of romance.

The 2014 Exeter Novel Prize was another push in the right direction for Kind Hearts, when it was one of the runners up. Enormous thanks to Cathie Hartigan, Margaret James and Sophie Duffy for organising the competition, and Broo Doherty for judging the finalists. A great experience!

Much appreciation to my patient editor, Alexandra Davies, and everyone else at Accent, especially Bethan James, Emily Tutton, Hazel Cushion, Helen Evans, Rebecca Lloyd, Joe Moore, David Norrington, and Zoe Foster for her fab cover designs. And not forgetting Peter Newsom, who my husband also thanks, for saving him from being the only man at the Dubai launch for Sitting Pretty!

I must mention Jane Northcote and the fantastic staff at the Dubai World Trade Centre Club, where I now spend a couple of afternoons a week as Writer in Residence. It's a wonderful place to write.

Huge hugs for my supportive writing pals, Sue Mackender, Terri Fleming, Tessa Shapcott, Denise Barnes, Adrienne Dines, Lynne Shelby, Jenny Haddon, Marie Frances, Anne Bennett, Sharmila Mohan and Linda MacConnell. You've all helped me more than you know.

Thanks and love to my family, who've been there at every turn and done everything they could to help me on my way.

And last but not least, my husband, Andrew, whose home-made pasta just gets better and better!

# CHAPTER ONE

My eyes blurred as Mum's coffin slid back, the curtains closing seamlessly around it. Did that sob come from me? Someone on my right pressed a clean handkerchief into my hand and I relaxed my grip on the soggy tissue remnants in my pocket. I should have known one packet wouldn't be enough. So, that was it. She was gone. I blew my nose, wiped the tears from under my eyes with my knuckles, and made my way back out into the harsh sunlight. Another kind lady waited and walked by my side. I think she might have been one of Mum's neighbours.

The pub had put on a decent spread. Mum's friends and neighbours kept bringing me things I didn't want to eat. I hid them so I didn't appear rude – behind glasses, in a pot plant – in a sort of sausage roll and Scotch egg treasure hunt for the cleaners later.

I'd wanted to do the food myself. It seemed the least I could do for her.

'Don't be daft, love,' Mum had said. 'I don't want the last thing you ever cook for me to be for my wake. Make me something now, while I'm here to enjoy it.' I'd made her favourite; Cumberland toad in the hole with onion gravy. She'd managed two small mouthfuls. That was the day she'd given me the letter and made me promise not to read it until after.

Charles Hetherin! Of course I knew the name – almost

every school leaver in Netley Mallow must have done a summer waitressing, changing beds, or working in the gardens at Hetherin Hall. But Mum had been so determined I go to Westminster to do my City & Guilds. I'd always just put it down to her fondness for Jamie Oliver.

But why let me grow up believing my father had died just before I was born then drop this bombshell on me? I needed answers, and there was only one person who could give them to me now. I drained my glass and put it down on the bar.

In the morning, I was going to Netley Mallow. And I was going to look him right in the eye. If he knew Mum was pregnant and just dumped her … if he had any idea he was my father … I'd know. And believe me, Charles Hetherin would wish I'd never been born.

\* \* \*

Back in my almost-big-enough-to-swing-a-cat Peckham flat, I put the kettle on – what is it about us Brits and the good old cuppa? I switched my tablet on and flung my red coat over the back of the chair. Yes, red. Mum had wanted people to wear bright colours and for there to be happy music and party food today. No black clothes or sad faces, she'd said. I'd followed her instructions as closely as possible.

Connecting to Google, that annoying phrase, *Who's the daddy?* popped into my mind. It got short shrift there and slunk away with its tail between its legs as I banged about the kitchen, warming the teapot, opening a brand new packet of Jaffa Cakes and inhaling the rich, tangy aroma. I rammed the first, slightly dented, one whole into my mouth. The shower of crumbs on the counter could stay put for now – I had more important things to think about.

By the time the tea was made, Charles Hetherin's self-satisfied face was once again looking at me from the screen. I must have done this a dozen times since I'd read her letter. It was the same picture I'd seen before – from the paper, when he'd hosted some big charity fund-raiser at the Hall. He looked well-fed and smug and his right eyebrow was slightly arched –probably busy congratulating himself on the tax-deductibility of the occasion. Meanwhile, poor Mum was buying dented tins and scouring the reduced shelf in the supermarket and giving herself tiny portions so I would have enough to eat. Why did she never tell me?

My eye was drawn back to the arch-villain eyebrow – Oh God, I do that too. And always the right one. I couldn't actually do it with the left. There's a photo somewhere of me pulling that same face, I was sure. Maybe it would be in Mum's things. Come to think of it, he'd got my eyes too, or I suppose I'd got his – they were exactly the same almond shape and shade of green. He didn't have my smattering of freckles though, unless he was wearing makeup for the camera. But we had the same coppery hair, only mine was long and ringletty and his looked like he was wearing one of Donald Trump's castoffs. Did that sound bitchy? Probably, but for now, I felt it was allowed. Normal, happy-go-lucky, smiley service would resume tomorrow. Or the day after. Maybe.

Munching on another Jaffa Cake, I found myself drawn like a magnet back to the Hetherin Hall website. Classic Georgian country house nestled between the three picturesque Netley villages. Tranquil landscaped gardens with tennis courts, croquet hoops, private spa, and access to the nearby golf course and stables. P.G. Wodehouse would have loved it. Twenty-two individually furnished, en-suite bedrooms with garden or woodland views, award winning àla carte restaurant, function rooms, licensed for civil ceremonies – well, aren't we fancy.

There was a slightly smaller version of the Hall – Hetherin House – up in Yorkshire, in Harrogate. And when I clicked on Hetherin International I found a couple of French versions too, in Paris and Saint-Émilion, Italian ones in Rome and Tuscany, and one in Switzerland. There were plans for one in Austria too, apparently. Was Charles Hetherin planning to take over western Europe, a couple of boutique hotels at a time? And if so, what did he have against Spain, Portugal, and Greece? Too 'package holiday' for a Hetherin establishment?

They all looked posh and expensive and lovely, but I was only really interested in the one where he lived – the one where I would find him. I studied the Hetherin Hall restaurant pictures and sample menu for what must have been the twentieth time. That menu was imprinted on my brain by now and I knew exactly what I would order as a diner there. The pan-fried local trout for a starter, followed by the pressed, slow-roasted shoulder of lamb with organic spring greens. For dessert, the bitter chocolate and orange liqueur tart with honeycomb dust – just the thought made me reach for another Jaffa Cake. This was my territory. Real food made with locally sourced ingredients; everything free-range, organic, happy, and sustainable – just how it should be. My kind of food, unlike the pretentious, how-it-looks-matters-more-than-what-it-tastes-like fare we produced at The Honor & Oak, my current restaurant. If they'd had any jobs going, I'd have been seriously tempted. Well, I might have if circumstances had been *very* different. But as things stood, it would be a ridiculous idea – unless I was planning to poison the family. I could bump them all off and make myself sole heir to the Hetherin Empire, like in that old black and white film – what was it called – *Kind Hearts & ...* something! A chocolate-orange flavoured snort of laughter escaped my throat. I'd clearly gone from the sublime to the ridiculous, only without the sublime bit first.

Picking up my cup of tea, I took a sip and immediately spat it back in the cup. It was cold. I reached for another Jaffa Cake to take away the taste but the packet was empty. Blimey! Had I eaten them all? No wonder I felt a bit sick.

I treated the cheese plant by the window to the contents of my cup – Mum had always watered her plants with whatever was left in the teapot and this big, green monster in particular was partial to cold tea dregs. It probably thought it was Christmas, getting a whole cup's worth.

Glancing out, I could see a gang of teenage school kids in scruffy half-uniform shuffling into the kebab shop across the road. I heard myself sigh. Why would anybody want to eat that crap? I'd rather chew the skin round my fingernails. I leaned my head against the cool glass and let my eyes wander unfocused over the grotty high street.

In the kitchens at Hetherin Hall, delicious ingredients, textures, aromas, and flavours would be brought together to make wonderful meals. If I were a Hetherin, I thought a little bitterly, I should be there. That was my birth right, wasn't it? I stared into the busy, noisy street, thinking about what I was going to do. Would Mum approve of me going down there and confronting him? She must have expected me to do something like that otherwise why write the letter now? I guessed she wouldn't want me to be alone in the world, not if I had family out there.

He had two children – a girl and a boy. I had a sister and a brother who didn't even know I existed. There were no pictures of them on the website, no mention of their names. I wondered if that was their choice or his.

Taking my cup back into the kitchen, I got a bottle of Sauvignon Blanc out of the fridge, then put it back. Not on top of Jaffa Cakes. I really would be sick.

Wandering into the bedroom, I opened the wardrobe door and wondered what I would wear to go to Hetherin Hall the next day. I knew it was a ridiculous thing to worry about, but how do you dress to confront a multi-hotel-owning millionaire who might or might not know he's your father? There was nothing suitable at all. I felt a wave of Jaffa overload sickness as I imagined him thinking I was some gold-digging con-woman and throwing me out on my ear.

Well, you know what, Charles Hetherin? I've just said goodbye to the only parent I've ever known – the only person who's always been there for me. And if you don't want to know me, that's fine. Nothing about meeting you can be as painful as these last months have been.

So, *Daddy*! You'd better get a good night's sleep tonight, because I'm guessing you won't be getting one tomorrow.

# CHAPTER TWO

I'd barely fallen asleep when the alarm went off. The temptation to hurl it across the room and snuggle down under my duvet was almost stronger than I was – after all, I was going to call in sick, anyway. Then the arch-villain eyebrow appeared in my mind, nudging me from groggily half-asleep to groggily half-awake.

An hour later, I'd lied my head off to Sheila, our one-woman admin department and any other title she cared to give herself, at the Honor & Oak, and taken as long as I could over breakfast to miss the rush hour traffic. While I worked my way through the twenty-seven point shunt I always had to do, whatever time of day it was, to ease my little Honda Jazz out from between the closely parked cars, I wondered if this was what battery hens felt like.

The roads became wider and less congested the further out of London I got. I didn't know if Surrey really was greener or if it was my imagination, but it felt as though I was driving through one of those films, shot in real time then sped up. Spring seemed to be doing its thing on fast forward. By the time I hit Hampshire, it had well and truly sprung.

There were cute little woolly lambs gambolling in a field. Feeling warm and sunny, I opened my window, and then quickly closed it again, holding my breath. I hadn't noticed the cows. Or was it bulls? It certainly smelled like bulls, but what did I know?

The radio reception was getting hazy, so I tried for another station. I couldn't find one that wasn't playing classical music or droning on about sport and was still fiddling with it when I noticed a police car flashing from behind.

'Bugger!' I pulled over, into the shade of a picnic lay-by, and slowed to a stop between a camper van and a tandem, its green-cagouled riders glancing up from their thermos flask and Utterly Butterly sandwich box. Great. An audience. Not embarrassing at all.

I was sure I hadn't been speeding. Had I been veering about when I was messing around with the radio? As if going to confront a wealthy and powerful complete stranger and tell him he's my long-lost father wasn't enough to worry about for one day. That was all I needed – and I'd managed so well to lull my apprehension into a peaceful, sleepy state. Well, at least I thought I had. It was wide awake now.

The police car pulled in and one of the boys in blue climbed out – except he was more stout middle-aged man in blue. He ambled across the tarmac towards me, just a little out of place against the backdrop of daffodils nodding their heads in the light breeze like guitar-strumming hippies. Even the camper van was sunshine yellow. I wound down my window and awaited my fate. At least I seemed to be the right side of the wind where the bulls were concerned.

'Good morning, miss.' He bobbed down and smiled in a fatherly way I really wasn't expecting. 'Did you know your right brake light is broken?'

'What?' I got out and went round to look. 'Oh, you're kidding,' I sighed. Bloody Peckham. You couldn't park within a mile of your own home and when you did find a space, you couldn't leave your car for five minutes without someone doing something to it. Unless I'd done it myself, shunting back and forth to get out of the parking space and had been in such a dither I hadn't felt the crunch.

'Have you got far to go, miss?' He could certainly give London policemen a lesson in how to speak to the public. I couldn't imagine him performing a stop and search. No, he'd be the one visiting primary schools, handing out lollipops and green cross code stickers – if they still had those now.

'Just to Netley Mallow,' I said. 'To Hetherin Hall, actually. I'm going there to … er … see someone …' I tailed off, realising I was talking too much. What is it about security guards, customs officers, and policemen that means I always have this compulsion to justify my movements and prove myself to be law-abiding?

We were attracting an up-close audience now, courtesy of the sunshine yellow camper van. Little feet in scuffed trainers scuttled around the side of the car and two small boys of about five and six in matching Spiderman T-shirts grinned at me through ice-cream covered mouths – one strawberry, one chocolate.

'Netley Mallow's the next village, miss. It's not far.'

'Thanks,' I smiled. Well. it would be rude to say '*Yes, I already know.*'

'There's Coopers'' garage there. Take you about ten minutes or so to get there.'

'Oh, right. Thanks.' I didn't know about the garage, but then it was years since I'd been near the area and I hadn't passed my driving test back then.

'They'll fix your light for you. Best sort it out now, don't want to have an accident.'

'Thank you.' I smiled at him again, thinking I must look and sound like the village idiot. In London I'd have got a fine or points on my licence or at least a snotty lecture about road safety.

'I can drive that way if you like – show you the way. Don't want to get lost.'

'That's very kind of you.' Now I was waiting for someone to leap out from behind a bush with a hidden camera. He couldn't be a real policeman, surely? Or had I just lived in London too long?

'Well, follow me then.' He strolled to his car and folded himself back in. Tandem Man shook open a map while Tandem Woman held his plastic cup. And from the corner of my eye, I could just see the two little ice cream boys breaking through a gap in the hedgerow, probably on their way to water the daffodils.

* * *

'Your back light's gone.' The salt and pepper-haired mechanic at A&A Coopers' scratched his head. 'Alan!' he called over his shoulder. 'Over 'ere, son.' He looked me up and down with what I assumed was curiosity, while a younger, slimmer, fair-haired version of himself came over, wiping his hands on what looked like the remains of an old T-shirt. 'What you reckon?'

'Back light's gone.' Cooper Junior didn't look at me at all.

'Reckon you can fix it for the young lady? She's on 'er way to Hetherin Hall.' He over-pronounced the H's dramatically.

'Nah Dad – whole casing's cracked. Need to get a new one from the Honda garage for that. Then we can fix it.'

'And where's the nearest one?' Cooper Senior scratched his head again.

'Reckon Southampton,' Cooper Junior answered, stuffing the T-shirt rag in his pocket. He still hadn't acknowledged my presence – maybe he was shy.

'Better give 'em a ring.'

'I can do that,' I jumped in. 'if you could just give me the number. Oh, and the number of a taxi to get to the Hall, please.' They were grinning at each other. What had I said?

'Reckon you'd best leave that to us, miss – all part of the service. We'll call you at the Hall when it's ready. And you won't be needin' any taxi to get there – it's just a five minute walk.'

\* \* \*

Before I knew what I was doing I was walking, in what was hopefully the right direction, having left my car with the Coopers. I had no idea how long it was going to take to get my light fixed or how much it was going to cost. What I *did* have was the feeling that they saw me as some kind of damsel in distress – clearly amused at the thought of me calling the Honda garage myself. The feminist in me wanted to be offended by the way they'd assumed I wouldn't know what I was doing, but somehow, I couldn't. They'd been so sweet, doing their best to help a stranger.

The sun seemed to switch itself to a higher heat as I walked. The Coopers' idea of five minutes was definitely longer than mine, but then I don't suppose they went in for court shoes much. Cooper Senior had given my feet a bit of a funny look when I got out of the car, but surely he must have realised I was driving in my stockinged feet and had just put my shoes back on. They were my smartest pair and had been clean and shiny when I left Peckham. They were quite dusty now.

Part of me felt as if I'd taken part in a sketch on a comedy show, or on one of Mum's Two Ronnies DVDs. I'd been half expecting them to break into a song and dance routine and I'd have to start dosey-doeing or whatever it was around the forecourt between them. But another part of me felt a kind of warmth that was nothing to do with the sun. People here were kind. Just look at the policeman too – kind and caring.

Maybe it was a good omen for what was to come. I hoped so.

# CHAPTER THREE

erin Hall breathless, dusty, and sweaty thanks to the fifteen minute walk in the warm sunshine.

'Good afternoon!' the voice from behind the reception desk greeted me. I looked towards it and my heart skipped a beat; it was like looking in a mirror, only one of those slightly distorting ones you find at the funfair. The young woman smiling at me had the same mop of copper curls, albeit a considerably tidier version. Her eyes, too, were the same colour and shape as mine, and if I wasn't very much mistaken, there was a smattering of freckles under that perfectly applied makeup. I could be looking at my twin. Or a waxwork dummy of me. Except she was talking and smiling and moving and I was just standing there, unable to come up with a thing to say, which if I came to think about it, made me the dummy.

She was still speaking as if nothing about me struck her as at all unusual. How could she not see it?

'If you'd like to go through to the restaurant,' she carried on, gesturing to her left with a beautifully manicured hand, which was where our similarities abruptly ended, 'they're waiting for you in there.'

My feet seemed to have lost whatever tenuous connection they usually had with my brain, as they followed her instructions without a moment's hesitation. My hand was already reaching for the door by the time some of the grey cells started to catch up and wonder who would be waiting for me – and why anybody was waiting for me at all.

How could anyone have known I was coming? It just wasn't possible. There was nothing when I googled Charles Hetherin about there being any kind of psychic powers in the family.

As I stood there with my hand in mid-air, a girl with a sulky face and pierced eyebrow shoved her way out of the restaurant, narrowly avoiding whacking me in the face with the door. She didn't look like the sort of customer or staff I would expect to see at a place like Hetherin Hall. She'd look far more at home in Peckham – I mentally gave myself a Basil Fawlty slap on the wrist. Nobody likes a snob, Polly.

'Don't just stand there,' a bored but gorgeous man barked from his seat at the one table in the room which wasn't covered in crisp, white linen. He had the kind of thick, dark hair that wouldn't look out of place on a pirate or a gigolo, and the way he was eying me up made it obvious he wasn't impressed. 'Come on in,' he commanded. 'You're half an hour late. You must be Sally.' He looked down at a piece of paper in front of him. Sally? Blimey! How many of us were there? And what was this, some kind of long-lost daughter audition?

'Er, no actually, I'm Polly ...' I started to explain, without really knowing what I was going to say next.

'Hi, Polly,' came a friendlier voice from the corner of the room, as a chef's jacket topped with a mop of long, almost dreadlock-like ginger curls popped up like a finger-puppet from behind the bar. I caught myself doing a double-take. He was the spitting image of that singer Mum liked back in the nineties, who sang a song about 'coming home to you' and the video was of him singing it on a fairground ride. I forget what it was called.

'It says Sally here,' Mr Bored-But-Gorgeous sighed. I peeled my eyes away from Singing-Chef-Puppet and refocused in time to see the grumpy one scribble something on his piece of paper – probably renaming poor Sally, whoever she was.

'Maybe I should ...' I started again.

'Take a seat, Polly. He doesn't bite.' Singing-Chef-Puppet came out from behind the bar with a large jar of pickled gherkins in each hand and a grin on his face. 'Well, not hard. Hi, I'm Will.' He held out his right hand, noticed the pickles, cradled the jar in the crook of his left elbow, and held his hand out again. I shook it with caution. 'And this ray of sunshine is Oliver. I'll be in the kitchen if anyone needs me.'

'I'm sure we'll manage without you,' Oliver muttered.

'Well, just try to manage keeping your hands off my gherkins,' Will called over his shoulder, before disappearing through what looked like the kitchen door.

'City and Guilds?' Oliver rolled his eyes and looked at me expectantly.

'Er, yes.' I was mightily confused. What did catering qualifications have to do with anything? Could you only apply to be a member of the family if you had the right skills set?

'How much experience do you have?'

'Experience?' I was doing that village idiot thing again.

'In the industry,' he sighed, looking like he was trying very hard not to roll his eyes. They were hazel, I noticed, with little amber flecks.

'Six years, But –'

'Six years? Well, you must know what you're doing then. Why did you leave your last place of employment?'

'My what?' The penny had taken rather a long time to

find the slot, but it was finally starting to drop. 'I think there's been some kind of mistake,' I jumped in before he started measuring me up for a uniform. 'I've come to speak to Mr Hetherin – Mr Charles Hetherin.'

'Mr Charles Hetherin doesn't conduct staff interviews,' Mr Bored-But-Gorgeous frowned at what he clearly thought was my gross stupidity. 'There's a chain of command, which you should know if you've worked in the hotel industry for six years. I'm in charge of the interviews,' he gave a poor imitation of the Hetherin eyebrow thing, 'what with me being the restaurant manager.'

'Yes, I'm sure you are, but if I could just speak to Mr Hetherin ...'

'That won't be possible,' he sighed. 'Mr Hetherin is away on a business trip in Europe and ...'

'Europe?' I interrupted, disappointment getting the better of my manners.

'Yes, Europe. You know – France, Italy, Switzerland, that kind of thing.' He was looking at me as if I'd asked what a potato was – talk about a bad first impression. 'This isn't his only hotel. He won't be back til the weekend, so I'm afraid, Sally, Polly, whatever you'd like to be called, if it's alright with you, you'll have to make do with me. Now,' he gave me a kind of Anne Robinson look that would have silenced anyone, '*if* you were to be offered the job, when would you be able to start?'

I felt my brain do a double take. Had this man, who clearly thought I was an idiot, just offered me a job in my own father's hotel?

'Obviously I'd need your NI number – we don't do cash in hand here. Do you have your P45 with you? Oh, excuse me, I need to get this.' He picked up his ringing mobile and marched over to a big picture window with it close to his ear. Saved by the bell. Quite literally.

My little grey cells were manoeuvring themselves like a newly-shaken kaleidoscope in my brain, trying to make sense of what was happening. I'd driven all that way to see Charles Hetherin, who was going to be away until the weekend – I hadn't even considered the possibility of him not being there. I wondered which of the hotels he was visiting, but asking Mr Bored-But-Gorgeous-Restaurant-Manager-Almighty clearly wasn't an option. Did I just drive back to Peckham, once my brake light was fixed, then call in sick again at the weekend and come back?

Or what if I were to call in sick again the next day – which I might need to anyway if I had no way of getting back to London. I could say I was much worse and needed the rest of the week off? I could get him to offer me this job and pretend to take it, just for a few days, couldn't I? After all, I was a trained chef – how hard could waitressing be? I'd have to fudge a bit about my P45 – pretend I'd left it behind and would get someone to send it to me. Who remembers their National Insurance number anyway?

Could I get away with it? It would give me somewhere to stay until I got my car back and some extra money to pay for the repair. It only needed to work long enough for Charles Hetherin to get back.

Mr Bored-But-Gorgeous, or Oliver as I should probably start calling him, had finished his call and seemed to be studying me with cool, professional interest. I hoped he wasn't a mind reader. But he'd thought I was called Sally, so maybe not. He'd returned to his chair and was leaning back in it, stretching his arms up and linking his fingers behind his head. His cornflower blue shirt sleeves were rolled up and the hairs on his arms were dark and thick. They were strong-looking arms. You'd know what was what if you felt a pair of arms like that around you. And this was a really inappropriate time to think things like that. What was wrong with me?

He seemed about to say something when a wraith-like old lady in a long, lilac cardigan, with wispy silver hair escaping from a half-hearted bun tottered in through the French windows. She was followed by a fluffy-haired, elderly man sporting a tan corduroy jacket with patches at the elbows, who immediately reminded me of one of the characters from *Dad's Army* – the quiet one who lived with his sisters – Godfrey? He was carrying an old-fashioned, vinyl shopping bag which didn't look heavy but was clanking with the sound of empty bottles.

'Oh, there you are, Jemima dear,' she said in my direction. I looked over my shoulder, but there was no one else there. 'You really must do something with that hair, dear,' she carried on. 'You'll never get a man to look at you twice if you go about looking like you've been dragged through a hedge backwards.'

My hands went automatically to my head. I realised that while she was talking to whoever she thought I was, her hands were busy, picking sugar cubes out of a neat row of sugar bowls on a waiters' station at the side of the room. It looked like she was taking two or three out of each bowl and stuffing them into her pockets. Then she carried on through one of the swing doors into the kitchen, closely followed by her partner in crime and his clanking bag. I looked at the strong armed restaurant manager, who didn't seem to think it was anything out of the ordinary. Right then it wouldn't have surprised me if the March hare had run past with a big watch. Well, I had already been told I was late.

'She seems to like you,' he commented. 'Do you live locally, or would you need staff accommodation? If I offered you the job, that is,' he turned and asked me, folding the sheet of paper he'd had in front of him and standing up. He was tall – a good head taller than me.

'Who were they?' I couldn't help asking.

'Mr and Mrs Hetherin Senior,' he said, placing his chair back under the table so it was exactly the same distance from the table as all the other chairs. Once a restaurant manager, always a restaurant manager. 'They live in a cottage in the grounds and have the run of the place. Mr Hetherin likes to take care of them but for them to have their independence at the same time.' He looked as if he was waiting for me to ask another daft question, so I was determined not to. That'd show him.

'Oh. That's nice,' I said, somewhat lamely. It didn't really sit with what I'd imagined of Charles Hetherin. Maybe it would be useful to spend some time here and get to find out about him from people who actually knew him before invading his world at the weekend.

'You didn't answer my question.' He looked at me. 'Would you need staff accommodation? We have a staff block behind the spa for full-timers. There are a couple of rooms available at the moment, although I can't guarantee what state they'll be in. Their last occupants both left in something of a hurry, leaving me two down in the restaurant, which is why we're rather desperate …'

'Thanks!' I laughed.

'I didn't mean it like that,' he said crisply, as he gathered up the papers on the table and folded them together. 'So, really, when could you start?'

'It looks like I'd better start at once.' I held my hand out and he shook it briefly but firmly. A wave of confusion washed over me and, convinced I must be doing the Hetherin eyebrow thing, I put on my straightest face. 'After all,' I added, 'you did say you were desperate.'

He didn't reply.

# CHAPTER FOUR

'Will, you've met Polly, our new and very experienced waitress.' Oliver rubbed his hands together as he introduced me. 'Whatever you do don't call her Sally – apparently she doesn't like it. Polly,' he looked at me, 'this is Will, our head chef. You can call him anything you like as long as you don't criticise his food or borrow any of his ingredients for behind the bar. He *really* doesn't like that.'

'Hi again,' Will nodded to me over the pass, while a couple of commis chefs lifted their heads from their tasks just long enough to see if I was worth checking out. 'Ignore Jack Dee there. Have you had a good look at the menu? If there's anything you're not familiar with, or anything you haven't served before, give me a shout, yeah? Don't try and wing it. I'm happy to explain. We always have a quick run-through of any specials before service, so don't worry about them. Welcome aboard.' Then he smiled and turned back to his work.

Neither of them seemed to notice I hadn't said a word, so hopefully neither of them had noticed me scrutinising Will. Just like the receptionist earlier, it was like looking at a version of me. And his hair was much more like mine only where I worked in the kitchen with mine scraped into a bun, his was now pulled back and bound into a rather rakish ponytail. This must be my brother!

'Earth to Polly.' Oliver handed me a clean glass cloth

and pointed me towards the tray of cutlery that had done its round with the dishwasher and now needed polishing. I took the cloth and looked round for an ice bucket. 'You'll find an ice bucket and hot water in the still-room,' he said, as if he'd read my thoughts. I didn't need this particular task explained – although shiny cutlery wasn't high on the Honor & Oak's list of priorities. Most of the restaurants I'd worked in had usually had the waiting staff standing around doing this prior to service.

I soon had three white linen napkin-covered trays lined up and was dunking and polishing while I ran through the dinner menu in my head. *Alresford watercress soup, spring chicken and vegetable broth, and soup of the day*. They wouldn't be any problem. Just carry the bowls from the kitchen and put them in front of the right diners without splashing them over the sides. Simple. *Buttered asparagus with a softly poached quail's egg, New Forest wild mushroom tartlet,* and *Local buffalo mozzarella and tomato salad*. Ditto – just putting plates in front of people. Interesting – buffalo in Hampshire – who'd have thought!

Zooming my way through steak, fish, and butter knives, salad, fish, and cake forks, dessert, soup, and teaspoons, I was amazed at how quickly I was getting through them. My mind started focusing on the seafood starters. *Pan-fried Hampshire trout* – my personal favourite, *potted prawns served with Melba toast,* and ...

'What are you doing?' Two blonde girls who'd come in carrying polythene-covered black skirts and white blouses with thin black stripes on them, on hangers, dashed over with horrified expressions on their faces.

'Hi, I'm Polly.' What was I doing wrong? 'Oliver told me to do these.' I looked from one to the other. 'I'm new ...'

'I'll bet you're bloody new,' the plump girl on the right grumbled.

'We make that job last an hour,' the wiry one on the left joined in with a stage whisper. 'What are we gonna do now?' They looked at each other and then at me.

'Quick!' the plump girl grabbed the nearest tray to her and tipped it to the floor with a clatter. 'Or do you want to spend the next hour scrubbing the hors d'oeuvres trolley?'

They both darted through the still-room door as Will came out of his office. I could see the girls and I were going to be good friends.

'Oh dear,' my unknowing brother grinned as he leant over the pass and caught sight of the cutlery on the floor. I could feel my insides curl up with embarrassment. 'They're going to have to go through the washer again.' He looked towards the staff door. 'The kitchen porter should be here any minute, but they really need to be done right away.' He came round to my side and knelt down, helping me scoop them all up. 'I'll show you how to work our dishwasher. You don't make a habit of throwing things on the floor, do you?'

'No, I don't.' I could feel myself blushing. What a great introduction to my long-lost sibling. Why didn't I just climb onto the tray and get in the dishwasher with them – my face probably couldn't get any redder.

'Should hope not,' he chuckled. 'That'd be a bit messy in a professional kitchen!' Was it my imagination or did he wink at me? He quickly picked up the now refilled dishwasher tray and carried it away. Head chefs didn't chuckle and wink – they shouted and belittled – well, at least the ones I'd worked with did – especially if you had the sheer effrontery to be a woman working in their kitchen. And none of them would stop what they were doing to help a clumsy member of waiting staff ... not unless she was wearing a very short skirt. It was nice to know my long-lost brother wasn't that kind of chef.

I slid the door of the washer open and he rolled the tray inside, closed the door, and pressed the on switch. He looked at his watch and raised his eyebrow. 'The others should have come in by now. Don't let them leave everything for you to do. They're a lazy bunch – they think we don't notice.'

'Thanks for the warning.' I bit my tongue not to tell him I'd already seen that much for myself. I didn't know where blonde and blonder were hiding out, but it was a bit much leaving the new girl to do all the work. A firm hand was going to be needed, even if I wasn't planning on pretending to work here that long.

As if my thoughts had conjured them up, the pair sauntered innocently out of the still-room. While Will went to the other end of the kitchen, they both came over, looking as if they'd never set eyes on me before. Maybe they were drama students at Wintertown Tech – they'd been getting a new Theatre Arts course up and running about the time I went to train at Westminster and I could imagine these two on it.

'Thanks for that!' I whispered to them. 'My first service and Chef thinks I'm some kind of clumsy idiot.'

'Hello!' The plump one made a big show of introducing herself to me, indicating with her eyes that Will was still watching. Breathing mint and chocolate over me, she carried on. 'I'm Mel. This is Lulu.' Lulu nodded at me, picking up a cloth and starting to polish a butter knife with the speed of an arthritic snail on a very cold day. 'First thing you've gotta learn in a place like this is you don't do anything too quickly, right?' Mel gave me a crafty wink as she imparted this great wisdom. 'The quicker you get your work done, the more work they find for you to do. See? And the last thing you want to happen is to end up cleaning the hors d'oeuvres trolley.' Both girls visibly shuddered.

\* \* \*

'Right you lot,' Will called into the restaurant as I was propping up the last of my perfectly folded Bishop's hat napkins on the last of the tables. 'Gather round for the specials.'

I followed Mel and Lulu into the kitchen, along with Oliver, who'd come back dressed in a well-cut black suit, looking stunningly handsome for a grumpy so-and-so. There were two waiters already there that I hadn't set eyes on in the restaurant yet – perhaps they considered themselves too manly for fiddling around with napkins.

'OK,' Will indicated the dishes lined up on the pass. 'Soup of the day is still roasted cherry tomato and courgette. For the benefit of Polly, who wasn't with us at lunchtime, Mel will give us a demonstration of how beautifully she serves this.'

Grinning, Mel came forward, picked up the empty soup bowl, and put it down at the little makeshift place setting. Then she picked up two small jugs and carefully poured the red and green soups from opposite sides of the bowl, ending with a turning movement that left a little swirl on the top of the colourful dish. I was impressed.

'Think you can manage that, Polly?' Will smiled encouragingly, and I had to remind myself that he didn't know I was a Westminster-trained chef. 'Here.' He handed me two more jugs and put a fresh bowl down. Feeling Oliver's eyes on me, my swirl went a little bit crooked, but they both seemed happy enough.

'A bit wiggly, but not bad,' Mel passed judgement, the cheeky madam.

'Fish of the day is different from lunchtime, as it sold

out,' Will looked round at us, 'so you'll all need to pay attention. Grilled fillet of bream,' he announced, 'infused with lime and coriander and served on a bed of crushed potatoes with a selection of steamed greens.' As he spoke, he placed a fresh, white, oval plate down, picked up the vegetables, and placed a teardrop-shaped serving of potatoes on one side of the plate and the same, pointing the opposite way, of vibrant spring greens on the other. Then he scooped up the fillet of fish and placed it at a slight angle across the top of the potatoes, spooning some of the juices in a zigzag across the plate to marry the dish's components. 'Voila!' He looked around. 'Anybody anticipate any problem with that?'

'No, Chef!' the little group chorused. I joined in, just a beat behind the others, before he singled me out again.

*  *  *

OK, I can do this, I thought, looking at the platter, an hour and a half into service. I'd cooked this dish enough times, years ago at college. It was delicious. It hadn't been on the menu anywhere I'd worked since, but I'd seen it being served by enough trainee waiters, both well and badly, to remember how it was supposed to be done. I was ignoring the fact that I had never actually served it myself.

'Come on, you can do this,' I whispered to myself. Out of the corner of my eye, I could see Will watching me. That would be all I needed, him coming over and drawing attention to me. Again.

Trying my best to look like I did this sort of thing twenty-seven times a day, I lifted and manoeuvred the hot platter, balancing it with a thick napkin on my left arm. So far so good. I picked up the serving cutlery with my right hand, took a deep breath, and steered myself through the 'out' door into the restaurant and towards table eight.

'The Dover sole?' I smiled at the smartly-dressed

couple at the table, sending up a silent prayer that I wouldn't drop anything on them. I'd served their soup perfectly but didn't think now was a good time to get cocky. The lady nodded at me and I stepped towards her. That dress looked like it was dry clean only. No, I thought. I will not splash hot butter on that dress.

I'd placed the piping hot plate in front of her. All I had to do was fillet this damn fish one-handed and place the fillets, right side up, tidily on her plate.

I picked up the fish knife, felt for the bone with it, and scored down along it. Again, so far so good. If this fish had been cooked perfectly, it should come away from the bone in one piece. I pressed harder on the knife and cut properly, then slightly lifted the flap of fish. Yes! Perfect. Thank you, Chef!

Cutting the head off and scraping away the edges with all those little pin bones in them, I finally had two perfect fillets. I placed them aside, skin side up, as gently as possible. Then I lifted the back bone out of the remaining fish and managed to make short work of the edges of the bottom two fillets. Now I had to pick them all up without dropping or breaking them.

I didn't even realise I was holding my breath until the last fillet was finally on the plate and in perfect position, the garnish had been placed to its side, and the drizzle of hot butter sauce had gently met the plate. Trying not to grin like an idiot, I made my way back to the kitchen, thinking how ridiculous it was to feel quite so pleased with myself. I'd filleted and served a Dover sole, big deal – the chateaubriand for table twelve would probably be ready and that needed carving at the table too, although thankfully with both hands.

I transferred the platter to my right arm and pushed at the door to the kitchen with my left hip, like I'd seen the other waiting staff doing. But instead of opening towards the kitchen, the door came flying out at me, accompanied by a waiter with a tray of hot plates.

Time seemed to stand still as everything flew into the air and landed with a crash in the doorway. I had wondered if anyone ever got the in and out doors mixed up. Now I knew the answer.

# CHAPTER FIVE

What was that smell! It woke me up at three in the morning from a dream about being trapped in a laundry basket full of dirty socks and an old kipper. Or it might have been a Dover sole. It was when a mangy-looking ginger cat appeared and started fighting me for the fish, turning to yawn a mouthful of fetid cat breath in my face that I woke up. Maybe it hadn't been a dream – just my nose trying to wake me up.

I hadn't noticed it the day before when the girl from Housekeeping had shown me to the staff block and told me to take my pick of the two tiny rooms, their windows open to the warm spring afternoon. I hadn't noticed it when I got back from the laundry with a set of staff-grade bed linen and put the sheets on the narrow bed. And I hadn't noticed it as I tried on the selection of restaurant uniforms they'd given me, hanging up the ones that fitted me before returning the others.

As it had been warm, it hadn't occurred to me to close the window before going to do the dinner service – my first shift as a pretend waitress in my father's hotel. Acting waitress, if you will. I'd only closed it when I got back to the room after the shift had ended. The cool Hampshire night air had seemed a little chillier than the Peckham version – probably all that extra space it had to float about in. So after I'd scrounged a blob of toothpaste and cleaned my teeth with the end of my finger and used the wet wipes and miniature tube of hand cream I always have in my bag to cleanse and moisturise my face, I'd closed the window just before getting into bed. But by three o'clock the room must have warmed up enough for the putrid pong to percolate its way into my nostrils and wake me up.

Where was it coming from? I'd thrown out the old pizza box with its treasure trove of dried out crusts that had been hiding behind the curtain on the window ledge. Ditto the one unwanted dirty sock with the hole in the heel that had been lying by the plastic rubbish bin, as if it had managed to climb out but had injured itself in the process and not made it any further. I'd also emptied the contents of the bin, at arms' length, into one of the skips behind the kitchens, not wanting to know or have any contact with whatever lurked beneath the King Size Mars Bar wrappers, the crushed Red Bull cans, the toe nail clippings, and the soggy dog-ends. So where the hell was it coming from?

Opening the wardrobe door, I could see nothing but two clean uniforms at one end, the skirt from tonight's shift – I was wearing the blouse to sleep in as I hadn't had the foresight to put a pair of pyjamas in my handbag – and the clothes I'd arrived in at the other, half a dozen empty hangers in between. I pulled out the drawers in the little dresser. Both were empty apart from a bit of fluff which I was going to clean out before I put anything of mine into them – oh, and a shirt button in the top one.

It suddenly occurred to me that I hadn't looked under the bed, something I probably should have done during daylight hours – who knew what monsters might be lying in wait under there.

Half squatting, half bending as low as I could (the thought of kneeling on that carpet with my bare legs made my stomach turn) I could just about make out a bundle shape before the blood rushed completely to my head and I had to straighten up. It was too far under for me to reach without lying on the floor and sticking my whole arm under, and that wasn't about to happen. Curiosity aroused, I slowly pulled the bed away from the wall. It looked like the room's previous occupant had left in such a hurry he, or she, but I'm guessing he based on that revolting old sock, had left his bag of dirty washing under the bed. I didn't care to hazard a guess how long those soiled clothes had been festering in that plastic bag or just how filthy they might have been to start with. It wouldn't have surprised me if there'd been a dead dog rolled up in weeks-old sweaty socks somewhere among the grubby contents.

I quickly pulled tonight's skirt back on, shoved my feet into my shoes, picked up the bag between my finger and thumb, and, my arm extended as far as possible, made my way out and down to the rubbish bins outside. No one in their right mind and with a normally functioning sense of smell would come back for that stuff. There was no way I'd be able to get into Housekeeping at this time of night for some antibacterial spray and a can of air freshener, so I headed back.

The smell couldn't have been as bad now I'd removed the cause of it, but it was stuck in my nostrils. There was no way I was going to be able to get back to sleep, but it was three hours before I had to go down to start breakfast duty. I opened the window a little, turned the light off, and sat by the ledge, looking out at the night sky.

What would Mum think of what I was doing? I took her letter out of my handbag and sat looking at the envelope – I knew its contents word for word. She had obviously wanted me to get in touch with Charles

Hetherin, but would she approve of this waitress subterfuge? Actually, knowing her, I thought she'd probably be quite tickled by the thought. Had she known anything about his other children? Will seemed so nice, much nicer than any other head chef I'd ever worked with. I wondered how old he was. He looked younger than me, by a few years I'd guess. He was young to be a head chef but I suppose if your dad was the boss, your feet didn't have to hit every rung of the ladder. Anyway, he would have to be younger as Mum would never have had a thing with a married man. And what about that receptionist who could be my sister? She looked younger still, but she wasn't spending up to sixteen hours a day in a hot kitchen. Plus, she looked like someone who cleansed, toned, and moisturised properly. And exfoliated, which was a habit I'd tried to get into from time to time.

That reminded me, an emergency trip to Netley Magna was on the agenda for the next day as I'd arrived woefully unprepared. I would have to go at the very first opportunity –hopefully between breakfast and lunch service if I promised to be as quick as possible. A chat with Mel and Lulu had been very helpful. Apparently Netley Magna, the biggest of the three Netley villages, had a Boots so I could get a toothbrush and whatever else I needed. It wasn't the nearest village and they said it would be too far to walk, so if my car wasn't ready I'd have to order a taxi to get there and back. But there was a clothes shop too called Sara's, where I could get some underwear and pyjamas. Thank God Hetherin Hall provided a full clean uniform every service.

Luckily I kept a phone charger in the car, so keeping my mobile charged wouldn't be a problem. That reminded me, I had to call Sheila at the Honor & Oak and let her know I was going to need the rest of the week off. They probably weren't going to be too pleased. The management had been very good about me having time off when Mum's condition had started to get worse towards the end but I could imagine their patience starting to wear a bit thin.

I looked at my watch – two and three quarter hours til breakfast service. Would this night never end?

# CHAPTER SIX

I was jolted awake by the sound of one of the commis chefs slamming the bathroom door. It took me a moment to realise where I was and what I was doing – asleep in a creased waitress blouse, my head on my arm, leaning on a window ledge by an open window. My neck was stuck in that position and made sure I knew about it when I tried to move. It took a while to coax it upright and a lot of rubbing before I could move my head around. I stood with the shower aimed directly on it for as long as I dared in our shared bathroom before getting into a clean uniform and following the others down. I must have looked a fright with frizzy hair where I hadn't had the time or the shampoo to wash it and dark circles under my eyes.

The breakfast service was easy compared to the silver service required at dinner. Just as well, as I'd hardly had a good night's sleep and my brain felt like it was on a five second delay. The guests helped themselves to whatever cereals and fruits they wanted from the little buffet set-up against one wall while we served their teas, coffees, and the various juices being freshly squeezed in the kitchen. We took orders for and served their choices of hot breakfast – the local farm's organic bacon and sausages and free range eggs being the most popular, for which I was thankful. The smell of kipper first thing this particular morning might tip me and my neck over the edge. Then there was just the toast and warm bakery items to dispense and it was over.

Once we'd finished clearing away, it was time for staff breakfast, and despite thinking I couldn't face a cooked meal, I found myself ploughing through a plate of scrambled eggs on toast as if I hadn't eaten in a week.

'Enjoying that?' Will teased as he plonked his mug of builders' tea and extra thick bacon butty on the table and took the seat opposite me.

'Best scrambled eggs I've had in ages,' I enthused, hoping to cover my embarrassment at being caught stuffing my face quite so energetically, by distracting him with praise.

'I'll give your compliments to the chef.' He raised his eyebrow as he took a huge bite out of his sandwich, making me laugh. I was glad I'd managed to swallow what was in my mouth, otherwise he might have ended up wearing bits of it.

Just then, the receptionist from yesterday who was possibly my sister sat herself daintily in the seat next to him. She smiled at me as she placed her bowl of fresh fruit salad and her grapefruit juice in front of her, and then looked at the remains of his bacon sandwich as if it might bite her.

'Good morning, Polly.' She turned back to me. 'I'm Jemima. How are you settling in? I hear you had a smashing time last night!' Her grin was infectious. It was just the sort of daft joke I would have made.

'Wait til you see what I've got planned for today,' I laughed.

'Wish I'd been there to see Ollie's face. It must have been a picture.'

'Unfortunately I missed it.' Will was clearly doing his best to look serious. He'd heard me offer to pay for the damage but, to my relief, Oliver had been insistent they didn't treat staff like that at Hetherin Hall – well, not first offenders, anyway. I hadn't been sure if he was joking about that last bit. He wasn't smiling when he said it. For the rest of the shift, every time I looked up I found him watching me.

'So, what's happening with your car?' Jemima spooned up a blueberry and half a strawberry and popped them into her mouth. No wonder she had such lovely skin. Maybe I should take a leaf out of her book. I watched her, fascinated. Jemima – of course! That was what the old lady had called me. So Grandma Hetherin had already mixed me up with my little sister – she could see the likeness. I knew I liked that old lady.

'Sorry! What did you say?' I noticed them both looking at me and suffered a moment of blind panic. *Had I been thinking that in my head or had I said the words out loud?*

'Your car?' Jemima repeated. 'You left it with The Two Ronnies.'

'Don't tease her, Jem.' Will picked a piece of red apple out of her bowl and looked at me. 'She means Coopers' garage. A and A Cooper?' Clearly seeing the look of stupidity on my face he added, 'They're both called Alan – Alan and Alan Cooper.' He tossed the apple chunk into his mouth.

'Oh, I see.' I hoped my face wasn't giving away the fact that I didn't, but I was saved by the arrival through the French window of Grandma Hetherin, complete with long, lilac cardigan. Grandpa shuffled in after her, sporting a beige cardigan over a checked shirt and minus his shopping bag this time. This should be interesting.

'Hello, Grandma.' Will stood up – what nice manners my brother had. 'Are you and Grandpa ready for breakfast?'

'Oh, William dear,' she homed in on him, 'I did make some nice porridge, but somebody must have put the salt in the sugar tin and it's salty. I couldn't give that to poor George, not with his blood pressure.'

'Come and sit down, Grandpa,' Jemima called loudly and clearly to the elderly man, getting up and pulling out a couple of chairs.

'Go and sit down with Jemima, George dear,' Grandma repeated, heading for Will, who was holding the kitchen door open for her. 'William can help me make more. He's such a good boy.'

Jemima stifled a giggle as the door swung shut behind them. Grandpa just smiled pleasantly at us. We smiled back. He was lovely – I couldn't even begin to equate this sweet, elderly couple with the people my mother had been afraid of telling she was pregnant.

'What'll really happen,' Jemima said to me *sotto voce*, 'is Grandma will tell him how to do it while he's doing it and then when he brings it in, she won't take the credit but she'll say what a big help he was to her. She's not a daft as she looks.' I bet she wasn't.

'Actually, Jemima,' I thought I'd ask while I had her on her own, 'I need to get to Netley Magna rather urgently. I came here yesterday, not expecting to be taken on straight away like that and I didn't bring anything with me – toiletries, clean underwear, anything.'

'Oh,' she looked quite shocked, 'you should have said. Housekeeping could have given you any toiletries you needed. I could have given you some bits and pieces from the spa.'

'The spa?' I'd never come across this kind of generosity from employers.

'Yes. I manage the spa and I'm always getting new product samples in with my orders. I usually give them to regular clients or use them when I go on holiday.' She must have caught the dopey look on my face. 'You didn't think I was the receptionist, did you?'

'Well, I suppose I did. You were on the reception desk when I walked in.'

'Just standing in,' she rolled her eyes. 'I seem to do a lot of that. You've probably realised how difficult it is to get reliable staff out here in the sticks.' She thought a moment. 'Let me ring Coopers' and see if your car is ready. It'll be quicker to go and pick it up than wait for a taxi.' And with that, she went to the restaurant manager's desk and picked up the phone.

At that moment, the kitchen door swung open again and Oliver walked in with an even thicker bacon butty than Will's and a mug of strong-looking coffee. That'd put hairs on his chest. I caught myself wondering if his chest was covered in the same thick, dark hairs as his arms. In a spotless white V-neck, which I firmly ordered myself not to look at to find out, and dark blue jeans, he looked younger than he had in his smart clothes. His hair was wet and looked as if he'd combed it back with his fingers. He looked sexy, in an Italian way. A bit of an Italian stallion, I wondered, feeling myself blush and forcing myself to look out of the window. I was, after all, here to find my father, not to get the hots for the local stud.

'Morning everyone,' he greeted the table. 'Morning, Grandpa,' he said more loudly. 'Waiting for your porridge?'

'Mmm, yes,' Grandpa nodded and smiled before looking at the empty plate in front of him.

'You didn't fancy a bacon sandwich?'

'Oliver, behave.' Grandma commanded from the kitchen doorway. 'You know he isn't allowed, not with his blood pressure.'

'Careful, Ollie. She'll put you on the naughty step,' Jemima chuckled, coming back to the table with a Post-it note which she handed to me with a smile.

'Don't worry,' he winked at her, picking up his mug, 'I'll leave a space for you.'

My chest tightened. A voice in my head wondered if there was something between the two of them. Of course there was, look how close they were! To cover my confusion, I picked up the little corner of toast I'd left on my plate and put in my mouth as I looked down. The words on the yellow paper blurred as the toast attacked the back of my throat and I started to choke.

# CHAPTER SEVEN

Oh my God! Oliver was Jemima's boyfriend! I sat, parked in a lay-by with my forehead on the steering wheel and my eyes shut, cringing inside. I'd nicknamed him Mr Bored-But-Gorgeous. I'd noticed his hair and the ambler flecks in his eyes and the hairs on his arms. Oh God, I'd thought he had strong-looking arms. And he was my long-lost sister's boyfriend. How icky was that? I'd practically drooled over him. It was less than twenty-four hours since I'd met Jemima and I was already officially the worst sister in the world.

What if I just turned the car round and drove back to London and forgot all about confronting my father? Why shouldn't I? After all, the first twenty-seven years of my life had been fine without him, why should I need him now. I could head straight back to Peckham. I could call Sheila and tell her I was suddenly feeling much better and then I could go back to work tomorrow and it would be like none of this had happened. Yes! That was what I'd do.

Turning out of the lay-by, I went back the way I'd come, passing Coopers' garage. Cooper Senior saw me and waved, so I had to wave back. His son still hadn't looked at or spoken to me once, even while I'd picked my car up and paid. I could see what Jemima and Will meant about them being like the Two Ronnies. After all, yesterday they'd reminded me of Mum's old DVDs.

Reaching the turning which would take me in the right direction for the M3, I suddenly didn't know what to do. I pulled in and sat a moment, gripped by indecision. It was silly to turn tail and run back to London without doing what I'd gone there to do. And for what? Because I'd thought Oliver was attractive? Big deal! I thought Colin Farrell was attractive. And Richard Armitage. And whatever the actor's name was from *Monarch of the Glen*. OK, none of them were in a relationship with my little sister, but ...

What was I, a strong, independent woman or a timid mouse?

The appearance in my rear-view mirror of an enormous green tractor with yellow wheels trundling towards me helped make up my mind. Instead of turning off, I drove on down the road and used the first lay-by to turn back round. Then, following Jemima's advice, I drove to Netley Magna. There, between a florist called – I kid you not – Oops-a-Daisy and the smallest Boots I'd ever seen, was Sara's Ladies' Wear, a rather old fashioned-looking clothes shop.

A little bell actually tinkled over my head as I opened the shop door and a woman – possibly Sara herself – knitting behind the counter which ran along one whole wall, put down her work and smiled at me. I waited for her to tell me this was a local shop for local people.

'Are you looking for anything in particular? We've some lovely new wool in.'

'Is it alright if I just browse?' Although it might be quicker if I told her what I wanted, I didn't want her hovering while I rummaged through her underwear.

She smiled at me. 'Just let me know if you need any help.' Then she went back to her needles.

There was a rail of mumsy cotton nightdresses and

matching dressing gowns I wouldn't even want to be buried in, but I needed to get something to wear to bed. I couldn't keep sleeping – or trying to – in my uniform shirt. A pair of mauve pyjamas with sheep all over them with the words *Dreaming of Ewe!* splashed across the front caught my eye. They were quite cute in a hideous kind of way. Beyond the nightwear, I could see a stand of knickers that looked like they could be turned upside down and used as family-size tents. There had to be something better.

Sara's policy must be to display the most unattractive stock in front of the stuff that was actually relatively alright, I was thankful to realise. Grabbing a three pack of something white, cotton, and far too small for a family of six to sleep in, I went to interrupt the knitting again.

'They're very popular, them pyjamas,' the woman cooed as she rang my purchases up in an old-fashioned till. I half expected the price to come up in shillings. 'I'll have to get Sara to order some more.' So she wasn't Sara. 'You visiting?'

'Something like that. I've just started working at Hetherin Hall,' I mumbled, a bit embarrassed to hear myself saying what I was doing out loud.

'My eldest worked a summer there before she went to college. Waitress, she was. Said it was a nice place to work ...'

'Yes, it is,' I interrupted before she gave me her daughter's career history. 'Thanks very much, but I have to get back. I don't want to be late when I've only just started.'

I just had time to pop into Boots for a toothbrush and a few other bits, before driving back to the Hall and getting ready for my first lunch shift. It felt so good when I went to get changed into my uniform to be able to give my teeth a proper brushing – a blob of cadged toothpaste on the end of your finger was one thing, but I'd been worried about opening my mouth too wide when I spoke to people in case I had something stuck between my teeth.

* * *

The restaurant seemed to be in the grip of a go-slow when I got there a couple of minutes late. I was happy not to run straight into Oliver although not surprised to see Mel and Lulu sitting at one of the tables chatting, their shoes off and feet up, while they half-heartedly folded their napkins in his absence.

'Hi, Poll.' Mel waved a wonky Bishop's hat at me, which immediately unfolded itself back into a plain square of linen. Lulu just nodded.

'Where is everyone?' I asked, definitely *not* meaning Oliver, as I walked over to join them. Apart from two piles of unfolded napkins, the table top was awash with little squares of green and silver foil. Lulu's jaw was going round and round like a washing machine and I had a little bet with myself that when she finally spoke, her breath would be really minty. And chocolatey.

'One of the commis chefs cut his finger off. Then he fainted. It'd take too long for an ambulance to get here so Oliver and Chef have driven him to the hospital,' Mel announced, as if this were a normal midweek occurrence.

'What!' I looked from one to the other, wondering if this was a wind-up.

'It's alright,' she shrugged. 'I think they stuck it in ice and took it with them, so they'll probably be able to sew it back on.'

'Right.' I wasn't quite sure what to say, so I headed for the kitchen, fully expecting to find the full complement of commis chefs busily working on the lunch menu, each with ten digits intact and to hear a cackle of laughter

46

behind me.

But they weren't, and I didn't. In fact, the kitchen resembled the Marie Celeste. Pans, whisks, knives, and chopping boards – everything seemed to have been abandoned. In the vegetable prep area, a stainless steel bowl of cauliflower florets in lemon water sat by a green chopping board. In the middle of the board, the remains of a roughly hacked cauliflower head sat in a puddle of blood. A chef's knife, far too large for what it had obviously been used for, lay where it had been dropped, the heel covered in blood and splashes and a smear of blood a few feet away. I could see exactly what had happened. Poor kid – what a price to pay for using the wrong knife.

I didn't know what to do for the best. Where the hell was everybody else? The other line chefs? The commis chefs? There was no one around to ask if this had gone into the accident book. I suspected there hadn't been time, but I couldn't just leave it like this – we had to get ready for lunch service and this was a safety hazard in itself. Hoping I was doing the right thing, I took pictures of the scene on my mobile, then I started to clean up the mess.

The guests would start coming in in a little over half an hour and what staff did we have – two waitresses who were too slow to catch colds, and me. I went into Will's office and rang Reception.

'Jemima!' I didn't give her a chance to speak. 'We've got a situation in the restaurant. I need your help. Now!'

# CHAPTER EIGHT

The looks on Will and Oliver's faces when they walked through the kitchen door were priceless. Whatever they'd expected to come back to, I'd be willing to bet it wouldn't in a million years have involved Jemima and myself running the show. In fact, I couldn't be sure they weren't slightly disappointed the place hadn't fallen apart in their absence.

Jemima had been wonderful, tracking down the remaining kitchen staff, curtailing their extended cigarette break, and chasing them to where they should be. After their initial surprise, they had all pulled together and helped me work out what was in an advanced enough state of preparation to stay on the now slightly limited menu. Luckily for me, I had plenty of experience running a lunchtime service without the interference of a head chef. And while I took over in the kitchen, Jemima made her presence known in the restaurant. She was brilliant at getting Mel and Lulu motivated and moving. Ten out of ten to the Hetherin girls!

'I don't believe it!' Will looked at the two servings of cauliflower and cheese fritters with roasted red pepper salad I'd placed on the pass as today's vegetarian special. Mel whisked them away to serve to table two like a real professional waitress.

'I double don't believe it!' Oliver looked at Mel's retreating back and then at me. 'Have we come to the

49

right place? I thought you were supposed to be a waitress.'

'Never mind that.' Will saved me from having to think of a reply. 'Possession's nine tenths of the law, or something like that, and she's behind my pass in my kitchen so I guess she works for me now.' He had the cheek to wink at me.

'In case you two haven't noticed,' I put on my best sous chef voice, 'we have a dozen mains to get out. And that's before we start on desserts. So if the pair of you could stop squabbling and help, Jemima and I would very much appreciate it.'

* * *

Will put the tray of coffee for four on the table as Mel and Lulu left to go home until the evening shift.

'I don't know how waitresses do that every day,' Jemima sighed in relief, tossing her dainty wedge sandals aside, folding her right foot into her lap, and rubbing her toes.

'And I don't know how you do that at all,' I laughed, nodding at her foot while I unfastened my borrowed chef's jacket.

'Yoga – you should try it. Er ... should you be doing that in here?'

I caught the twinkle in her eye, waited a second, and then flashed open the jacket with a 'Ta dah!' as all three of them stared at me.

'Very funny,' Jemima chuckled. 'You must have been hot with that on over your waitress uniform.'

'I thought I'd better keep both on in case I had to serve anything.' I peeled the jacket off. 'Phew, that's better. It was a bit like working in a sweat suit.'

'So.' Oliver managed to put a lot of meaning into that one word. He picked up his cup while we waited for him.

'Am I right in assuming that you are, in fact, a professional cook?' He managed to make it sound like he was accusing me of being a pick-pocket. He'd obviously come back to earth first, and was definitely going to be the one to ask the awkward questions.

'I'm a sous chef ...'

'Yes!' Will cheered, looking like his team had just scored the winning goal. I could have hugged him.

'I don't get it,' Jemima looked from me to Oliver and back to me. 'Why interview for a waitressing position if you're a chef?'

'That's exactly what I'd like to know.' Oliver inclined his head. He had the look of a long-suffering headmaster, albeit a young and hot one, who was prepared to wait all day for the naughty child in front of him to admit to whatever misdemeanour had been committed.

I knew I had to be very careful what I said. I couldn't tell them the truth, not until I'd had a chance to speak to Charles first. That wouldn't be fair to him. But I couldn't tell them any actual lies. That wouldn't be fair to them. And I hadn't told any so far – I was City and Guilds trained. And I did have six years' experience in the catering industry, just not as a waitress.

'The thing is,' I started, reaching for my coffee cup and taking a sip to give my brain a few more seconds, 'the thing is, I've been working in a restaurant in London, but I'm not very happy there.' I looked at Will. 'It's not the sort of place you'd be proud to work in – nothing is organic or free range, or even remotely local.' I was thankful to see him nodding in understanding. 'The clientele are all either East London wide boys or City types who want to be seen to be eating whatever's trendy, whether they like it or not. As you can imagine, flavour doesn't play a big part in the meals we produce. They just have to look the part. We could probably make them out of Lego as long as they looked right.'

'Sounds awful,' Will said. Jemima nodded her agreement.

'Yes, but there must be thousands of restaurants in London.' Oliver was like a dog worrying at an old slipper. 'You're obviously good at what you do – well, as long as you don't have to walk through doors without dropping things – so why not leave and work at another restaurant? And why pretend to be a waitress, which let's face it, you're quite erratic at ...'

'Ollie, don't be horrible,' Jemima butted in, standing up for me in a sisterly fashion. If only she knew.

'It's OK,' I smiled and returned to my hopefully adequate explanation. 'I grew up in Wintertown,' I continued. 'I left when I was sixteen to go to Westminster, to train to be a chef and do my City and Guilds ...'

'You trained at Westminster!' Will sounded as if his team were gearing up for another goal.

'Yes. My mother and I were huge fans of Jamie Oliver and she was determined I study there rather than go to Wintertown technical college.'

'I don't blame her,' Will nodded, while Oliver just rolled his eyes.

'This is a lovely trip down memory lane, but I still don't understand why you were pretending to be a waitress.' Oliver was going to wear that slipper out.

'My mum died ...' I hated saying those words. Hearing them come out of my mouth made it seem more real, that she truly had gone and wasn't at her flat, at the end of a telephone, waiting to hear all my news.

'Oh, I'm so sorry,' Jemima put her hand on my arm. 'She must have been young.'

'Yes, she was.' I could feel myself welling up and I

didn't want to do that – I wasn't after sympathy. I swallowed. 'The funeral was the day before yesterday and afterwards, I needed to get away.' I ignored the looks of surprise I could feel, rather than see, on their faces. 'The next day, I got in the car and drove down to Hampshire. I was on one of the local roads when a police car flashed me to pull over.'

'Because of your brake light?' Jemima asked.

'Yes. He was so nice about it. He drove to Coopers' garage so I could follow him ...'

'And you came here for a coffee or something while you worked out what to do and I went and stuck my oar in and sent you to a job interview.' Jemima shook her head as if in disbelief. 'You must have thought I was a nutcase.'

'But why did you take the job?' Oliver asked, gentler now.

'What does it matter why?' Will heaved a sigh. 'She's here now and just look what she pulled out of the bag for us at a moment's notice! If Polly wants to stay, I think she'll make ... no, scrap that, she's already made a great addition to the team.'

'Yes,' Oliver said. 'Your bloody kitchen team. And meanwhile, the restaurant is down two waiters and I'm left with two dumb blondes who do nothing but eat their own body weight in after dinner mints every shift.'

'Actually, that's not quite true.' I didn't know why I was standing up for Mel; I certainly didn't owe her any loyalty. I think I was just relieved I'd slipped off the number one topic of conversation slot and was hoping to keep it that way. 'They actually eat each other's body weight in after dinner mints.'

'Thank you, Polly.' Oliver glared at me in a sexy Heathcliff kind of way that made me feel a bit hot and goose-bumpy. 'That's very helpful.' He put his cup down and stood up. 'If you'll excuse me, I need to go and advertise for more waiting staff. Again.'

'Hey, Oliver!' Jemima called to his retreating back, grinning conspiratorially. 'Why don't you see if Sally is still available?'

# CHAPTER NINE

OK, *Lord Nelson's pie* – shouldn't that be Admiral Nelson? I worked my way through deveining the crate of fresh prawns in front of me. I wasn't sure; History wasn't my strongest subject at school. *Dover sole, filleted by hand at the table* – yes, I'd already reacquainted myself with that dish, thank you. *Beer battered cod, hand-cut chips, and minted fresh peas* – well, almost every British restaurant had that classic on the menu. *Fresh-caught fish of the day* – no problem. If it's a whole fish, baked or steamed. If it's a fillet, pan-fried, grilled, or roasted. Piece of cake. Hey, I thought, fishcake. I should suggest that to Will for a lunchtime special.

My first full day as a member of the kitchen team saw me prepping the seafood items on the menu. As my career so far had involved me working in all sections of the kitchen rather than just the pastry kitchen which seemed to be where female chefs were expected to want to work, I didn't have a speciality. From being a floater in a few kitchens, the sous chef position was one which I appeared to have fallen into because I seemed to like organising people. It could also possibly be because I was a bit bossy.

Will hadn't had a sous chef working under him when I'd first arrived. The Hetherin Hall kitchen wasn't that big, so when his last sous had been seduced away to a flash restaurant in Basingstoke, he told me he just hadn't bothered replacing him. He'd had line chefs in charge of meat, fish, vegetables, and garde manger – the one in charge of cold savouries, buffets, and things like that. And, of course, there was a pastry chef, doing his puddings and pastries in his own little room next to the still-room. Each of these had a commis chef working under them.

If the meat chef hadn't been called away to an emergency of his own, while the unfortunate nine-fingered commis and his severed digit were being driven to hospital, I probably wouldn't have had the chance to show them what I was capable of. But luckily, the remaining chefs were so busy arguing over who should be in charge that none of them actually got round to doing anything. Plus, I think the novelty of having Jemima and the "new girl" taking charge had piqued their interest – and, more importantly, if it all went wrong it wouldn't be any of their faults.

\* \* \*

I finished prepping my prawns and started on the crabs for the Hamble crab salad, keeping my distance from the newest and youngest commis who was scaling a box of beautiful fresh bream and covering himself and his work-space in a confetti of white scales. If the fish chef wasn't going to show him how to do it properly, I'd sort him out the next day – I didn't want to tread on anyone's clogs, but he couldn't go on like that.

I was more than happy with the arrangement Will and I had come to. He was going to have me working my way round the different sections of his kitchen, getting to know each item on the menu from the ordering of ingredients to the plating up and serving of the finished dishes. It was luxury compared to the thrown-in-at-the-deep-end approach that I and every other chef I'd ever worked with were used to.

'How's it going, Poll?' Will appeared at my elbow, a clipboard stuffed with paperwork and receipts tucked under his arm.

'Good thanks. Although,' I nodded my head towards the boy by the sink, 'there seems to be something fishy going on over there.'

Will groaned. 'With that sense of humour you'll fit right in.'

'Do you want me to take him in hand?' I asked.

'Later, but yes, definitely.' He tapped the clipboard. 'I need to start going over these with you first. As soon as you've finished what you're doing, give me a shout and we'll go to the store room and make a start on them.'

* * *

Oliver seemed to be in and out of the kitchen a lot in the run up to lunch service. The tap-tap of his shiny shoes against the muffle of our clogs on the kitchen floor made my stomach lurch and my pulse do funny things. It was almost as if he were checking up on me. Was he expecting me to turn out to be a rubbish chef as well as a rubbish waitress? I'd show him. Not that I cared what he thought of me.

'Away! One watercress soup, two asparagus and quail's egg, and a crab salad for table three. Service!' I called over the pass as Mel trotted in, grinning at my less than glamorous appearance. If she thought my shiny forehead looked amusing with my fringe obliterated under my white skull cap, she should have seen me in the awful paper forage hats we had to wear at the Honor & Oak, where I had to attach a second half to one to accommodate all my hair. She'd have wet herself.

'Don't you have a dining room to take care of?' Will enquired of Oliver from over my shoulder. 'She's not going to start juggling with the serving platters however long you stand there.'

'Just checking the right things are coming out,' Oliver mumbled, following Mel back into the restaurant.

'Away! Two soup of the day, one asparagus and quail's egg, and one potted prawns with extra toast for table five. Service!' I called.

'Funny that.' Will looked at me.

'What?' I took a new order from Lulu as she came to pick up table five's starters. 'Order! No starters. One Dover sole to be filleted in the kitchen, one fish of the day, two spring lamb. Table seven and they're in a hurry.'

'Oliver's never felt the need to check up on things before.'

'He doesn't believe I'm up to the job, does he?' I tried not to feel cross as I took an order from one of the snooty boy waiters whose day off it had been yesterday and whose name I couldn't remember. 'Order! Starters: one asparagus and quail's egg, and one chicken livers on toast. Mains: two spring lamb. Table twelve.'

'Somehow I don't think that's the reason he's doing it.' Will raised his eyebrow and my hand missed the order board and ended up throwing table twelve's order slip onto the floor. I bent down, scrabbled to retrieve it, and straightened up, red in the face as Oliver walked back in with another order. *Bugger!* I snatched it out of his hand without touching him. *Buggerbuggerbugger!*

'Order!' I croaked. 'Starters: two asparagus and quail's leg. Mains. One spring lamb, one vegetarian fish of the day. Table eight.' *Buggerbuggerbuggerbuggerbugger! I should have just kept driving yesterday. Why didn't I just keep driving? I'd be in London now. And I'd never have to set eyes on my sister's sex god of a boyfriend again.*

The board rattled as I slammed the order slip onto it. Why was everyone looking at me like that? What had I said?

# CHAPTER TEN

Roll on Saturday, I thought as I lay in bed, wide awake at half past three in the morning. Again. Couldn't even blame a ghostly kipper nightmare or anyone's stinky laundry this time. It was my own mind, flopping round and round like a pair of tights in a tumble drier, getting more and more tangled with every thought that was keeping me awake.

No one had said in front of me what time Charles Hetherin was due back, and why would they? To them, I was just another employee. I hadn't felt able to ask, but I had managed to eavesdrop and find out he was in Italy. The sooner he was back, the sooner I could meet with him. Once I'd had the chance to tell him about Mum and find out if he knew she was pregnant, I'd be able to get back to London and my proper life. I couldn't stay here. Even if they were my family and they welcomed me with open arms, I had to get away.

Jemima was lovely. I felt as if she and I could be friends even if we weren't sisters. I hoped we would be friends when she finally knew we were. Will was sweet, although I got the impression that, not knowing who I was, he might fancy his chances with the only female in his kitchen. He'd asked me earlier if I had a boyfriend pining away for me in London.

'Don't be daft,' I'd told him, hoping the blush I could feel on my cheeks didn't look as bad as I imagined. 'You know what chefs' working hours do to personal relationships.'

'Yeah, but a pretty girl like you ...' he'd started to say.

'What about you?' I'd interrupted before he said anything he'd be mortally embarrassed about later.

'Ah, but I'm not pretty,' he'd started again.

'Oh, I don't know,' I'd jumped in, thankful he'd unwittingly given me a way to turn the conversation around. 'You have very pretty hair.' That had done the trick. I might as well have asked him how many times he'd been to see *The Wizard of Oz*.

It wasn't personal. It happened a lot in the male-dominated world of chefs and their kitchens and I'd become quite good at deflecting unwanted extra-culinary advances. But Oliver? That was a whole other kettle of not particularly fresh-smelling fish. Although I wasn't planning on having any more inappropriate Heathcliff fantasies about my sister's boyfriend's arms, it was bad enough that I'd had some to start with. Not that I'd known they were inappropriate at the time, but that wasn't the point. I could feel my face blushing in the darkness at the memory, and this time I knew my face would be as red and hot-looking as it felt. No, I couldn't be around Oliver. While I was stuck here waiting for my prospective father to make an appearance, I had to avoid Oliver like the plague.

Thank God I wasn't working in the restaurant any more. At least in the kitchen I wouldn't have to keep catching his amber-flecked eye.

There was going to be a wedding reception at the Hall on Saturday in the ballroom – the largest of the function rooms. Like everyone else in the kitchen, I would be up to my eyes in canapés all morning, and that suited me perfectly. In my experience, anybody who wasn't butterflying, rolling, stuffing, topping, or garnishing several things at once wouldn't even be allowed in the kitchen. I would throw myself into making sure we served the best damn canapés the Hall kitchens had ever made. That would keep my hands occupied and my mind off my problems.

Having turned my pillow over for the umpteenth time while trying to stop wondering what time Mr Hetherin would get back and how long it would be before I could feasibly introduce myself to him, I gave up trying to sleep. I grabbed my tablet and waited, feeling like some kind of low-level addict, for the internet to connect so I could get another fix of looking at the pictures of Hetherin International.

I clicked on Rome. Villa Hetherin Rome – an eighteenth century architectural delight, set in one of Rome's most desirable locations, a stone's throw from the Spanish Steps. Once again, I gazed at the pictures of its imposing pillars, its secluded alcoves where busts of people whose names I didn't even know sat on antique tables, and its polished marble, and felt as if I'd taken a step back in time. I half expected Audrey Hepburn to be standing on that wonderful staircase, long cigarette holder in hand, looking stylish and sensational. It made me want to watch *Roman Holiday* again.

When I'd had my fill of Rome, I clicked on Tuscany. Villa Hetherin Viareggio – an art nouveau villa with impressive turrets and intricate balconies, set back from the seafront promenade. It managed to look posh while at the same time so beautifully Tuscan – which I'd always thought of as rustic – with flowers everywhere. There were massive terracotta pots of them, window boxes, hanging baskets, strategically placed oversized olive jars, and what looked like gigantic sinks on colossal stone plinths.

I couldn't stop myself clicking on the restaurant menus. At home, if I couldn't sleep, I'd go and sit in the kitchen and look through my cookery books – it could be the most relaxing thing in the world – as long as I didn't start getting over-excited by all those delicious Tuscan dishes and ingredients. *Crostini with liver pate* – yes, please. *Cacciucco* – a gorgeous seafood soup and Tuscany's answer to *Bouillabaisse*. *Panforte di Sienna* – the richest cake I'd ever eaten. How Italians weren't all the size of an opera house, I'd never understood. I sighed happily as I looked back down Villa Hetherin Viareggio's current sample menu. *Log off, Polly. Log off and go to sleep. At this rate you'll have bags under your eyes the size of an opera house by Saturday. That's not a good look.*

# CHAPTER ELEVEN

First thing Saturday morning, Will, Greg the buffet chef, Steve the pastry chef, and I grabbed a coffee, synchronised our lists, and set to work. Everyone else was on breakfast duty and joining us straight afterwards, and all the advance prep that could have been done had already been done and ticked off in quadruplicate.

The round and boat-shaped pastry cases were ready and sitting on their respective trays waiting for their wild mushroom or fruit and crème patisserie fillings. The blinis were cooling to be topped and garnished just before serving. The bite-size salmon en-croute were waiting for the miniature smoked haddock quiches to come out of the oven so they could go in.

'Polly!' Will yelled from the other end of the kitchen. 'Ollie's only sent eighty shot glasses. Organise another forty, will you?' Honestly, I thought, trying to ignore that clenching feeling in my stomach at the thought of speaking to Oliver. Make yourself indispensable just once and yours is suddenly the only name anyone remembers. That was a task any of the commis chefs would be capable of accomplishing, and in defiance I snaffled the least busy-looking one and sent him for the glasses. The chilled spicy gazpacho shots had not been my idea and I'd argued against them. It would only take one clumsy guest, one slip of the hand anywhere in the vicinity of the bride, and her day – never mind her dress – could be ruined. But

Greg had been adamant and Will had agreed with him. I just hoped I'd be proved wrong.

I picked up my clipboard of lists and went to check the fish section. The bucket of crab salad was chilling in the walk-in fridge, waiting to be spooned into the delicate cucumber cups still being scooped out with melon ballers by a couple of commis chefs. On the shelf above the crab mixture, the sausage-shaped smoked salmon and dill roulades were firming up nicely, ready to be sliced. Prawns were in the process of being wrapped in filo pastry, and goujons of sole were being bread-crumbed ready to deep fry just before serving.

'Polly!' I heard as I went to check the fridge for the fresh tartare sauce. Oliver. *I'm not here!* I went hot and cold as I ducked inside and tried to pull the fridge door closed behind me as quietly as possible. *There! You can't see me!* I thought I was doing a pretty good job of blending myself in with the contents until I heard the door swing open. 'There you are!' He tapped me on my arm and I jumped as if I'd been stung, nearly knocking the tartare sauce to the floor. 'Didn't you hear me? There's been some kind of disaster with the cake. We need you now!' I wished I'd climbed inside the freezer instead of the fridge. He'd never have followed me there.

'You need a pastry chef,' I challenged him. 'I'll get Steve.'

'Steve's too busy, and anyway, you're good in a crisis.' Three cheers for me, I thought. I'm really going to have to stop doing this being good in a crisis thing – it seems to cause me no end of trouble.

'Do I need to bring a piping bag or something?' I asked him as he ushered me out of the kitchen.

'What?' His face was a blank.

'Has something fallen off the cake and needs sticking

back on with icing?' I offered as the possible cause of the cake disaster.

'How the hell should I know?'

I managed to silence the words on the tip of my tongue, which were something along the lines of 'Maybe you should know because you were the clown who'd told me about it', only slightly less polite. The less I said to him the better.

The bride had made her own wedding cake – that much I did know. There were all sorts of things that could have gone wrong, but the most likely one would be that one or some of the decorations had fallen off in transit and needed reattaching. As long as they weren't broken, it was no problem. Some royal icing in a piping bag and it'd be as good as new.

Oliver strode into the ballroom with me scurrying behind him, looking anywhere but at those denim-clad legs, my eyes definitely not gliding upwards ... I stopped dead when I saw the cake. The bottom tier looked very pretty, if you ignored what was sticking out of it at a drunken angle. As I stepped forward, I could see the love, practice, and hard work that had gone into piping all those pink, purple and cream gerbera daisies round the sides to match the bridal bouquet, the buttonholes, and the table centrepieces. But what I imagined had probably been a lovely smooth top looked like it had been attacked by three inebriated imps with imp-sized pneumatic drills.

The middle and top tiers were being held as carefully as if they were made of nitro-glycerine by Mel and Lulu, whose faces were a picture of silent movie anxiety. At any other time it would have been comical. Next to them, however, an exquisitely-dressed woman who had to be the mother of the bride was having what I believe used to be called a fit of the vapours. I could see what had happened.

The round tiers should have been supported by four pillars and dowelling rods, set evenly apart. For some reason only three had been used, and they were far too close to the centre of the base tier to be much support to the middle one. The middle tier had only needed to be placed slightly off-centre for its weight to tip it, pushing the pillars and rods in the other direction. How the top tier hadn't ended up smashed on the floor, I didn't know, somebody – Lulu, to be exact – must have been very quick or just in exactly the right place at the right time. That must have been a first. She'd milk it for months.

'Oh my God, poor Fiona! All her hard work. What will I tell her? She'll be so upset. What are we going to do?' The woman looked from one of us to the other in sheer panic. I thought she was about to cry. 'The one thing she asked me to do and I've ruined everything.'

'I'm sure there's something we can do. The icing and those lovely daisies didn't get damaged.' I tried to sound as reassuring as I could, hoping the flowers on the bit I couldn't see were still alright. 'Mrs ...'

'Mrs Sloan. I'm Fiona's godmother ...'

'Well, Mrs Sloan, leave it to us. We have a lot of experience with this kind of thing. I promise you, it'll be fine. Now, would you like a glass of water?' I looked round to Oliver to ask him to fetch one, but he'd disappeared. Typical – the one time I actually needed him.

'All those months of cake decorating lessons – that was my wedding present to her, you see,' Mrs Sloan explained as I walked round the other side of the cake to inspect the damage. 'Fiona and Craig already live together. They both have good jobs so they have a beautiful home and don't really need anything more to put in it. Their wedding list was full of things like theatre tickets and lunch at that lovely Marco Pierre White's.'

'What a good idea,' I smiled, wishing she would go away. She seemed lovely and genuinely horrified at what she'd done to her goddaughter's cake, but I would be able to concentrate on hiding the damage much better without an audience.

'She did so well with it, too.' Mrs Sloan carried on talking. 'After every class she brought home something beautiful she'd done. Some of them were so lovely it seemed a shame to cut into them.'

'Well, we'll soon have this one back to looking beautiful.' I looked at my watch. 'What time is the ceremony?'

'Oh my goodness, I have to get a move on or I'll be late.' She looked doubtfully at the cake. 'Are you sure?'

'I promise you, Mrs Sloan,' I gave her what I hoped looked like a smile of confidence, 'by the time the bridal party arrive, no one will know anything happened to the cake at all.'

'Thank you so much … er …'

'Polly,' I said, gently shepherding her towards the door, thinking the quicker she went the more time I would have.

'Can you really fix it?' Mel asked once the door had closed.

'Would you two put those cakes down on the bar before you drop them?' That would be the last thing I needed. 'One of you needs to stay with this and make sure nothing else happens to it until I come back.'

'Yeah, but can you fix it?' Mel repeated.

'Of course I can.' I gingerly touched one of the pillars. 'Whether I can fix it in time is another question.

Oliver insisted on helping me carry everything I thought I would need to the ballroom in a couple of carrier bags and one of the hotel's picnic cool boxes he'd found for me. Steve hadn't been happy about me taking up valuable space in his pastry kitchen to make a big batch of royal icing. He'd been even less happy having to give me access to his supply of cake paraphernalia. There hadn't been any pillars that matched the six existing ones on the cake, but that had been an exceedingly long shot. If there'd been more time, I would have been able to cut eight new ones to the size the bride had obviously wanted them to be, but getting them all exactly the same took time and patience and I had a limited supply of both.

Mel was guarding the three tiers when we got back to the ballroom and reluctantly went back to her own duties. I'd decided fixing it in situ was the only option – there would be no more moving this cake until the bride and groom had been photographed cutting into it. Then they could do whatever they wanted with it.

'What can I do to help?' Oliver asked for the umpteenth time. I gritted my teeth and laid out my wedding cake repair kit

'Don't you have your own stuff own to do?' Hopefully he'd remember something vital that needed his attention elsewhere.

'Everything's on schedule,' he shrugged. 'Anyway, the most important part of a wedding reception is the cake – especially if the bride has made it herself, so this gets top priority.' *Blimey*. I couldn't help but be impressed – a straight man who understood the importance of wedding cake. Lucky Jemima. Lucky, lucky Jemima.

Like a surgeon with a trainee scrub nurse by my side, I gently removed the remaining two pillars and rods and put them aside, while Oliver hovered, clearly thinking I might need him. I half expected him to mop my brow, horrified with the thought of him touching me and horrified with myself for wanting him to. *Concentrate, Polly, just concentrate. You can beat yourself up later.* I took a deep breath and tried to block his presence out of my mind. It wasn't easy – his aftershave was subtle but so definitely there, warm and sandalwoody and … *The cake, Polly, concentrate on the cake.*

The very moist fruit cake – the bride had been a little over-generous with the brandy – was easy to squish back into place to fill in the holes. Covering the top with some of the fresh icing, I set to, smoothing it with an angled palette knife.

I worked out where the cake would be firmest, to stick in the four rods I'd brought from the pastry kitchen. There was no time to be timid. With Oliver handing them to me one by one, I plunged them into the cake and followed with the pillars. Now I had to leave the icing to firm up, so I started the same process with the middle tier, which was much easier because apart from a couple of petals which had had their ends snapped off in the collapse, it wasn't actually damaged.

Mel, Lulu, and the others were quietly milling around, attending to their own duties while I was doing this and I was faintly aware of the gentle clink of glassware. Every so often I could feel one of them stop briefly to watch my progress, but they were smart enough not to distract me. When I felt it was time to put the tiers in place, Oliver was patience itself, squatting and looking from all angles to see I wasn't about to place the middle off centre. What strong-looking thighs he had. My hands shook and my mouth was dry but that was down to the cake, it really and truly was. It was a hairy moment when, under Oliver's scrutiny, I actually let go of it, and it took me a moment to be able to step back. When nothing bad happened, I picked up the top tier and put that in place too.

'That's amazing,' Oliver breathed. His smile sent my

pulse racing and I had to look away. 'You've worked your magic again, Polly. No one would ever know what had happened to it.'

'The bride might notice there are four pillars between each tier instead of three,' I said. My voice sounded breathless and I tilted my head and studied the cake to take the attention off myself. 'And she might wonder why the bottom pillars have grown a couple of inches.'

'No way! She'll be too happy to notice,' Mel sighed. 'You've done a brilliant job.'

'She certainly has.' Oliver's voice boomed over my left shoulder while his hand settled on my right. I froze, the fabric of my chef's jacket no protection against his touch. 'Well done, Polly.' He patted my shoulder. 'You've saved the day again.'

'Thank you, but I need to get back to the kitchen,' I mumbled, tearing myself away from him.

Hurry up, Charles Hetherin, I thought as I raced away from the ballroom. I just wanted him to get back. This was all getting a bit too much. I really needed to tell him who I was and get the hell out of there.

# CHAPTER TWELVE

I could feel Oliver's hand on my shoulder for the rest of the day, as if I'd been branded. If this was the turmoil he put me in just by touching my shoulder – and not even my bare shoulder – just imagine the effect he could have on me if ...

I don't know how I got through lunch and dinner service. At least being divided between the wedding reception and the restaurant meant I was too busy to think. Though he didn't help by coming into the kitchen for replacement canapés or to check on things for the sit-down meal. Why did he have to be such a control freak? And why did he have to keep smiling at me like that? And where the hell was Charles Hetherin? He was supposed to be coming back today.

It was late. The bride and groom had departed for their honeymoon and everyone else had left, and the bride's godmother wanted to thank me for sorting out the cake. Oliver came to find me and accompanied me to the empty ballroom as if I might have forgotten where it was.

'Thank you, thank you so much, Polly,' she ever so slightly slurred, clasping my hands between her own well-manicured ones. 'I don't know what would have happened if it weren't for you.'

'It was my pleasure, Mrs Sloan.' If my voice trembled and my smile became a little fixed as Oliver's hand found my shoulder again, she didn't seem to notice.

'I'll be writing to the hotel to tell them how marvellous you were,' she beamed at me, and then at Oliver. Before either of us could reply, her husband appeared at her side, nodded his thanks, and led her away.

There were waiting staff clearing up, but it felt as if Oliver and I were suddenly alone. The sandalwood of his aftershave was subtler, but still there. And his hand was still burning my shoulder through my jacket.

'Fancy a night cap?' he asked, looking at me with a grin. 'I think we've earned one.' He started to steer me towards the bar as Jemima wandered in. I wanted to shrug off his hand before she saw it, but didn't want to draw attention to it.

'Oh, there you are.' She seated herself daintily on a bar stool. 'I hear you were a star with the wedding cake, Polly.' She did the Hetherin eyebrow thing as she grinned at me.

'Er ...' Was I hallucinating? Oliver hadn't moved his hand from my shoulder and Jemima wasn't the slightest bit bothered. In fact, the only person bothered was me – extremely hot and bothered. I perched myself on the stool next to her, taking my hat off and tossing it onto the bar.

'She certainly was.' Oliver finally removed his hand and went behind the bar. 'Now, I know what Jemima likes.' He reached into the chilled cabinet for an open bottle of the house white and a blue bottle of fizzy water. 'What about you, Polly?' He looked me right in the eyes. 'What's your pleasure?'

My mouth was so dry I couldn't speak. My treacherous shoulder was crying out for him to put his hand back on it. I was surprised neither of them could hear it.

'You look exhausted.' Jemima put her hand on my

arm. 'It's been a really long day, hasn't it?'

'Would you rather just go to bed, Polly?' Oliver's face was perfectly innocent as he asked. I had to stop seeing double meanings in everything he said. Especially with Jemima sitting there. What kind of long-lost sister was I?

'Actually, I'm rather tired.' Jemima gave a theatrical yawn and picked up the drink he'd barely finished pouring for her. 'I think I'll take this with me. Goodnight, you two.' And she was gone.

'That sounds like a good idea,' I heard myself squeak. 'I think I'll be heading off too.' I went to stand.

'Don't go, Polly.' He placed two glasses of wine on the counter and came round to my side. 'Have a drink with me. We haven't had a proper chat yet.' Then he sat on the next bar stool. It was too close for comfort, but he didn't move it – he just plonked himself down and smiled.

I couldn't speak. I could just about breathe. He rested one foot on the rung of my stool, right between my own feet. I was so aware – too aware – of his charcoal trouser-clad ankle, just centimetres from my own blue and white checked ones. Almost touching but not quite. He didn't seem to notice.

'Cheers!' He picked up his glass and chinked it against mine. I had no choice but to do the same, but I angled mine so our fingers wouldn't touch – there was only so much temptation a girl could cope with. 'You're a very talented chef, Polly. How come you don't have your own restaurant?'

'I … I …'

'Not that I'm complaining, of course. I know it seems you and I got off on the wrong foot, but it was our lucky day when you wandered in. I really admire you, Polly.' As he sipped his drink I took a gulp of mine, coughing as it hit the back of my throat. That brought tears to my eyes.

'Steady on.' He edged slightly closer, making me anything but steady. 'Don't need to down it all in one.' If he only knew ... 'I was wondering, Polly – have you and Will arranged when your day off is?'

*Oh my God!* My stomach jolted. I could almost feel my blood pressure shooting up like one of those things at the fair that people hit to see how strong they are. Was he asking me out?

'I don't think you should be asking me that.' My voice didn't sound squeaky anymore – just panic-stricken.

'Why not?' He looked confused. 'You don't have a boyfriend, do you?'

'No, but you have a girlfriend.' And I'd gone back to squeaky again.

'No, I don't.' He gave me a slightly puzzled look.

'Yes you do.'

'We're starting to sound like a couple of pantomime characters,' he chuckled. 'I don't know why you think I have a girlfriend, Polly, but I can assure you I don't.'

'What about Jemima?' Had I got the wrong end of the stick? My pulse was starting to do a little dance.

'Jemima? No.' He shook his head, chuckling. 'She doesn't have a girlfriend either. Or a boyfriend, which I imagine is what she'd prefer.'

'But I thought ...' The little dance was turning into a jig.

'Is that why you've been off with me?' There was a definite twinkle in his amber-flecked eyes. 'You weren't jealous, were you?'

'You've got a very high opinion of yourself,' I sniffed, picking up my glass and taking another gulp.

'No, I just know that if I thought you had a boyfriend, I'd be jealous.'

I put my glass down before I dropped it. Then I nearly

jumped a foot in the air as his hand closed itself lightly round mine. The jolt was so powerful, I don't know how the glass didn't shatter. Then his fingers moved ever so gently over the back of my hand and it was as if the rest of the ballroom just faded away.

'So – about this day off of yours,' he murmured. I had to lean a little closer to hear him. I hoped he wasn't waiting for an answer – right then I couldn't have even told him my name. 'I know this lovely place on the way to Brockenhurst. Fabulous food, we could drive over there for lunch or dinner. You'd love it.'

Not trusting myself to speak, I nodded. He was single. He wanted to take me out to dinner. He'd have been jealous if I'd had a boyfriend! Just minutes ago I wouldn't have believed this possible. I watched him refill our glasses. He was gorgeous and so sexy. He had a sense of humour. He worked in the industry, so he understood the time constraints of my job and he was still interested in me. Had I found the perfect man?

'So,' he whispered, handing me my glass even though it was closer to me than him. My fingers brushed over his and slotted into the gaps between them. He kept hold of it far longer than necessary, looking into my eyes. Then he picked up his own glass and held it against mine. 'Cheers.'

'Cheers,' I whispered back, taking a sip then putting my glass down. He followed suit and our fingers found each other's again. Had I moved closer to him? Or had he moved closer to me? His subtle sandalwood scent enveloped me and my stomach did a little flip as his free hand stroked my cheek. I couldn't take my eyes off his lips.

'Polly,' he breathed my name, cupping my face with his free hand. Then he gently pulled me those last few inches closer, his lips brushing against mine, teasing us both with breathless, wine-flavoured kisses until neither of us could take any more.

My arms wound themselves round his neck. I could feel his hands in my hair as we kissed harder, pulling me further into him. A bar stool toppled – I think it was mine. The sound brought us briefly back.

'Not here,' Oliver murmured into my cheek.

I was only half aware of him taking my hand and leading me out of the ballroom. Outside in the darkness, he pulled me to him, our mouths seeking each other's. I couldn't breathe and I didn't care. Somehow, we edged our way back into the main building, my heart beating so hard I thought it might explode. If there was anybody around to see us, I didn't care.

We stumbled through his bedroom door, his hands finding the buttons on my chef's jacket. A gasp escaped me as his fingers brushed my skin, melting my insides. I started undoing his shirt, ruffling the dark hairs on his chest with eager fingertips. He smelled so good.

'Oh God, Polly,' he breathed, his lips on my throat as he peeled my jacket off. A brief flash of panic hit me – which bra was I wearing? Of all the times for this to happen, I was in my chef's whites with my white sensible underwear underneath – and at the end of a long, sweaty day in the kitchen. But he didn't seem to care as he slid my bra straps down, his lips finding my shoulder and working their way down to my breasts, my momentary panic dispersed by the fireworks rocketing through my veins.

We fell onto his bed, me pulling his shirt off, my clogs making a muffled thunk as they hit the carpet, his shoes tumbling to join them. 'I want you so much,' he whispered. 'I've wanted you since the moment I saw you.'

I muffled the sound in my throat, burying my face in his chest, my fingers tracing the hairs which narrowed from his chest to his taut stomach.

While he undid his belt buckle, I pulled my trousers off and stretched out. His duvet was soft. The cover felt luxurious against my skin. Turning my head to watch him, I caught sight of a photograph on his chest of drawers.

'Is that you and Jemima?' I sat up.

'Mm,' he mumbled, turning his attention back to my breasts.

'When was it taken?'

'Mm ...'He was stroking my skin but I batted his hands away. 'What?'

'When was that photo of you and Jemima taken?'

'I don't know, eight years ago, maybe nine – why?'

An icy coldness ran down my back – the closeness between them I'd mistaken for a boyfriend/girlfriend thing.

'Is Jemima your ... your *sister*?' I had to force the word out – they could have been childhood friends, couldn't they? But the chill in my stomach told me I knew the answer already.

'Yes,' he shrugged, unknowingly opening the door to a nightmare. 'I thought you knew.' He went to touch me again.

I leapt off the bed, pulling my straps up and grabbing the rest of my clothes. 'I have to go.'

'What's wrong?' He looked confused.

A wave of nausea washed over me as I picked up my clogs and ran from the room. I couldn't speak. And even if I could, what could I say? How could I tell him the girl he'd been kissing – the girl he'd been undressing on his bed – that girl was probably his sister?

# CHAPTER THIRTEEN

*No, no, no, no, no!* The word ran on a loop inside my head. I stood under the shower head, the water running as hot as my skin could stand it.

Why had I been so convinced that Will was Jemima's brother? Just because he had the same hair colour? There must be millions of people in the world with red hair – they weren't all bloody related. I was stupid, stupid, stupid.

What if I hadn't seen that picture? What if my loved-up brain hadn't made the connection in time? The thought made me want to turn the hot tap higher. Another few moments and he – I couldn't even bring myself to say his name – he and I could have … I wanted to scrub his fingerprints off my skin. But how would I ever scrub the memory of what we'd been about to do from my mind?

The door handle turned a couple of times and then someone banged on the door.

'Hurry up,' a voice whined. 'I'm gonna bust a vessel.'

'Sorry.' I turned the taps off and got out. I'd rather have stayed in there all night. Winding my towel round myself and bundling my dirty clothes together I reluctantly opened the door.

'Freakin' hell, Polly.' A commis chef in boxers and a stained White Stripes T-shirt ran past me. 'What's with the sauna?' He didn't wait for an answer.

Back in my room my mobile was silently ringing, *his*

name on the caller display. I rejected the call and switched it off, squirming at the contact of even touching the phone while he was ringing it.

I dried myself roughly and pulled my pyjamas on. Why couldn't Charles Hetherin have come back today like he was supposed to? What was it with the men in this family – did they just float around on their own little cloud, with no concept of how their actions might affect other people?

My hair hung round my shoulders in soggy clumps. Washed without conditioner, it would be hell to get a comb through. Maybe I should just shave my head. I was just trying to get my fingers through a section of it when footsteps came bounding up the stairs. On a reflex I locked my door and turned the light out. Seconds later, a discreet knock made me jump.

'Polly!' His voice was a stage whisper. He was clearly torn between wanting to speak to me and not wanting the others wondering what he was doing here. I held my breath, hoping the latter want would win out and he'd go away. 'Polly, what's wrong?'

I closed my eyes. Whatever kind of wrong he might be thinking of would be nothing compared to the wrong that had nearly happened.

If I could have disappeared, I would have. But if I left without speaking to Charles, then what had this all been for? I had to wait until he came back, then I would leave. Hopefully I could have some kind of long-distance relationship with my father, and Jemima and I could meet in London or Winchester or wherever. At least I could be certain that once *he* knew who I was, he would be just as desperate to stay away from me as I was to stay away from him.

# CHAPTER FOURTEEN

After a night of much tossing and turning and very little sleep, I called down sick for the breakfast shift and spent the time quietly packing for a quick getaway once I'd spoken to Charles Hetherin, ignoring phone calls and deleting unread text messages from you-know-who. I arrived for the lunch one with a determination to be too busy to speak to anyone, and with my best *don't-mess-with-me* face on for good measure. I deftly avoided *him* on three separate occasions, by which time he looked as if he might be starting to get the message. I'd heard the phrase *time of the month* uttered just within earshot and quite frankly, if that was what was keeping everyone from bothering me, that suited me just fine.

The spa had no bookings that afternoon so I hid out there with Jemima between lunch and dinner, sipping green tea with peppermint, my toes tingling from the tea tree oil foot mask she'd insisted we both apply to our weary feet. Thankfully she didn't ask me anything about last night and I felt a rush of sisterly love for her.

'No wonder your hands look so nice,' I said, peering up at a shelf of aroma-therapeutic massage creams. 'Moisturising people with lotions and potions all day. I bet when you're eighty you'll have the hands of a twenty-something.'

'I hope you won't have the hands of someone who

squelches them around in animal entrails all day,' Jemima chuckled, raising her eyebrow. It looked so cute when my sister did it. I started to wonder how come she'd picked up our father's habit but *he* hadn't, at least not very well, then shook that thought straight out of my head.

'Preparing a box of chicken livers does not count as squelching about in animal entrails!' I tried to sound indignant and missed by a mile. She'd walked into the kitchen on Thursday, seen what I was doing, squealed, and walked straight out again. 'I was only doing it to get to know how all the dishes on the menu are prepared. That's normally a job for a commis chef.'

'Well, pardon me, your royal chefness!' She threw a lavender-scented neck cushion at me which I caught and shoved between my head and shoulder.

'Ah, that's better,' I sighed, wiggling my green gunk-covered toes and reaching for my tea cup.

I'd been far too busy earlier to allow myself to be disappointed that Charles Hetherin's return from Italy had been delayed. Making sure I was as busy as possible to avoid *him* had kept my mind occupied. Charles was now due back later today – I just hoped he was actually going to make it this time.

We were going to do cod Provençal for the dinnertime fish special, so in between tasks I got on and started peeling and deseeding the tomatoes for the sauce. It smelt delicious by the time it was finished and would smell even better after a few hours.

Jemima had wandered into the kitchen when I was just about finishing up and her offer of a cuppa back at the spa was much more appealing than going back to my room to ignore phone calls and pretend I wasn't there. We'd meandered across to her little kingdom, which actually wasn't that little once you got inside – a kind of ylang-

ylang and clary sage scented TARDIS but without the requisite doctor. The relaxing atmosphere had started wafting over me the second I walked through the door; the lavender, lemongrass, and marjoram candle she lit working its magic on my weary limbs and mind. Now, herbal tea in hand, lavender pillow on shoulder, and green gunk on feet, my eyelids wanted to close and treat my eyes to some much-needed sleep.

'Hey!' Jemima's voice put a stop to that. 'Don't zonk out yet. I'm not washing your feet for you. Here.' She passed me a pair of paper socks to put over my feet.

'Spoilsport!' I sat upright, yawning, and took them. 'Don't think these'll catch on.'

'You'd be surprised what kind of people slip them in their bags when they leave, always the ones with the most money. Can't imagine what they do with them.' She stood up gracefully and hauled me to my feet. 'Let's get this washed off. Is there anything decent to eat in the kitchen?'

'Be a pretty rubbish hotel if there wasn't.'

'What was that lovely tomatoey thing you were making earlier?'

'Provençal sauce.' I could see where this was going. She'd lulled me into a matey sense of mellowness and now she wanted a teatime snack, and a healthy teatime snack at that, not even something fun like a chip butty. Sneaky. I was going to have to watch her.

* * *

Ten minutes later, we padded our lovely fresh feet, mine stuffed back into my work clogs, into the empty kitchen.

'I don't want anything with it,' she'd said as she locked up the spa, like she was going out of her way to make things easy for me. 'Just pour a bit in a bowl, like soup.' *I'll give her soup!* I was actually quite enjoying being lightly irritated by my little sister. Not only was it a new and unexpectedly heart-warming experience, it was doing a good job of keeping my mind off other things. Well, mostly.

I was just lifting the big pan off the shelf in the walk-in fridge when I heard Jemima shriek. Heart in my mouth, I let go of the pan, which was more than half way over the edge. Before I had time to realise what I'd done, most of the contents had sloshed themselves down my front.

'Dad!' I heard her cry, 'you frightened the life out of me! I thought you weren't coming back til later.' *Dad? Oh my God!*

'I managed to get things wrapped up a bit quicker. How have things been here? Did the wedding reception go alright?' *Oh my God! It's him. He's here!*

'Everything went really smoothly. Oh, the wedding cake fell apart but Polly managed to put it back together and nobody even knew anything had happened. She was amazing.' *OhmyGodohmyGodohmyGod!*

'Yes, I've been hearing from your brother about this wonderful Polly – a bit of a modern day Mary Poppins I gather.' *What! Why? When?*

'But with much nicer hair,' Jemima informed him. 'Well, usually.' *Cheeky.*

'I'm looking forward to meeting her.' *No! Not right now! Not like this! No!*

'Well, she's just in the fridge; we were going to have a little snack.' I could hear her dainty mules padding towards me. *Go away!* 'Hey, Polly! Come out and meet my dad.' *Please go away, please!* I looked down at myself. It wasn't a pretty sight. Was there anything big enough for me to hide behind? Maybe I could imagine myself smaller and squeeze into the big pan – after all, I'd just tipped about half the sauce out of it.

'Polly?' The fridge door swung open and there, open-mouthed, stood Jemima. And just behind her, was my father.

*  *  *

'Mr Hetherin?' I straightened up and looked for the very first time, at the man my mother had sent me to find. How clean and smart and business-like he looked – not a single auburn hair out of place even after a day of meetings and a long journey home. And how typical I should be covered in olive oil, bits of caper, and tomato sauce. I hoped that wouldn't turn out to be an omen.

'Hello. You must be Polly.' He shook my hand warmly, seemingly oblivious to my wearing the wetter ingredients for cod Provençal down the front of my whites. 'I've been hearing wonderful things about you.

'Thank you.' I just stood there staring at those green eyes that were so like mine only with crinkly lines at the corners. After all the things I'd imagined saying to him, all the speeches I'd practised in my head, that was all I could manage to say? *Thank you*?

'Would you like to come out of there?' he asked with a perfectly straight face, opening the door wider. 'You must be getting a bit cold.'

'Er, yes. Thank you.' Thank you again? I should sack my inner script writer – she was useless.

'The boys tell me you took over the kitchen and kept things running the other day. They're both very impressed with you,' he said, unwinding a huge roll of industrial kitchen paper and handing some to me. 'And Jemima too, and it takes a lot to impress her. Initiative! That's an admirable quality. Welcome to the team, Polly.' He nodded towards me and turned to go. *Speak up! What happened to "What am I, a strong, independent woman or a timid mouse?" Speak up or squeak up and do it now!*

87

*You're already covered in sauce, how much worse could you possibly make it?*

'Er, Mr Hetherin?'

'Yes?' He smiled and for a moment I could feel Mum behind me.

'I wondered if I could talk to you ... about something ...'

'Yes, of course. I've got a conference call shortly but if you'd like to come along to my office at the end of dinner service, bring a pot of coffee and something sweet to go with it and we can have a little chat.' He turned as if to go and then stopped. 'Oh, and Polly,' he raised his eyebrow and I could see a twinkle in his eye, 'I'd put that jacket in to soak if I were you.'

'Yes, yes, I will. Thank you.' And I watched him go. A chat? A chat sounded cosy, like something two ordinary people would do, sitting in comfy armchairs set either side of a toasty fireplace, warming their toes and sipping hot chocolate. And neither of those two people would feel sick with nerves at what they were about to say to the other. Maybe I should have told him it wasn't going to be a chat but one of those life-changing conversations where somebody gets told something that leaves them feeling as if they've been kicked in the stomach.

I went back to the fridge and started clearing up. My soggy front was making it feel even colder than usual. It was a good job I didn't need to concentrate – all I could see in my mind was Charles Hetherin's face as that door opened. How could that moment have turned out to be the very first time my father set eyes on me? Of all the stupid things I could have been doing, hiding in a walk-in fridge looking like an escapee from an explosion in a Heinz factory had to be amongst the stupidest.

# CHAPTER FIFTEEN

I was first in the kitchen for the dinner shift after going to sort out my stained jacket then hiding up in my room going over and over in my head my very first meeting with the man who was going to be my father. He could have turned up when I was saving the wedding cake but no, of course not, that wouldn't have been half as much fun. I did my best to block the memory out, or at least rewrite it a little in my head, then got on with a second, smaller batch of Provençal sauce to add to the remains of the first. It was on its way to being ready by the time Will sauntered in.

'Hello.' He peered over my shoulder. 'Am I having one of those what's-it moments where you see something you've already seen? I could have sworn you made that earlier.' He picked up a teaspoon and dipped it in. 'Hmm, not bad. Would've been better if it had been made early enough to …'

'Give the flavours time to develop – yes, I know,' I jumped in, snatching the spoon from him. 'And yes,' I snapped, 'I did. But it was so much fun I decided to do it again. And it's called *Déjà vu*.' I stirred my pan with determination. I would never have dared speak like that to any other head chef I'd worked with. It amazed me that I'd fallen into thinking of Jemima and Will as family so easily that it had already affected the way I spoke to them. Only Will wasn't family, was he? If only he had been

Jemima's brother rather than …

The other kitchen staff were drifting in. There was a certain amount of knuckle cracking as they switched things on to heat up and sorted out their mise-en-place for service. Mel and Lulu wandered in and out of the still room, fetching the ice-bucket of hot water and probably shovelling as many after dinner mints as they could into their mouths before hauling over the trays of cutlery to be polished. All the while I stirred my sauce and kept an eye on the clock, willing the hands to move quicker.

At the end of dinner service, he'd said – that meant three and half hours to go. I felt queasy and wondered if my hands would shake if I stopped holding the pan with one hand and stirring it with the other. I wasn't about to find out. If anybody wanted me to stop and do something else, they could whistle.

The motion of moving my arm round and round was therapeutic. Probably. I still felt the need to go over in my head what I was going to say to him, as if I hadn't thought out that conversation over and over again since the day Mum gave me that letter. But the dialogue in my head had changed many times since my arrival at the Hall. My anger at and suspicion of Charles Hetherin had been tempered by the things I had learned about him from his family and his staff and, just a little while ago, by his kindness towards a clumsy chef who'd wasted a whole load of delicious ingredients. He was a popular man. I was very glad he hadn't been there when I'd arrived – I might have gone steaming in, full of blame and accusation and that probably wouldn't have ended well.

A trickle of sweat ran down my back as the kitchen got warmer. The sounds and smells of meals being cooked carried on around me. Nobody bothered me. It was as if I were invisible. I vaguely registered Will expediting the orders when they started coming in and, when service was over, the quietening of the kitchen brought my attention back to the clock.

* * *

At precisely one minute past ten, in a clean jacket, I stood outside Charles Hetherin's office door with a tray of coffee and a slice of bitter chocolate and orange liqueur tart from the sweet trolley balanced on my arm. *Take a deep breath.* I put my hand in my pocket and touched Mum's letter. I felt faint and my heart was racing, but if there was any fainting to be done, it might as well be done on his side of the door, so I knocked on it before my brain could talk my hand out of it.

'Come on in,' I heard and I opened the door, feeling how I imagined a Christian would have entering the Coliseum. 'Oh, coffee, lovely,' he smiled and indicated a pair of neat leather armchairs. 'And choc-orange tart – my favourite! Do sit down, Polly. Now, what did you want to talk to me about?' He started to pour the coffee. 'Do you take milk and sugar?'

'Just milk, please,' I said as I sat on the edge of the chair. I could feel my pulse hammering through me and wished I'd brought decaf – a caffeine hit might just finish me off right now. I took a slow, deep breath.

'My mother,' I started. 'I wanted to talk to you about my mother.'

'Your mother?' He handed me my coffee and indicated the tart.

'No thanks.' I'd be sick if I tried to eat anything – I wasn't even sure coffee was a good idea. I looked at him and he smiled, encouraging me to go on. 'Yes. Her name was Rosie Hanson. She grew up in Wintertown. She went to the technical college there in the late eighties. At the weekends and holidays she worked at Netley Magna

91

Country Club, where she met a boy. He was called Charles ...'

'Rosie?' He looked as if he'd just arrived in memory lane and wasn't sure which direction to walk down. 'Rosie? Good Lord! Rosie Hanson! There's a blast from the past. She was a lovely girl. Of course I remember Rosie; she was the very first girl to break my heart.' He gazed out of the window. 'I took her to see that film ... oh, what was it ... *Dirty Dancing*!' The smile on his face was warm. 'So you're Rosie's daughter. My goodness, how wonderful. How is she? Is she in back the area? Does she still like to dance?' The eagerness in his voice made what I had to say all the more painful.

'She ... she died.' I felt my voice break. It was so much harder saying the words to someone who had known her. I blinked back the tears – I didn't want to cry in front of him.

'Oh, my dear, I'm so sorry.' He leant against the edge of the desk. 'Was it recent?'

'A couple of weeks ago,' I croaked.

'I'm very sorry, Polly,' he put his hand on my arm. 'Was it an accident or illness?'

'Cancer,' I whispered, hating even the sound of the word.

'I'm terribly sorry. I hope she didn't suffer.' He sighed. 'And ... and your father? Is he still alive?'

That did it. As the tears spilled over, I hid my face in my hands and sobbed. Mum had wanted me to find my father and here he was, kind and supportive without even knowing.

He slipped a handkerchief into my hand, much as someone had done at the crematorium. This one had been ironed, and smelt of citrus – limes, and I knew that whatever happened, wherever I went, the smell of limes would remind me of this moment, and what I was about to tell this man. I blew my nose and took a sip from the glass of water he handed me. He was being so kind.

'Not long before she died, she wrote me a letter.' I took another sip and a deep breath. 'Mum brought me up on her own. When I was little, she told me my father had died just before I was born. She did her best to be both parents. She worked very hard, sometimes two jobs at a time to make sure I never did without.' I saw him nod as if he understood. 'I never questioned what she told me about my father.' I couldn't help looking at him for some sign he might have guessed what I was going to tell him.

'So he hadn't died?' His expression was one of interest in an old friend, nothing more.

'No.'

'Well, she must have had a good reason for telling you he had.'

'She thought she did. Apparently he came from an important local family. He was a few years older than her and destined for a wonderful business career. She was afraid if his family found out she was pregnant, they would try and make her get rid of me.'

'So she was scared and alone? Poor Rosie.'

'She went to stay with an old family friend in Southampton while she was carrying me – I don't know who. But when I was born she decided to tell my father about me. It was too late for anyone to stop her, and she thought he had the right to know. She didn't want anything from him.'

'What happened?'

'She didn't get to tell him. It turned out he was in Switzerland, doing some hotel management course and by the time he came back, he was engaged to one of her friends.'

'Switzerland?' He looked confused. 'What year was this?'

'Nineteen eighty-eight.' I could see the thoughts whirring through his head.

'I was in Montreux in eighty-eight.'

Time seemed to freeze as we looked at each other. It didn't look like panic on his face, or anger or denial. He looked baffled – genuinely confused. I opened my mouth but no sound came out. Sitting in front of him, knowing for sure he'd had no idea, I couldn't form the words to tell him.

'Polly?' When he finally spoke, his eyebrows were still furrowed. 'Have you come here because your mother's letter said that ... that I'm your father?' The words seemed to be causing him pain and I wished I were somewhere else – anywhere else but here. He didn't want me to be his daughter. He didn't want the scandal. I should never have come.

'Yes.' I could barely hear my own voice.

'Polly ... I'm so sorry, but ...'

I stumbled blindly from my chair and made for the door. I couldn't sit there and hear him say it. Mum had been right, in the first place. She should never have written that letter. Why had she done that? Had the cancer affected her memory?

'Polly!' I heard him call my name as I hurtled along the corridor, out of the building, and towards the staff block. His voice rang in my ears as I grabbed my things, mostly already packed in the Sara's Ladies' Wear carrier bag, snatched up my handbag, and ran to my car.

The rain didn't start falling until I'd almost reached the lay-by where the policeman had pulled me over. By the time I got to Peckham it was torrential.

# CHAPTER SIXTEEN

My flat seemed so cold and dark with the rain lashing at the windows. I put the kettle on and the water heater, thinking a bath would be both warming and soothing. The milk in the fridge had gone off of course and there were no Jaffa Cakes. It was too much effort to go back out in the rain so I settled for hot Ribena.

While I waited for the emersion heater, I took Mum's letter out of my bag. Half of me wanted to tear it to shreds, something the other half of me would never let me do – it was the last thing Mum had ever written to me, and whatever the outcome, I wanted to keep that piece of paper she'd touched and the words she'd put on it. Her face looked out at me from the photo frame on my book case, smiling into the camera on her fortieth birthday. The cake I'd made was in front of her and she was lifting a fork-full to her mouth. She'd been so happy – so healthy. Neither of us had had any idea of what was to come. Next to it was the Easter egg I'd bought her just a couple of weeks ago – she never got the chance to open it and I hadn't been able to bring myself to eat it. I stifled a sob and went to run my bath.

The water had started to get cold when the doorbell rang. I opened my eyes and sighed. It was probably Sheila from the Honor & Oak, wanting to check I'd be in work the next day, though she could have just phoned. The last thing I felt like doing was talking to anyone so I ignored it and ducked my head under the water to rinse off the conditioner I'd put on and forgotten about. When I resurfaced, the bell rang again. *Oh, just go away. Leave me a voicemail and leave me alone.* I ducked under again just to block out the noise, but it didn't work – it just made it sound like the bell was ringing next to my head.

Taking my time getting out of the water, I wrapped myself in a bath sheet and my hair in a small towel. With a bit of luck, she'd have given up and gone by the time I was decent enough to open the door. There was no entry-phone for my flat, so pulling my dressing gown on over my towel and tying the belt firmly, I went to the living room window and looked down to the street door.

I couldn't believe who was standing there, without a coat or an umbrella, his auburn hair plastered to his head like a soggy Red Setter. Charles Hetherin! What was he doing outside my home? How the hell had he found me? Of course! The form I'd half-filled in when I'd started at the Hall. My home address was one of the bits I'd thought would be safe to complete. As he started to turn away, I shrank back from the window in case he looked up and saw me. If I hadn't wanted to stay and listen to his reasons for why I was surplus to requirements in his family, why would he have thought I'd want to hear them here?

'Polly!' He had a commanding voice – it carried over the rain. I stepped back further. 'Polly, I know you're there, I walked past your car.' *So? That doesn't mean anything. I could have parked it and gone to a friend's place.* 'Polly, I saw the curtain move. Come down and open the door. We need to talk and I'm not going away until we have. So the quicker you open this door, the quicker I can leave you in peace.'

I peeped carefully out of the very edge of the window

and there he was, looking right at me. He raised his hand to acknowledge that he'd seen me. Why hadn't I just stayed in the bath? There was no choice now but to go down.

I left him in the kitchen with a hand towel while I went to put some clothes on. When I came back, he'd boiled the kettle.

'The milk's off ...' we both said at exactly the same time.

'I could go out and get some,' he offered.

'I was making do with hot Ribena. It's nicer than it sounds.'

'Alright, hot Ribena it is.' His smile was like that of an uncle trying to keep a small niece happy by taking part in her dollies' tea party. The kitchen felt even smaller than usual and he seemed to take up so much of it. I stirred the drinks and carried them through to the living room. At least we could both sit down in there. He noticed the photo of Mum and picked it up. His back was towards me so I couldn't see the expression on his face as he looked at her.

'Polly.' He turned round while I was still fumbling with my mug. 'Please sit down. We need to talk about this.'

'You mean you need to make me understand how inconvenient I am?' I knew I sounded like a stroppy teenager, but if he wasn't going to be my father he couldn't tell me off, could he?

'That's not what I ...'

'You don't need to worry. I won't cause a scandal for the Hetherin family. You didn't need to come all this way to make sure I'll keep quiet. I'm sure you can come up with a convincing reason to give everyone for why I had to leave in such a hurry. I'll stay away and no one will ever know. Mum didn't want anything from you and neither do I!'

'Polly, you've got this wrong. That isn't why I'm here.' He leaned forward and looked at me with something like sadness. 'Look, Polly, I haven't had a chance to get to know you, but from what Jemima and Oliver have told me and from hearing you talk about your mother, I rather think I would have liked to have been your father.'

'I don't understand.'

'The thing is, when I said your mother was the first girl to break my heart, I didn't mean she disappeared without a word and I never saw her again. I meant that while she was working at the country club, she went off with someone else.'

'She wouldn't have done that. She wasn't that sort of ...'

'I know. I wouldn't have believed it myself if I hadn't seen them together.'

'You must have been mistaken.'

'I hoped I was. His name was Martin. All the girls fancied him and he had developed a bit of a reputation, which was why I was so surprised to see Rosie with him.'

'What sort of reputation?' I knew I wasn't going to like the answer.

'He was a love-em and leave-em type.'

'And you think he and Mum ...' I couldn't bear the thought of someone treating my mother like that.

'I'm sorry, Polly. The thing is ... Rosie and I ... well, it was the eighties ... AIDS was big news. People were very careful about ... that sort of thing. We always used protection.' The poor man sounded as uncomfortable saying it as I felt hearing it. Every generation probably believes they invented sex. No one wants to think their parents ever did *that sort of thing*. 'There was just one time,' he was looking deep into his mug, 'I remembered while I was driving up. We had one accident – a condom split. Which means,' I could see him forcing himself to look me in the eye again, 'although there's a tiny chance I might be your father, there's also a chance I'm not.'

I didn't know what to say. This wasn't a conversation I'd ever envisaged having.

'But this ... what did you say his name was?'

'Martin.'

'Surely he would have taken the same precautions as you? I mean, Mum wasn't stupid, she'd never have taken risks like that.'

'No, I'm sure she wouldn't have. And I hope he would have been careful too. But he was very charming, one of those lads who could talk girls into ... I don't know, Polly. I really don't know.'

'I was going to show you Mum's letter.' I hesitated. 'If you wanted to read it. I thought it might be helpful for you to see it in her words.'

'That's a good idea,' he nodded. I handed it to him and went into the kitchen while he read it. I don't know why I did that – it wasn't as if I didn't know what he was reading word for word.

When I came back out, we sat there looking at each other, our drinks going cold. Neither of us seemed to know what to say.

'So what do we do now?' It sounded like a stupid question, but it was going round and round in my head until it just spilled out.

'Would you ... what do think about ... we could do one of those DNA, paternity tests?' He looked surprised, as if he hadn't expected to hear himself say that.

'A DNA test?'

'I believe they are quite accurate, if what they do on television is anything to go by. I could look into it. If that was something you wanted to do.'

'What do you think?'

'I think that if you are my daughter, I'd like to know.'

'I think I'd like to know too.'

'And if it turns out you're not?'

'Then I'll be no worse off than I am now.'

\* \* \*

After he left I sat in the gathering darkness, mulling over everything we'd said. It was like going over a scene from a soap in my head, and after a while I started to wonder if I was remembering things as we'd said them or if my mind was adding embellishments. One of the most important conversations of my life and it had started to take on a life of its own.

He'd offered to take me out to get something to eat before he left, or to order a takeaway for me. I'd said no thanks, that apart from the milk situation I had plenty of things I could make a meal out of. The truth was, I was far too churned up inside to eat. A DNA test! While my tablet got its act together I wondered what a test would entail. A prick of blood from my thumb? One of those long, cotton bud-swabby things poked around inside my mouth? A hair pulled out of my head? My only knowledge of DNA tests was what I'd seen on *Silent Witness*.

There were so many adverts for companies selling testing kits, I didn't know where to start. The first site I looked at said the most accurate results needed samples to be taken from mother, father, and child, but that a motherless test could be taken. What did that mean? How much less accurate would that be? I still had Mum's dressing table set, with her hairbrush, comb, and mirror. I hadn't been able to bring myself to get rid of them – I'd played with them as a little girl. Would a hair from the brush work? They use that sort of thing on TV. I kept on scrolling through website after website, but the more I read the less I understood.

If the test result was positive and Charles Hetherin really was my father, then I suddenly had a whole family – a kind and clever Dad, a funny and beautiful sister, a dotty kleptomaniac grandma, and a sweet old granddad who had to watch his salt intake – and that was before we even got started on the stepmother, the aunts, and uncles, and the cousins. There was also the brother I could never ever look in the eye ...

And then the tiny thought that had started out tip-toeing around in the back of my mind, so quietly I hadn't even noticed it, eventually elbowed its way forward, shoving and leap-frogging its inappropriate way to the front. If the test result was negative and he turned out not to be my father, what would that mean? Not just that Charles Hetherin wasn't my father, but that Oliver Hetherin wasn't my brother. And if Oliver wasn't my brother, he and I hadn't been about to commit ...

As silver linings went, it was a pretty mind-blowing one.

# CHAPTER SEVENTEEN

*Polly, I want you to know that whatever the result, you have a job with us at Hetherin Hall for as long as you want it.*

Those words replayed themselves round and round in my head as I drove back down to Hampshire a week and a half later. It had felt like forever, working my notice at the Honor & Oak and trying not to think about what my future might or might not hold. Thank goodness the menu there required so little actual attention that it didn't really matter that my mind was hundreds of miles away.

Deep down in my heart, I knew what the DNA result would be and so too, I believed, did Charles. And I was sure he wanted those results to confirm what my mother had already told us. There was no way Mum would have written that letter, telling me Charles was my father, if there had been any possibility that he wasn't.

The drive through Surrey to Hampshire had a sunnier, more positive feeling to it this time. However, every time I let my guard down, a cloud would descend, casting its sandalwood-scented shadow over everything. The first time I'd done this journey, I'd been angry and alone and more than ready to thumb my nose at the man who'd abandoned us. This time, he and I were in a kind of shared quest, the results of which had the power to change our lives – not just mine and his, but the entire Hetherin clan. Although I didn't want to think about Oliver, I felt desperately sorry for what a positive result would mean to him. Nothing about this was his fault. As far as he was concerned, he'd had the hots for a female member of staff and she'd reciprocated. Then, just when they were getting to the juicy bit, she'd had some kind of meltdown and run off with no explanation and had gone on to successfully evade every attempt to find out what had gone wrong. I hoped that when he found out what it was, he had a stronger stomach than I did. We could avoid each other around the hall, but any kind of family gathering would be a bit of a minefield.

I turned my attention back to the road. The flowers in the hedgerows looked even brighter and prettier than they had last time. I couldn't help smiling as I passed the place where I'd opened the window and copped a pungent lungful – I wasn't going to make that mistake again. Then there was the picnic lay-by where the policeman had pulled me over. The daffs were still there, but sharing their space with other flowers now, primroses and bluebells and some little stripy ones I didn't know the name of. A group of half a dozen motorbikes and mopeds were parked there, some of their riders laughing and joking with each other while others nipped through the hole in the hedgerow to relieve themselves. I remembered the two cheeky little boys with ice-cream on their faces. Not far to go.

The Coopers were hard at work on the forecourt of their garage when I passed. One of them was flat out under one car with his grey overall-covered legs and battered trainers sticking out. The other was bent double with his head buried in the engine of another, looking like a pair of grey overalls from the waist down with a pair of comfortable old moccasins at the end. It was only their footwear that gave me an idea of which was which and even then, I could have been wrong.

As I turned into the driveway to Hetherin Hall, there was an unexpected feeling of coming home, which half of me scoffed at while the other half argued that it wasn't ridiculous at all and that when it turned out that I was in fact a Hetherin, this would actually be my home. In either case, Charles had offered me a permanent, full-time position as sous chef, so Hetherin or not, this would technically be where I lived. I'd given a month's notice on my flat, and while my car was packed full of clothes, Mum's cheese plant, and other essentials, I would have to drive back on my next couple of days off to empty it out and bring the rest of my things before handing back the keys to the landlord. I couldn't imagine how I'd accumulated so much stuff in the few years I'd been living there, but I suppose I did buy more kitchen paraphernalia than your average single woman. Thank goodness I had rented it furnished – at least I didn't have to worry about storing or disposing of furniture.

Charles' Mercedes was next to Jemima's sporty little number and I parked in the space next to her car. I wondered what she would say when she saw me. And Will, the most laid-back head chef ever – what was he going to say to his vanishing sous chef? I expected a scowl from Oliver, or to be completely ignored, which was fine by me. If we were going to have to co-exist as brother and sister, it might be easier if we ignored each other. Charles and I had talked the subject to death – apart from the Oliver episode which, if the test proved positive he could never find out about – and decided that until we ourselves knew the results of the DNA test, all anybody else needed to know was that I'd had to go back to London to work my notice at my old job and now I was back.

The reception desk was manned by a woman I hadn't seen before but who seemed familiar. She looked to be in her mid to late forties, was immaculately made up, and had the kind of hair which looked like each strand had been individually highlighted, low-lighted, and commanded as to which direction it needed to go in. She wore what looked to be designer clothes and not the sort you got in the Designers at the Debenhams sale. She must have been from a very posh agency – Snooty Temps 'R' US perhaps? Stuck Up Staff 4 U? I stifled the urge to giggle. Anyway, she looked far too la-di-dah to be a receptionist, even in a place like Hetherin Hall. I had been going to go straight through to Charles' office, but she had a territorial look about her that made me feel the need to explain myself.

'Good afternoon.' She looked me up and down so subtly I was only just sure I wasn't imagining it, and she clearly found me wanting.

'Oh, good afternoon,' I replied, wishing Jemima had been standing in like she had when I'd first come here. She was much more welcoming. I hoped she wasn't new permanent staff. 'I wanted to speak to Charles ...'

'*Mr Hetherin* is busy at the moment.' She looked like she wanted to tell me off for being cheeky and I almost felt as if I should apologise. 'Do you have an appointment?'

I was about to say no when I realised what I actually *did* have was an open-ended appointment to see Charles whenever I wanted, for which I certainly didn't need this woman's approval. 'He's expecting me,' I said as forcefully as I could while not wanting to sound rude, and started making my way towards his office.

'Just a minute...' she started as Jemima came round

the corner and rushed up and hugged me.

'Polly! I'm so glad you're back! I couldn't believe it when you disappeared. Mum!' She looked at the woman at the desk. *Mum?* 'This is Polly. Remember, I told you about her?'

*Did she just say Mum? This was Polly and Oliver's mother?* That must have been why there was something familiar about her. I didn't hear what she said to Jemima, I was too busy trying to come to terms with the fact that I might have just met my wicked stepmother. Charles hadn't said anything about her being here. She was going to hate me. Scratch that, she already did. I could see it in her eyes. She was busy thinking what a common, bad-mannered, unsuitable friend I was for her daughter. I wondered what she'd think if she had to be told I was actually her daughter's step-sister. She'd probably have kittens and not the cute and fluffy kind.

Jemima walked with me to Charles' office, chattering away about goodness knew what. I was just glad to get away from her scary mother.

'Polly! Hello, Jem.' Charles stood up from his desk and came forward. He kissed Jemima on the forehead, turned to me, and then stopped in his tracks, obviously realising just in time that he couldn't do the same to me. He stood there a moment looking awkward and my urge to giggle had to be re-stifled. 'So, how are you? Good trip down?'

'Yes, fine thanks.' I could feel one of those terribly British conversations about the weather coming on, which might have been too much for my inner giggle box, especially when all I really wanted to know was about the battle-axe stepmother in Reception.

'Good weather for moving,' he smiled. 'I've told Will to expect you in the kitchen for dinner service tonight. Is that alright?'

'Yes, that's fine, thanks.' I wondered if Jemima thought it odd that he was being so flexible with me, but she just looked genuinely happy that I was back. I felt a rush of fondness for her and hoped she would be as happy to be told that we were sisters.

'Do you need a hand unloading your car, Polly? I can call one of the boys.' His hand was already on the phone.

'No thanks,' I jumped in quickly. I'd worked with enough commis chefs in my time to not want any of them having access to my bags and thinking it would be funny to walk into the kitchen tonight wearing my knickers on their heads. 'I'll just drive round the back and offload. It's all light stuff. I really don't need any help.' My mum's cheese plant was probably the heaviest thing I'd brought on this trip and I wasn't entrusting that to anyone but myself.

Jemima met me at the entrance to the staff block and I was amused to see that although she genuinely wanted to help, she picked up the lightest-looking bags to carry upstairs. I left the cheese plant until last, as things had been packed in around it to keep it from moving about on the journey. I was just edging it out of the boot when a slight scent of sandalwood wafted around me and the aforementioned shadow fell across my shoulder. My stomach both flipped and turned, even before the hands reached in to help me. They were strong-looking hands and were attached to strong-looking forearms with thick dark hairs on them and cornflower blue shirt sleeves rolled up to the elbows. *Go away, please, just go away ...*

'It's alright, thanks. I've got it.' I was aiming for friendly but firm and missed by several miles. My voice sounded shrill even to my own ears.

'Don't be silly.' Oliver sounded pedantic. 'It's heavy.'

'Well, I managed to get it down the stairs and into the car all by my weak little self,' I snapped, tightening my grip on the plant pot.

'And this time you'll be carrying it *up* the stairs,' he moved his hands round to stake his claim on it.

'Thank you, Professor Know It All,' I tugged the pot towards me. 'I'm fully aware of how stairs work.' I knew I sounded childish but I couldn't help myself.

'I don't know why you insist on seeing a simple offer of assistance as a personal slight.' He pulled the pot back towards him and started to lift it out of the boot. 'Or maybe you're just afraid of being forced into an awkward conversation.'

'I don't see it as a slight,' I scowled, moving my hands further round the pot and pulling it back. 'I see it as a complete unnecesser ... unnecessary ... un ... oh, you know what I mean. I don't need your help and I don't want to have a conversation with you, awkward or otherwise!' He still wasn't backing off and it was infuriating. I actually wanted to slap him but I had my hands full right then.

'Just let me carry the damn thing!' He moved his hands round and as they touched mine a jolt of electricity made me let go. Everything seemed to go into slow motion as my beloved cheese plant plummeted towards the ground, my hands not quick enough to catch it before the pot hit the edge of the boot and tumbled, hitting the gravel with a crunching crash.

'Oh no!' Jemima poked her head out of the door. 'Your lovely plant.'

'Yes,' I hissed, glaring at Oliver. 'My *mother's* lovely plant.'

# CHAPTER EIGHTEEN

'Order!' I called, feeling as if I'd never been away from this particular spot in this particular kitchen. 'Starters: two soup of the day, one mushroom tartlet, one chicken livers on toast. Mains: one Nelson's pie, one cod and chips, two spring lamb. Table one.'

'Happy to be back?' Will grinned at me from the other side of the pass. He was more than happy for me to have come back that day as it meant he could have the evening off to go into Winchester for a friend's birthday drinks.

'Happy to be back, Chef!' I saluted him with a soup ladle.

'Just try not to throw everything all over the floor.'

'How about I settle for not letting any of the commis chop their fingers off?' I ducked as he pretended to throw a peppermill at me. 'Watch it,' I teased. 'That counts as harassment in the workplace with a pepper grinder – very serious offence that is!'

'See you at breakfast,' he chuckled, and disappeared through the restaurant door.

'Order!' I called again as Mel deposited an order slip in front of me. 'Starters: two potted prawns, one trout, one crab salad, and one mushroom tartlet. Mains: two cod and chips, two spring lamb, and one shepherdess pie – that's for a vegan so strictly no cheese topping, not even the vegetarian stuff. Tables seven and eight combined.'

'Well?' she said, looking exasperated. Mel and Lulu

had been desperate for gossip as to why I'd disappeared for the best part of a fortnight and suddenly come back. I'd tried telling them to mind their own business but that hadn't worked. I'd tried telling them a work-related variation of the truth but that had apparently been too mundane. Now I'd taken to telling them ridiculous tales; at least while they were working out whether these were true or not, they were quietly getting on with their work.

'Look,' I whispered, doing my best to look shifty, 'I had to go and give evidence in a court case. But it's all hush-hush, there are people under witness protection whose lives could be in danger if you start blabbing about it.'

'Really?' Her eyes were huge and I could tell this was more the sort of thing she'd been hoping to hear. I didn't think she'd ever been to London, but I imagined she would be very disappointed when she finally did. She seemed to have the impression that there were gangsters round every corner and that the Queen actually hung her washing out in the grounds of Buckingham Palace.

'Away! This is one of yours,' I looked at Mel, 'so don't go disappearing. One watercress soup, one soup of the day, and one trout for table five. Service!'

As Mel trotted out to the restaurant with her starters, Lulu slunk into the kitchen. I could see she didn't have an order slip and that she was torn between coming to me for a bit of gossip or heading to the still room for an Elizabeth Shaw chocolate mint fix. We really needed to find a better place to store the after dinner mints – that girl wasn't going to have any teeth left by the time she was thirty. I made her decision for her. 'Any volunteers to give the hors d'oeuvres trolley a bit of a once over?' She shot into the restaurant as if the kitchen were on fire.

* * *

112

We were wiping down the kitchen at the end of service when Jemima came in. I hadn't seen her since she'd helped me gather up Mum's poor cheese plant and then brought me a pot she must have evicted some other innocent plant from for me to put it in.

'And what can I heat up for you?' I asked.

'Anyone would think I only come here when I want food.' She did her best to look indignant but we both ended up laughing.

'Well, that is kind of the point of a kitchen. Can I tempt you with some delicious twice-cooked, hand cut chips?' I laughed as she shuddered at the thought of eating anything fried. 'What about some fish pie? There's one portion left, we could share it. Go on,' I teased. 'You know you want to.'

'Could I just have some of the fish part without the mashed potato?'

'Luckily for you, the mashed potato is my favourite bit. How about I heat it up and get two forks, then we can dig in?'

'Mm, that sounds great. Is there any green salad left?' She followed my eyes to the fridge and came back with a bowl of cucumber, watercress, and lettuce. I was seriously going to have to take that girl in hand – she was far too health-conscious for her own good.

'So,' I started as innocently as I could while we shared our supper at the desk in Will's office. 'I didn't realise your mother worked here.'

'Mum? God, no!' Jemima snorted with laughter. 'She turns up every now and then and pootles around for a while in Reception. Or my spa if I can't get rid of her.' Jemima rolled her eyes. 'Don't get me wrong, I love her to bits but she completely rearranged everything in there once and I couldn't find anything for a month. She soon gets bored and goes off again. She doesn't like to be tied to one place. Dad ...' She tailed off as the door opened and Oliver came in. He'd clearly been avoiding me since his display of testosterone-fuelled man-handling had nearly destroyed my beloved cheese plant, and he'd managed to keep out of the kitchen for almost the whole of dinner service. It was almost worth it to have been left in peace for most of the evening.

'Oh.' He looked almost wary when he saw me. 'I thought Will might be back.'

'You're joking, aren't you?' Jemima put her fork down daintily and patted her mouth with a napkin. 'The first evening he's had off in almost a month? They'll be at the Slug and Lettuce until throwing out time and then they'll go back to the birthday boy's house. Will won't be back this side of breakfast and if he is, he won't be in any fit state to even smell it being cooked let alone serve it.'

This was the first I'd heard about being left in charge for breakfast service. I didn't mind – it wasn't exactly taxing, watching over a kitchen of chefs while they cooked breakfast for fifty or so guests. But the fresh fish deliveries usually coincided with breakfast service, and quick decisions had to be made about what to take for the lunch and dinner specials. This was definitely Will's territory. I hadn't taken charge of that here yet and would have liked a bit of warning. I didn't know what the budget allowed for, and didn't want the delivery man trying to pull a fast one when he saw me rather than Will. Would it look too pathetic if I asked Charles to be there – it was his hotel, after all. Yes, I decided. It would look completely pathetic and not at all Hetherin-like.

'If you're worried about the fish delivery, I could take charge of that. I know you haven't had a chance to do it yet.' As if he had read my mind, Oliver stuck his very

114

unwelcome oar in. I wanted to snap it in half and whack him over the head with it. That would put an end to any more mind-reading shenanigans from him.

'I don't know what makes you assume I'm not capable of dealing with a simple delivery.' I put on my most confident voice. The cheek, assuming I didn't know what I was doing. This was the man who, as a professional restaurant manager, had hired a sous chef to work as a silver service waitress. Yes, I thought, I could manage perfectly well without his help. He'd probably drop them all over the floor. Alright, so that was a bit pot, kettle, black coming from me, but I'd never damaged anything that was of great sentimental value to anyone – at least not that I knew of.

'I wasn't assuming anything, Polly,' he sighed and I was disgusted with my stomach for doing another of those flips at the way my name sounded when he said it. That couldn't keep happening. That absolutely and definitely could not keep happening. 'I was just trying to be helpful. Although after this afternoon, I really don't know why I bothered. You don't need anybody's help. You clearly don't need anything from anyone.' And with that, he turned and marched back out into the restaurant. Now it was my turn to sigh. *That's right, little brother – let's just keep annoying each other as much as possible. Let's irritate each other so much that we spend as little time in each other's company as we can. That way we'll all be happier.*

# CHAPTER NINETEEN

Of all the mornings for me to oversleep, the one when Will wasn't going to be around was probably the worst. And how annoying that Oliver was in the kitchen, looking like he was sucking on a lemon, when I rushed in half an hour late with my hair escaping in all directions from my hurriedly pulled on skull cap. At least he had the sense not to say anything before turning and taking his sour face back out to the restaurant. He'd be curdling the milk and putting the guests off their breakfasts if he wasn't careful.

I did the rounds of each section quickly; everyone was fine and getting on with their prep. I was just thinking I would grab a quick cup of coffee when the fish man arrived at the back door looking for Will. I assumed what I hoped was my most professional expression and went to speak to him.

'Hung-over, is he?' The man seemed to know what was what before I'd managed to get a word in edgeways. 'Thought as much.'

'I'm the sous chef,' I was determined to tell him something he didn't think he knew. 'I'm in charge this morning.'

'Oh, I've heard all about you.' He smiled as if he expected me to think that was a good thing. 'Dab hand with a wedding cake, so I hear.'

'Thank you.' Maybe he wasn't so annoying after all.

'Bit clumsy with everything else, though. Heard you

had a smashing time on your first night.' He guffawed until he was red in the face, which didn't take long.

'We've already had that joke, thank you,' I sighed. Then, determined to get the order sorted and get rid of him, I carried on, 'Now about the order for today …'

'Oh, don't you worry yourself about that. All sorted.' He tapped the side of his nose in a way that made me want to shut the door and tell him we didn't want anything today thank you.

'Why don't you unload the regular order while I take a look at what else you've got?' I suggested, hoping he'd leave me to look in peace. Fat chance.

'I've got some lovely fresh sardines for you,' he winked. Much more of that and I wouldn't be able to stop myself slapping him with a kipper.

'I prefer to look for myself, thank you,' I said as firmly as I could.

'Well, that's up to you of course, but Will …'

'William isn't here this morning,' I said, sounding like Grandma H, 'but I am, and I'll be in charge of today's order.' Really, did nobody here have any faith in my abilities to do anything other than float about with a piping bag saving wedding cakes? My eyes fell on some lovely looking salmon and my brain started conjuring up possibilities for the lunchtime special. 'Is that salmon wild or farmed?' That would show him I knew what I was doing. He'd probably expected my first question to be how much it cost.

'Lovely bit of salmon that, but these sardines …'

'I want to know about the salmon, please.'

\* \* \*

I was exhausted by the time he left. We'd haggled as if we were in some Middle Eastern souk and I was reasonably happy with the price I'd got the salmon for. Now to

118

prepare it for what I had in mind. Checking everyone else was alright and that the chef who was on the pass for this service was expediting the orders properly, I got a commis to start scaling them so I could get on with my own prep.

Salmon three ways was the dish I wanted to put together. I cut and weighed a tray of small fillets to be griddled and served with crispy skins, making sure each one was the same size and dropping the little trimmings into a large bowl for the fishcake component of the dish. Then I made a start on cutting and rolling the pieces for the ballotines in cling film, to be poached and topped with a coffee spoon-sized quenelle of dill butter. Every other scrap of fish went into the bowl for the fishcakes. I loved this part of my job – putting dishes together, matching up flavours, and getting the most out of beautiful ingredients – something I'd missed even more than I had realised at my last kitchen. By the time breakfast service was over and the chefs were getting the staff breakfasts out, my fillets and ballotines and herb butter were sitting in the fridge and I was cooling the mashed potato ready to mix with the trimmings.

At this point, Oliver came in and I caught him trying to have a furtive look at what I was doing. It was a good job he hadn't wanted to be a spy – he'd be rubbish at it. When he realised I'd seen him he gave me a quizzical look, but at least he didn't start questioning me or I might have tipped the bowl over his head.

Jemima wandered in shortly after that. She helped herself to a glass of freshly-squeezed pineapple juice and came straight over.

'Fish pie?' She took a sip of juice. She really didn't have the cooking gene – we didn't put salmon in the fish pie.

'Salmon fishcakes.' I rolled my eyes at her. 'One day you'll make some poor man a terrible wife!'

'Just because I don't spend my days messing about with dead animal bits doesn't mean I'll make a terrible wife.' She picked up a pinch from the little bowl of fresh dill the commis had chopped for me and sniffed it. 'Mm, anyway, who says the woman has to be the one doing the cooking? When I get married it'll be to someone who's happy to share the chores.'

'Good for you.' I nearly added *little sis,* but just in time I stopped the words that had so easily nearly slipped out of my mouth. It would be a relief when we had the DNA results and Charles and I could either tell the rest of the family who I was or ... well, that was the only way it could turn out, really. The other option just wasn't possible.

'Penny for them?' Jemima's voice interrupted my train of thought.

'Sorry. I was just drifting.' I gave her a smile that hopefully said *'we're getting to be good friends'* and not *'hey! I'm your big sister; you just don't know it yet.'* 'Could you grab me a glass of juice, please? I'll just finish this then I'll come out and have something to eat.'

She was tucking into her usual bowl of colourful fresh fruit salad when I plonked myself next to her with my hastily grabbed bacon roll. She did her usual thing of looking at it with comic disgust. Oliver was doing something at his manager's desk and I hoped he had already finished his breakfast. His was the last face I wanted to look at while I was eating.

\* \* \*

We were well into lunchtime service by the time Will surfaced, looking a little green around the gills. He made himself a cup of builders' tea and – seeming perfectly content that cheffy things were going on as normal and nothing was on fire – wandered into his office.

'Away!' I called. 'Mains: one spring lamb and two fish of the day for table seven.' I watched one of the snooty boy waiters pick them up as Oliver came in. He nipped round the pass and into Will's office.

Most of the tables were on their desserts or cheese selections by now, and we only had one more main course order to go out, which would use the last two portions of my salmon special. I was overly pleased it had been so popular, but had hoped Will might see one plated up before they all disappeared. It looked like I was going to get my wish, as I saw him and Oliver come out of the office and walk towards the pass. When they reached me, I hoped Oliver would keep on walking. He didn't.

'How's it been today?' Will asked.

'Good, thanks.' I glanced around to make sure nobody was doing anything they shouldn't be. 'We didn't do many soup of the day, but the fish specials have completely sold out.'

'There's still one order to go out, isn't there, Polly?' There Oliver went saying my name again. It was a name he wasn't going to be able to bear the sound of once he knew.

'Yes, that's right. It'll be ready in a couple of minutes.' As I wondered why Oliver seemed as keen as I was for Will to see what I'd done, snooty boy waiter came back in, in anticipation of his final mains order. A couple of minutes seemed to take their time to go by. 'Did you have a good time last night?'

'Yeah, great, thanks.' Will had the grace to look just a little sheepish.

'The Slug and Lettuce, wasn't it?'

'And the rest,' Oliver teased.

'Jealous, much?' Will shot back at him, grinning like an idiot.

'No squabbling on my pass, boys.' I checked the clock and the chefs behind me. 'Away! Last mains order. One Nelson's pie, one cod and chips, and two fish of the day for table five.' The dishes appeared on the pass and I was delighted to see everything plated up as precisely on this last order as they had been on the first. I wouldn't have expected anything less, but as I was eager for Will's approval it would have been typical for something to have been amiss.

Snooty boy waiter scooped up all four plates with a practised hand and whisked them away. I waited for Will to say something.

'So,' Oliver spoke instead. 'Tell us about the fish of the day, Polly.' Argh! Why wouldn't he go away? *Stop calling me Polly, stop interfering in the kitchen, and just bloody well go away.*

'Salmon three ways,' I said, directing my words towards Will and my coldest shoulder towards Oliver. 'Griddled salmon fillet with crispy skin, poached ballotine of salmon with dill butter, and salmon fishcake with tartare sauce, served with steamed new potatoes and asparagus.' I waited for my head chef to pass judgement, certain in the knowledge that I'd done the pricing correctly, every dish had sold, they had looked good going out, and all the plates that I'd had time to notice had come back empty.

'Sounds good.' Will nodded and a little cheer went off inside my head. 'The ones I saw looked and smelled good too.' *Yes! He liked it!*

'Thanks.' I couldn't stop a smile quivering around the corners of my mouth.

'Just one little thing though.'

'What's that?'

'Yeah, Will,' Oliver chimed in like a really annoying clock. 'What's that?'

'Well, the thing is,' Will cocked his head slightly, 'what the hell happened to the sardines I'd asked for?'

# CHAPTER TWENTY

The DNA testing kit arrived a few days later. Charles and I wanted to be able to read through the info that came with it, even though he, at least, must have known it all off by heart by then. Frankly, the more I tried to understand the ins and outs of how it worked, the more confused I became. It would have been much quicker and easier to have had it done privately by his doctor, but I understood his reluctance to involve any third parties. A postal test, using just my surname would be much safer.

Miranda, my soon-to-be wicked stepmother, had been on Reception when the post arrived, and had been consumed with curiosity about why I was receiving suspicious-looking packages at the hall. She had no qualms about interrogating me as to what was in it, as if she suspected I was some kind of drug dealer or into fencing stolen goods. I was half expecting her to demand I open it in front of her. If she'd seen me take the package to Charles' office and heard him lock the door after I'd gone inside, I think her head might have spun round on her neck then exploded.

The package contained three colour-coded envelopes, each with two of those cotton bud-type swabs, correspondingly colour-coded. There were instructions on how to perform the sample collection, consent forms for us to fill in, and a pre-addressed envelope to send the samples in. So far, so good. Whilst Charles read through the instructions, I looked through the consent forms. Although I basically knew what it meant, the words looked a bit daunting staring at me from their very black and white pages.

'Are you alright?' Charles put the instructions down and looked at me. 'We can always leave it for a few days if you don't feel ready yet.'

'No, I'm fine,' I smiled back at him. 'It just seems so formal when you have to start signing things.'

'We're doing the right thing, you know.' He sounded fatherly and wise, and that made me smile.

'I know.' I took a deep breath and looked at him. 'OK. Ready when you are.' I said, not moving.

'Do you want me to go first?'

I nodded. It was silly to be so apprehensive. Everything I'd read had stated that collecting the samples didn't hurt – not even when it was done to babies. And the outcome wasn't anything to be scared of. Well, certain aspects were, but there was nothing that could be done about that.

Charles took two clean whiskey tumblers from the drinks tray on the side table and placed them on his desk, then he opened up one of the envelopes and took out both swabs. He rubbed the first then the second around the inside of his cheek and under his tongue for what seemed like ages. It always looked much quicker on TV. Then he carefully placed them upright in one of the glasses, which he moved to one end of his desk. 'There you are,' he smiled, 'nothing to it.' He held out the other to me as if it were a bag of sweets. 'You did remember not to have anything to eat or drink for at least an hour, didn't you?'

'Are you kidding?' I didn't know about him, but I couldn't swallow a thing since I'd woken up, thinking today was more than likely going to be *the day*.

'Just checking.'

OK,' I breathed, taking and opening it. I started to do exactly what he had done.

'Don't forget it has to be at least ten seconds to collect enough for a proper sample,' he reminded me. Another thing they don't seem to take into account on television.

Once I'd finished with both swabs, I put them in the second glass.

'Now pop that on the side table just to be on the safe side,' he nodded towards it. 'We don't want to accidentally sneeze on it or something.' I did as I was told, then we looked at each other.

'So, what do we do now?' It suddenly felt a bit of an anti-climax and I wondered if he felt the same.

'We have to give them time to dry before we post them back to the lab.'

'On television they always just shove them straight back in,' I mused.

'Do you watch a lot of television, Polly?'

'You don't really have the time or energy to do much else between split shifts when you're a chef. At least, I don't.' I suddenly had a thought which made me want to giggle, but whether that was mirth or panic, I wasn't sure. 'Er ... we won't be putting these with the rest of the outgoing post at Reception, will we?' The image of Miranda being the one to send our DNA samples off was too much to contemplate.

'No, I'll take them myself to Winchester or Eastleigh. Unless you want to take them?'

The thought of escaping the rather claustrophobic atmosphere that had descended on Hetherin Hall with Miranda's arrival seemed very appealing. It was as if Charles could read my mind. 'I think you could do with a bit of a breather. If the kitchen can spare you, why don't you take a couple of hours for yourself? We're hardly busy at the moment.'

'Well, I've still got a fair bit of prep to do …' I started to say.

'I'm sure Will could get someone else to do that today.'

'I'll go back to the kitchen while the samples are drying.' I thought I'd be better off doing something practical for the next fifty-five minutes, rather than sitting in here watching the seconds tick by on the ornate clock on his mantelpiece.

'Good idea.' He stood up. 'I think I'll go and have a wander round the grounds, see if anything needs doing. I'll lock the door so no one else can come in. The samples will be quite safe.'

\* \* \*

An hour later, I was driving along bluebell and cow parsley-fringed lanes, the all-important envelope sitting on the passenger seat next to me. Charles wanted to send our samples Recorded Delivery but deemed the post mistress at Netley Magna to be too much of a busy body to chance taking the envelope there. I was glad of that as a drive through the narrow country lanes and a walk round somewhere different would make a change that was definitely as good as a rest.

I plumped for Winchester – it was a long time since I'd been there. It was a pretty drive and I soon found myself following signposts into the town centre. Charles had told me there was a post office in WH Smiths on the High Street now, so I aimed for there.

Standing in the queue, I felt like a secret agent doing a vital drop. I clutched the envelope to me, then, worried I might damage the swabs by holding them too tight, which I knew was ridiculous, I relaxed my grip on them a bit.

The three people ahead of me seemed to have saved several months' worth of post office requirements for this particular day. One middle-aged woman was renewing her car tax – probably not internet savvy, asking for information about Post Office bonds – short sighted, as she must have walked past the stand full of leaflets, and of course, buying stamps for all those letters she'd be writing instead of sending emails. A young woman with two toddlers in a pushchair was collecting some kind of benefit, then trying to pay a bill she didn't have enough money for. Then there was an older woman collecting pensions on behalf of at least three other people and who kept getting their pension books mixed up. I fully expected to finally get to the counter in time for the assistant behind it to say 'Sorry, we're closed', but she just smiled as she took and weighed the envelope. After I'd paid, I almost winced as she tossed it into a tray of other Recorded Delivery items. I sent up a silent prayer before forcing myself to walk away.

There were signs everywhere to the cathedral and although there really wasn't time for a sight-seeing trip, I followed them anyway. It was a lovely day and it would be nice to have a little walk in the grounds. It was a striking building and despite the number of people, very peaceful. I walked around the outside, past strolling couples, family picnics, and lounging students with open books, and found myself at the Refectory where I realised how hungry I was. After a quick look at their menu and an even quicker look at my watch, I ordered a jacket potato.

Will had been fine about me disappearing for a while, but I didn't want to take advantage of his kind nature. I wondered how he would feel about suddenly finding out his sous chef was another Hetherin. He'd probably be his usual cool, laid back self about it. If he'd been Charles's son he'd have been quick to welcome me into the family, I was sure, just like I was certain Jemima would be. Oliver wouldn't, and I wouldn't hold that against him. But as for their horrible mother, I'd have to watch my back where that particular Hetherin was concerned. I just knew it.

# CHAPTER TWENTY-ONE

'Hey, Poll.' Jemima knocked on my bedroom door the next day while I was on my afternoon break. She wandered in without waiting for an invitation. 'Fancy coming to Southampton with me? I've got to change a pair of shoes.'

'I've only got a couple of hours.' I put down the book I'd been trying – and failing – to concentrate on and looked up from where I was sprawled across my bed.

'That's fine, we won't be long. I've only got to go into West Quay.' She batted her eyelashes at me.

'I'm none the wiser. And fluttering your eyelashes won't work on me – I'm not a man.' I didn't move. The hotel was going to be quiet this week, and breakfast and lunch services today had dragged pitifully. It was much more tiring standing around doing next to nothing than working flat out – not a concept I expected Jemima to be familiar with.

'It's the big shopping mall in Southampton. Well, it's not that big, but it's where I need to go.'

'I don't know, Jem, I'm a bit tired.' I was more than a bit tired. I'd hardly slept, with thoughts of the DNA test swirling round and round in my head. My skin was starting to look awful.

'All the more reason to go out for some fresh air.' She clearly had no idea about my jaunt the previous day and I wasn't about to enlighten her.

'Yeah? Fresh, did you say? I opened my car window on my first drive down here, and fresh wasn't the word I'd have used to describe it.'

'I promise not to drive you past the pig farm.'

'It wasn't pigs – it was cows. Or bulls …'

'Oh, I know where you mean. We don't go anywhere near that farm to get to Southampton. Come on,' she started to wheedle.

'My calf muscles ache,' I grumbled.

'There's an outdoor food market,' she said with a completely innocent look. She was good at that.

'What sort of food market?' I suddenly felt ever so slightly less tired.

'International. You know, stalls selling Indian, Thai, Greek dishes, and ingredients, and all sorts of things.' The little minx knew that would get my attention. 'And it's in the main precinct, right by where we want to go.'

'Oh, go on then.' I swung my weary legs off the bed and grabbed the nearest pair of shoes that weren't my kitchen clogs. If I had known about this food market, I'd have gone to Southampton instead of Winchester yesterday. 'But it'd better be good.'

* * *

Southampton had changed beyond recognition since the last time I'd been there. C&A, where Mum had bought my school blouses, had still been around back then, so that shows how long ago that had been. What had been Plummers department store, where Mum had worked in the restaurant when I was a toddler, was now a university building. Woolworths had been replaced by TK Maxx and HMV, and there was a Primark where I was sure Marks & Spencer used to be. This West Quay place hadn't been there at all.

The food market Jemima had been talking about was right in the pedestrian precinct, although it looked a bit straggly. Maybe business was a bit quiet everywhere at the moment.

'Come on,' Jemima pulled on my arm. 'We'll change my shoes first then come back this way.'

'How about you go and change your shoes and meet me here?'

'Oh, come on, we can window shop – it'll be fun.'

'I'm alright for windows, thank you.' I could see where this was going. We'd be wandering around, looking at things I couldn't afford and neither of us needed, and by the time we got back out there wouldn't be time for me to look at the one thing I'd come to see.

'You're such a spoilsport,' Jemima pouted – she actually pouted at me. I wondered if I should buy her a lollipop.

'And yet you insisted on me coming here,' I risked the Hetherin eyebrow thing and she laughed.

'You look just like my dad when he's trying to be stern and disapproving,' she joked, fortunately not noticing the rabbit-in--headlights look I felt flitting across my face. 'Alright, I'll sort out my shoes and meet you here. But don't get me anything –'

'Fried, salty, sweet, high in calories, cholesterol or carbs,' I butted in. We both chuckled.

I watched my little sister walk into the mall. What would things have been like if we'd grown up together? Would we have this easy-going friendship that had sprung up so effortlessly, or would childhood squabbles have given us a different kind of relationship? Would things change between us when the DNA results came back and she found out I was her sister? I felt a rush of affection for Jemima and hoped for the umpteenth time that she wouldn't be angry with Charles and I for keeping her in the dark.

\* \* \*

'Oh my goodness, that was yummy!' Jemima chased a last stray grain of rice round her food container with her chopsticks and popped it into her mouth. 'What was it again?'

'Stir-fried morning glory with ginger, garlic, and red chillies and steamed jasmine rice.'

'And what was yours?'

'The same but with lovely crispy pork on top. I did offer you a bit …'

'It was delicious without the pork, thank you.' She licked her chopsticks and reluctantly put them down. 'I won't be able to eat for a week but it was so worth it. We must come here again.'

'Yeah, but when we've got more time to enjoy it,' I said, looking at my watch. 'Talking of which, we need to go.' I grabbed both containers and dropped them into the nearest bin. We headed off back to the car park, Jemima clutching her new shoes, me clutching a bag of kourabiedes, fresh and crunchy and liberally coated in icing sugar. I loved this Greek shortbread, although I was pretty sure the Greeks would insist that shortbread was our version of kourabiedes. Whatever – they were gorgeous. And I'd be hiding my biscuit tin in my room, far from the other chefs' greedy fingers. These babies were all mine.

# CHAPTER TWENTY-TWO

Wasn't it just Sod's Law that Charles wasn't there when the DNA results came back. The fact that they arrived a day later than we were expecting wasn't helpful, but how typical that the one business trip he couldn't cancel would be on that very day. Miranda rang through to the kitchen for me to go to Reception to sign for an envelope. If she could have wrangled it away from the courier before I got there, I believe she would have steamed it open. Her curiosity was killing her – I felt like offering her a saucer of milk.

After all the waiting, all the anticipation, now I had the results in my hands and I couldn't open them. Half of me wanted to run to a quiet corner and rip the envelope open and find out once and for all. The other half was too scared to face the results alone – just holding the envelope was making my stomach churn. Anyway, it wouldn't be right to open them on my own – Charles and I had to do this together. And in the meantime, I had to keep this important envelope safe and away from prying eyes. But where? It was too important to leave in my room – what if there was a fire and it got destroyed and we had to go through all this again? I also didn't trust Miranda not to make up some excuse to go and have a snoop around. That woman definitely didn't like me, and from what I could tell, she was winding Oliver up against me as well. Not that he would need much winding up after the way he must think I'd treated him. And although it was actually a very helpful thing at the moment if Oliver didn't like me, nobody wanted to feel they had actual enemies. There was going to be enough for him to get his head round if the result was positive and he had to be told that we were, in fact, too closely related to be doing what we'd been about to do. In any case, once my own head had finally got through to any other parts of me that still needed convincing that Oliver was my brother, it might be nice to be accepted as his sister. And that would happen much more easily if he didn't actively hate me.

It would be far safer to keep the envelope with me, but that was easier said than done. The pockets in my chefs' trousers weren't long enough to conceal a long envelope and if I folded it over it might pop itself out and fall on the floor without me noticing – it probably wouldn't, but this was one of those situations where a little paranoia was allowed, or at least I thought so. I'd have to fold it in three to get it into the breast pocket of my jacket, but then it could fall out while I was lifting something – it probably wouldn't, but my paranoia didn't want to take the chance of me fishing it out of a pan of soup. I'd seen enough mobile phones ruined that way. The most secure way I could think of would be to have it round my leg under a long sock. I hurried up to my room feeling – or imagining I could feel – Miranda's eyes on me as I went. My newest pair of tube socks would be the tightest and least likely to fall down while I was working, so I took off the pair I was wearing, pulled the new ones on, and slipped the envelope into the right one. Deciding that wasn't very comfortable, I took them off, put the old socks back on with the new ones on top and the envelope in between. That was much better, if a little warm. If I'd had a rubber band I'd have held it in place with that too. Then I sent Charles a discrete text message saying 'The eagle has landed', in case anyone saw it for any reason, and got myself back to the kitchen before Miranda had them sending out a pitch fork-wielding search party for me.

I was in charge of organising the specials now, since Will had managed to get over me messing up his precious sardine order. He had introduced me properly to the delivery people so they knew to bring their fresh goodies straight to me. As we weren't going to be busy, I was doing fewer portions than usual, but having great fun putting new dishes together for the menu. Today, inspired by our trip to the food market, I had decided on creamy Thai crab and coconut as soup of the day, and steamed sea bass with ginger, garlic, and loads of fresh coriander for the fish. In the absence of morning glory, I was doing a broccoli, ginger, garlic, and chilli stir-fry and serving it with egg fried rice or mushroom fried rice as a vegan alternative. We didn't have jasmine rice in the store room but I'd put some on order. Jemima said she was looking forward to trying it although I had warned her that it wouldn't be the same as what she'd eaten at the food market.

Oliver had picked today to start popping into the kitchen and stiffly but politely questioning me on the specials. I didn't know whether that was down to my choices, which his face seemed to indicate he thought downright odd, or if his mother had told him to keep an eye on me. Either way it was very unnerving and I wished he would leave me in peace. I'd already knocked over a tin of coconut milk after he'd appeared at my elbow without warning and made me jump. Much more and I'd be a nervous wreck.

\* \* \*

The lunchtime service came and went. It was quiet, although the few diners we had had eaten heartily. The chefs, it seemed, were looking forward to polishing off the remains of my soup for their lunch as it wasn't the sort of thing we could keep for another service. Maybe I'd do something more conventional the next day, the remains of which could be converted into something else, if bookings were going to be as low – I would check the reservations book, if I could get to it without having to go through Oliver.

I was ladling out, making sure I kept some aside for Jemima, when Will and Oliver came bustling past, clearly in the middle of some kind of dispute.

'I've already said yes,' Oliver was saying. 'Why does everybody at this hotel think they can ride roughshod over any decision I make?'

'I think it says more about your decisions than it does about the hotel,' Will retorted, his placid self unusually ruffled. He carried on walking but Oliver stopped dead in his tracks, his face like thunder.

'Well, it's too late,' he snapped at our head chef. 'They've already booked their transport and they're coming whether you like it or not.'

I was trying to decide whether there was any point in asking if there was anything I could do to help when Oliver flung himself round like a toddler having a tantrum. In one movement, he managed to knock both the bowl of soup I was putting down and the full ladle I was about to tip into another, and spill the piping hot contents of both down the lower half of my front.

My shriek must have been half shock, half knowledge that the soup was very hot and half annoyance. It really was a shriek and a half, and it certainly grabbed their attention and shut the pair of them up. So did my quick impromptu strip, as I kicked my clogs off and yanked my wet trousers down before the liquid could scald my legs. Thank goodness for double fronted chef's jackets or I would've had to whip that off too and put everyone off their food.

'You stupid idiot!' I yelled at Oliver. 'Do you know nothing about kitchen safety? Call yourself a restaurant manager? Why don't you throw a few knives at me and bash me over the head with a rolling pin for good measure?'

He stood there with his mouth open while I screeched at him like a half-dressed, angry fishwife, a crowd of curious chefs materialising behind him. Most of them were ungallantly looking at my unusually bare and unfortunately unshaven legs.

'What do you lot think you're doing, standing there gawping?' I turned my screechiness in their direction. 'Have none of you ever seen a pair of legs before? You must have all lead very sheltered lives!'

There was some mumbled and indecipherable muttering. 'Find yourselves something to do or this,' I indicated the soup, 'will all go down the drain.' They all suddenly became very busy. 'And you,' I glared at Oliver, 'you can bloody well clear up this mess!' Picking up my soup-splattered clogs and soggy trousers, I padded away to Will's office where I knew he kept spare chefs' whites. I closed the door fairly loudly and grabbed a fresh pair of trousers. They were a couple of sizes too big but they were clean and dry and would do for the walk to my room, where I could get changed properly and clean my clogs before they started to smell like a bad day at Billingsgate.

Although I could feel it, the first thing I did when I got to my room was check that the envelope was still safely tucked between my double layer of socks. Thank goodness that was where I'd decided to put it, although if there'd been more soup, it might have reached my socks as well. Things always seemed so much wetter when you didn't want them to be. I took it out and dropped it on the bed while I changed into my own clean trousers.

I sent Charles another text – *any idea when u r due back?* But as he hadn't replied to the first, I doubted he'd have time to answer this one either. I had just pressed send when there was a tap at my door before Miranda, without waiting to be invited, let herself in.

'I heard there was some kind of incident in the kitchen – and that you were running around the place in your underwear, *Polly*.' She managed to make my name sound like some kind of assumed identity. Her eyes were roaming all over the room like police searchlights. I hastily sat down on the envelope and started folding William's clean trousers over my lap whilst assuming what I hoped was an innocent expression. It occurred to me that as teenagers, Jemima and Oliver must have had an impossible time trying to get anything past her – their school homework must have always been in on time. I hoped the garde manger chef had concealed whatever it was he liked to smoke at the end of the day in a very good hiding place or she'd be up there next, pulling his room apart as if living out some kind of *Prisoner Cell Block H* fantasy. She might have been a sniffer dog in a previous life – I bet she'd have been a good one.

'I'd hardly call it an incident, *Miranda*.' I couldn't help giving her name the same treatment she'd given mine, but if she noticed my tone she ignored it. 'Oliver just knocked over some hot soup and it splashed down my trousers so I had to take them off before my legs got scalded – that was all. I'm not in the habit of taking my

140

clothes off in front of a kitchen full of chefs. Although,' I added, desperately trying to keep my right eyebrow under control, 'I should probably warn you that if they were ever to catch fire, I would feel obliged to remove them rather quickly.'

She looked directly at me for the first time since she'd entered my room. If she were a cat, the fur on the back of her neck would be standing up in great, spiky tufts. 'There's something about you, young lady,' she announced, 'that I neither like nor trust.' Her voice had gone all posh as if she were trying to sound like the queen. Half of me was waiting for her to bellow '*Orf with her head!*' then go and make some jam tarts and have a game of croquet with a flamingo. 'And I should tell you I'm not the only member of the family who feels like that.' That'd be Oliver then, but at least I could see where he was coming from. 'I suggest you get yourself back down to the kitchen and finish up whatever it was you were supposed to be doing.'

'I'll be there in a moment.' I waited for her to leave.

'I'll walk down with you.' She clearly wasn't planning on going anywhere until I stood up and went with her. Why had I taken the blasted envelope out of my sock? I didn't think I could stand up and walk out of the room without her seeing it and I didn't trust her not to have x-ray vision. She looked like a woman who was capable of doing anything just to be awkward – especially, apparently, where I was concerned.

'I just need to do something first,' I said, wondering what I could need to do that involved me staying exactly where I was until she left the room.

'What do you need to do that is more important than the job you are being paid for?' She'd make a great prosecution lawyer.

'I,' *think, Polly, think,* 'I er … took some laxatives.' *laxatives? Where did that come from?* 'And I need to er … be away from the kitchen for a while.' I was cringing inside. Really, was there no embarrassment I wasn't capable of heaping on myself?

'Laxatives?' She might have been that old lady in *The Importance of Being Ernest* saying '*A handbag?*'

'That's right.' I looked at her as if I'd just said the most reasonable thing in the world and couldn't imagine why she would want to question it.

'Then I would suggest you sit in the bathroom rather than in here,' she said, starting to move towards the door and away from me. Maybe she thought I might explode – not a pleasant thought given what I'd just told her.

'I'm on my way.'

'I'm glad to hear it.' Her look before she walked out told me that not only was she not glad to hear anything I said, she hadn't believed a word of it either. Something told me she wasn't going to be welcoming me into the family with open arms.

# CHAPTER TWENTY-THREE

When I went down for the dinner shift, the envelope firmly back inside my sock, I found out what Will and Oliver had been arguing about. Apparently, Oliver had taken it upon himself to plug the gap in bookings by doing a deal with some photographic society he'd come across in one of his magazines. They were arriving in time for last dinner orders, which meant that, after a quiet few hours, we were going to be rushing round at the last minute and staying on late. Personally, I didn't mind – to be honest, I felt he had a right to do what he could to boost business, but plenty of grumbling dissent could be heard going on in the ranks. The society would be staying overnight and going out on a rather tame safari in the morning, photographing New Forest ponies and deer and oak trees, that sort of thing. Then in the afternoon they were going to the Watercress Line to do the same with the steam trains. Rather them than me. I just hoped the breakfast shift had been warned about the extra work they should expect.

Actually, I thought it was rather enterprising of Oliver to arrange a whole block booking like that at what sounded like fairly short notice. He'd even limited the menu choices to make it easier on the kitchen staff. I was impressed, but of course I wasn't going to tell him. I just wanted to get this day over and done with, and for Charles to be back so we could get on and open this damned envelope. The temptation to find out that I really was a part of the family Mum had wanted me to find came at me in waves. Most of the time, I managed to treat it as if the envelope just contained something like exam results of which I was already pretty certain, and that they wouldn't be any different for holding on for a few more hours.

The photographic society seemed a charming group. Their chairman popped his head round the door and thanked us for keeping the kitchen open, promising to chivvy along any slow eaters. They didn't take long to order.

'Order!' I called the second Oliver handed me the slip. 'Starters: eight asparagus and quail's eggs, six mushroom tartlets, and four potted prawns. Mains: five Nelson's pies, six spring lambs, six venison bangers and mash, and one shepherdess pie. Group table.'

The starters were out in minutes and the mains would be ready to go as soon as the starter plates came back in. Whether by accident or on purpose, Oliver had picked the most time-friendly dishes on the menu to offer the group, and the grumbling had all but died away. He seemed to be in his element out there, chatting and joking. I'd gathered that he was into photography – he wandered around the grounds enough with his fancy camera and had even taken a couple of sneaky before and after pictures of the cake at that fateful wedding reception, but this was the first time I'd seen him so chatty and enthusiastic about anything. He looked really happy.

Jemima and her mother wandered into the kitchen in the hiatus between serving the starters and the mains. Miranda's sour face couldn't dampen my pleasure at seeing Jemima, however hard it tried.

'Feeling better, Polly?' Miranda smirked as if nothing would please her more than to embarrass me in front of the whole kitchen.

'What's the matter?' Jemima looked at me with concern. They really were two very different sides of the same coin.

'I'm fine, Jem ...' I began to say. The empty starter plates started coming back in at that moment and relieved, I called, 'Away! Five Nelson's pies, six spring lambs, six venison bangers and mash, and one shepherdess pie. Group table.'

Most of the photographers had cheese and biscuits and a few had the New Forest gateau or fresh fruit salad, the only sweet options they'd been offered. Coffee and after dinner mints, if Lulu and Mel had left any, were going to be served in one of the lounges so we could close up in the restaurant. I was just finishing up for the day when Jemima came back in.

'Hey.' She was smiling at me in the way she usually did when she was about to pester me for something to eat.

'Hey, Jem.' I studiously ignored the smile while I picked up the last of those cling film-wrapped odds and ends that were always left at the end of the day and put them on a tray to go in the fridge. They would do towards making the next day's staff meals.

'I don't suppose there's any of your gorgeous stir fry left?' Her voice was just the non-annoying side of wheedling and although I was tired, I couldn't help smiling. If she were a cat she'd been winding herself round my ankles and purring and I'd be reaching down to rub her head with one hand, grabbing a tin of Whiskas and a tin opener with the other.

'I can do you a quick one – you won't be wanting rice, will you?'

'Carbs! At this time of night?' She looked suitably horrified. She followed me to the fridge as I put the tray in and took out the bowl of prepared broccoli.

'I'm surprised you eat anything at this time of night. Tell me, who did you used to go to for your midnight snacks before I started working here?'

'Well, sometimes Will, but he can be mean if he's already put everything away. Sometimes I'd go and help myself to some fruit salad. And anyway, it's only ten o'clock – still naughty, but I don't go to bed until midnight and I subscribe to the belief that it's better to eat a little and fairly often than to have three big, stodgy meals.'

'I had noticed.' I heated up the oil in the pan before tossing in the vegetables. 'So, am I right in thinking you've only taken to these regular raids on the kitchen since I've been here?'

'Well, you make the nicest snacks ...'

'Yeah, yeah, I'm wonderful,' I shook the pan. 'It's got nothing to do with me being a big soft pushover at all.' I noticed she had the grace to blush a little.

I tipped most of the stir fry out into a bowl and picked at the remaining bits in the pan while she ate, both of us sitting on a work bench like naughty schoolgirls. I couldn't imagine getting away with this sort of thing in any other kitchen I'd ever worked in. But then, I'd never been part of the family before.

When we'd finished, I put the bowl in the dishwasher and the pan in the sink and ran some water into it. I was going to go out through the back door, but Jemima didn't like going through the tradesman's entrance so we walked through the darkened restaurant and into the big hallway. There was laughter and plenty of chatter coming from the lounge where the photographic society must still be having their coffee. Jemima swung round the doorway to have a look – I held back, dressed in my no longer very white whites.

'Hey, look at this,' she stage whispered, tugging on my arm.

'What?' I held back. 'I don't want them to see me – I'm all dirty.'

'You'll want to see this,' she pulled harder. 'It's Ollie!'

Something told me I very much didn't want to see whatever it was that Oliver was doing, but Jemima didn't give me much choice. My arm not being made of elastic, my head made it far enough round the door to see exactly where she was indicating. There, perched on the arm of one of the big, red brown Chesterfield sofas was Oliver, smiling at a stunningly pretty, arty-looking girl with long, glossy auburn hair, the sort you usually see being tossed annoyingly in adverts for very expensive shampoo. She was dressed entirely in black and looked chic enough to belong in front of the camera rather than behind it. He looked completely engrossed in what she was saying. Because the sofa was directly facing us I could see that she, in turn, was gazing up at him as if he were the most fascinating man in the world. Maybe she didn't get out much.

'Oh my God!' Jemima giggled. 'Ollie's pulled!'

'Don't be ridiculous,' I heard myself whisper. It suddenly felt rather hard to breathe.

'Just look at the way she's looking at him. She fancies him!' *Please shut up, Jemima,* a strange voice in my head begged as my stomach felt as if it was filling up with cold grey lead. But she carried on. 'I always knew somewhere in the world there must be someone who wouldn't think Ollie was a complete plank. I thought he might have to visit a few care in the community homes to find her, though. And here she is, sitting in our lounge. And she's gorgeous! Just look at that hair! Who'd have thought it?'

I felt cold all over. Jemima had no idea what her babbling was doing to me and how much I wanted to shut her up. But she could never know about the turbulence I was feeling and so I had to stand there and try not to listen as the words kept trickling out of her mouth, pushing down the feeling of nausea rising higher and higher towards my throat.

The girl was putting her hand on his arm now, her fingers gently curling round it. I swallowed. Their heads bent closer together as they shared some joke. He threw back his head in easy laughter. Her hand didn't move. I swallowed harder. *I won't throw up, I won't.*

A small group of the more middle-aged members came out at that point, and I shrank away from the door. They didn't appear to see me as they wished Jemima a good night and made their way to the big staircase. She seemed happy to stand there all night spying on her – our – brother. I'd seen more than enough. I just wanted to escape to my room, but the only way without going back to the kitchen was past that door. Not only did I not want to see anything more of what might or might not be happening, I most definitely didn't want anyone seeing me.

'Jem, I'm tired,' I told her. 'I'm going to bed.' I turned to go back towards the restaurant.

'OK, I'll fill you in on the goss in the morning.' She barely noticed me leave.

I felt my way back through the restaurant, thankful for the darkness while I tried to compose myself. How could I have messed up so spectacularly? I'd come here to find my father, not a new boyfriend. How had I managed to let myself get so distracted by a handsome face and a pair of strong arms? If it hadn't been for that blasted wedding cake, I'd never have found myself alone with Oliver that night, and we'd never have ended up ... I went through the door into the kitchen, where it was never quite as dark. Things could have worked out fine – I'd have met Charles, we'd have done the DNA test, and right now I wouldn't be feeling sick to my lead-filled stomach.

Reaching for the back door key, I found an empty hook. Which twit had locked it and not put the key back? Now I had to go back and pass the lounge. The urge to scream growing in my head, I went towards the door to the restaurant and froze. Somebody was in there. I stood closer to the out-door and listened, scarcely breathing.

'Cognac? Or something else?' *No!* My heart stopped as I recognised Oliver's voice. *No, no, no, no, no!* Another voice, female, of course, said something I couldn't make out, and then there was a gentle laugh and a tinkle of glasses and the sound of drinks being poured. Whatever was said next was drowned out by the clinking of two brandy balloons and then there was silence.

The silence was the worst. I couldn't breathe. I couldn't move. My insides were churning as if somebody had picked me up and shaken me. All my brain would allow me to do was torture myself, picturing what must be going on in that silence. And remembering, with a burning hot flush of shame.

I just made it to the still room and pulled the door behind me before I threw up.

# CHAPTER TWENTY-FOUR

Of all the sleepless nights I'd had at Hetherin Hall, that night had been the most miserable. It had been one thing being kept awake by a horrible smell, but being kept awake by a DNA result that's tucked under the pillow your head is trying in vain to rest on, tortured by images of the unsuitable man you've fallen for sharing passionate cognac-flavoured kisses with a girl who wouldn't look out of place on the cover of *Vogue* whilst you hid in your mucky chefs' whites with your hands over your ears trying not to be sick – that was just too much. Add the fact that the unsuitable man wasn't unsuitable because he had inappropriate piercings or a prison sentence for something unforgivable, but because he was your long-lost *brother* and I couldn't understand how my head hadn't exploded. I imagined it might still be a possibility. It certainly wanted to, as did my heart – I could feel them. They weren't happy. I put the pillow over my head in the hope that I might accidentally suffocate myself and not have to worry about any of it any more.

I was exhausted when I crawled out of bed in the morning. I still felt sick. My head was banging and my stomach felt full of lead. And now my heart seemed to have gone on a go-slow. I was too tired be angry with myself, although I knew I should be. What had I expected? That Oliver would be a celibate bachelor for the rest of his life? That he would go and hide himself away in a monastery? Of course there were going to be girls, and probably quite a few of them. Despite what Jemima thought of her brother, he was a very attractive man. *Stop that! Don't go there! That's what started this trouble in the first place.*

I should be happy for him and relieved for myself to see him getting friendly with a gorgeous girl. In fact, I should try and find that gorgeous girl's male equivalent for myself. I really had to get a grip, or else I would have to leave Hetherin Hall. Because one thing was certain, if I couldn't get my ridiculous emotions under control, there was no way Oliver and I could work under the same roof – even if that was possible once he knew who I really was.

This was the day Charles Hetherin and I were going to find out for sure if I was his daughter. We had gone over and over how we would tell the family and decided that if and when we had something to tell them we would play it by ear, rather than have some rehearsed speeches ready. Although I hadn't been able to stop myself worrying what some of their reactions might be and trying to work out what I could say in response. But as that had turned out to be something different each time I thought about it, that wasn't turning out to be much help. Anyway, I just wanted him to hurry up and get back here so I didn't feel so completely on my own. All that soppy stuff about a problem shared being a problem halved suddenly held new meaning. When Charles was around, my shoulders certainly felt lighter, but I would have to wait until lunchtime as he had a breakfast meeting to get through before he could leave. He was going to start it as early as he could – he had finally sent me a text to let me know.

\* \* \*

We were clearing away after the lunch service when my

phone beeped in my trouser pocket, announcing a text. It was Charles and he was back. I managed at once to knock over the dish of mixed herbs, pepper, and salt that had been unlucky enough to be near my elbow, sending the lot to the floor with a fragrant clatter and creating a little peppery cloud. Mentally calling myself some very unflattering names, I dashed for a dustpan and broom, swept it up with one movement, and dumped it unceremoniously in the bin before wordlessly vanishing through the back door and round the side of the building. Miranda was still haunting the reception desk and I couldn't cope with having to avoid an interrogation on where I thought I was going and whether or not I'd finished what I was supposed to be doing first. Charles's office had French windows and I would knock on those and get him to let me in.

My heart was hammering in my chest and echoing in my head as I half walked, half ran. By the time I got there my mouth was dry, I was breathless, and I wouldn't have been surprised if I'd fainted before I even managed to tap on the window. As it turned out I didn't need to raise my hand – he'd seen me coming and already had it open.

'Trying to break the four minute mile?' He poured me a glass of water and smiled awkwardly, looking as if he hadn't slept much either.

'Thanks,' I gasped after an unladylike glug. We both stood, looking at each other.

'It must have been hard not to open it.' He sat against the edge of his desk.

'Just a bit.' I sipped some more water and sat down. After racing to get here, neither of us seemed to be in such a hurry any more.

'Have you got it with you?'

'It hasn't left my sock since it arrived.' I bent over to

153

pull it out. 'Well, not for long, anyway.'

'That's a novel place to keep correspondence.' He did the eyebrow thing and, like a magic spell, it immediately dispelled some of my trepidation.

'It didn't seem like a good idea to leave it lying around.' I handed it to him and for a moment we both held a corner of it.

'You do know, don't you, that whatever this result, you are a wonderful young woman. Your mother must have been very proud of you, and I am so glad she wanted us to meet. Even if, she was wrong and you don't turn out to be my daughter, I will be honoured for us to be friends and, like I said, you will always have a job and a home here at the Hall.'

Unable to say anything, I nodded and let go of the envelope. I watched as he picked up his paperknife and started to slit the top. It seemed to take him forever to open it and pull out its contents. Time seemed to stand still. I couldn't have moved if I'd tried. I might not have even taken a breath, as he unfolded the pages that were more than likely about to change our lives. He smoothed them out with his hand and started to read.

'Charles?' Miranda's voice was shrill as she rattled the handle of the thankfully locked door. 'Are you in there, Charles?' The shrillness was punctuated by harsh knocks. 'I know you're in there. I heard you talking.' We looked at each other in silence. Did she have a key? Would she go to Reception and help herself to the master key? 'Charles, I want to speak to you about that *Polly* girl.' That made both of us jump in surprise and my face start to flush. 'She's walked out of the kitchen yet again without a word. William's furious. He's had enough, she's always doing this sort of thing. I think we should terminate her contract immediately.' Charles stood, placed the results face down on his desk, and marched across the room. He unlocked the door and flung it open in practically one movement. Miranda almost fell inside.

'Polly is here in the office at *my* request,' he growled. I'd never seen him angry and hoped I wouldn't ever find myself on the receiving end of it. 'She has never walked out of the kitchen without good reason. William is more than happy with her work otherwise he wouldn't have made her sous chef and more to the point, *I am very happy with her work.*'

'But ...' She glared at me.

'This is my hotel, Miranda,' he ploughed on. 'My hotel and my business and just because you deign to honour us with your presence once a month, it does not give you the right to make any decisions regarding the staff I or my children choose to employ.'

'But ...' She was still glaring.

'If I paid your bills by direct debit, Ollie and Jem would never even see their mother, would they? Now, go back and man the reception desk which *you* seem to have walked away from without a word to anyone before I decide *I've* had enough. I'll have no more of this interference from you – do you understand?'

Her glare had turned into a death ray stare and I heartily hoped that looks really couldn't kill. She left without another word, but I knew this vendetta against me wasn't over. And if she hated me this much now, well ... I didn't want to think about the many ways she could try to terminate more than my contract in the future.

'I'm so sorry about that,' Charles sighed, his face grave. 'Miranda has jealousy issues – she's probably envious of your friendship with Jemima.'

'It's fine, really.' I tried to sound reassuring. 'Do you think we can read these results now? I don't know how much more of this my nerves can stand.'

'Of course.' He picked up the pages and turned them back over. This time I stood at his shoulder and tried to read with him. There was a lot of writing about genetic markers and percentages and although I understood most of the words individually, I couldn't make out what they meant together.

'What does it say?' I heard myself whisper.

'I'm not sure yet. Hold on,' he said softly as he carried on studying what might as well have been hieroglyphics. I kept looking, as if some magical insight might suddenly come to me. It didn't.

He finally got to the end. He seemed to read the last bit a few times as if wanting to make sure he'd got it right.

'So?' My whisper sounded young and scared – little girl lost.

He put the pages on the desk and turned to look at me. There were tears in his eyes. 'Polly,' he croaked, taking my hands in his. A tear spilled over and ran down his face. 'I'm so sorry.'

# CHAPTER TWENTY-FIVE

I stumbled back onto the chair behind me. They'd got it wrong, they must have – Mum would never have put me through all this for nothing. She'd never have made such a monumental mistake.

'Twenty-seven years!' Charles Hetherin, my boss, the man I worked for, knelt at the side of my chair. 'I'm so sorry I haven't been there for you.'

Was this what the cancer had done to Mum? Mixed everything up in her memory so she'd forgotten about this Martin?

'All the things you've missed out on – all the sacrifices poor Rosie must have made when she could have just come to me ...'

What was I supposed to do now? How could I find this Martin? Should I even try to, or should I just give up? Did I really want to put myself through this heartache and disappointment again?

'All the birthdays and Christmases we've missed. Your first words, first steps, first day at school ...'

Could I even stay here? He'd said I could, but people just say things, don't they? Then they regret them later and wish they'd kept their mouths shut when they find themselves lumbered with something *or someone,* they don't really know what to do with.

'All the family holidays, all the things your brother

and sister got to do together while they were growing up ...'

Did I *want* to stay here? How much torture would it be to be around the family that was so nearly mine? To have Jemima keep coming to me for those cosy night-time snacks ... Oh God, Jemima – I'd been so sure she was my sister – she felt like my sister. There was definitely a bond between us.

'Jemima always wanted a little sister ...'

And now I'd have to get my head round her just being a friend.

'I reckon she'll like having a big one even better. I imagine Ollie will be thrilled too.'

And as for Oliver – I couldn't think about that right now.

'I think we should get them in here and tell them straight away, don't you? Polly!'

I jumped 'I'm sorry?' I'd vaguely heard him talking but I hadn't been paying attention.

'Don't you think we should tell Jem and Ollie?'

'Tell them what?' I asked numbly. What was the point in telling them – there was nothing to tell them.

'That you're their sister, of course!' Charles jumped up, looking at me as if I had suddenly sprouted wings and failed to notice.

'But I'm not ...'

'Polly, haven't you listened to a word I've been saying?'

'I think my ears disconnected after the *"Sorry I'm not your dad"* bit.'

'I never said that!'

'You said sorry and you were crying ...' Was it me who was going mad or him?

'I said sorry because I was ... no, I *am* sorry, *very*

158

sorry that I've missed the first twenty-seven years of your life.' His eyes were still wet and glittering, but he was smiling and my stomach did the biggest flip ever. My breath caught in my throat.

'So,' I coughed, grabbing the glass of water, taking another gulp, and spilling some down my chin. 'When you said sorry, you didn't mean that the result was negative and you were sad not to be my dad ...'

'No, you silly girl,' he laughed. 'I meant that the result says,' he snatched up the piece of paper again, 'the probability of my being your father is 99.99% and I was sorry about everything we've both missed out on until now. I suppose, in hindsight I could have put it better, so let me now be very clear.' He coughed and cleared his throat. 'Polly Hanson, Polly Hetherin, or whatever you would like to be called from now on – I, Charles Hetherin, am your father!'

I think it was me who squealed as I jumped up and hugged him. One of us certainly did. This was me, for the very first time in my life, hugging my father – the thought sang inside my head. This was my father, for the first time in my life, hugging me. This was what my mother had wanted and I could feel her smiling down on us. I couldn't remember having felt so warm, so protected since ... well, probably since I was a little girl. I might have been twenty-seven now, but the little girl in me didn't want this moment to stop.

The loud knock at the door barely caught my attention. I didn't care if Miranda came in brandishing a cast iron frying pan and hit me over the head with it. There was nothing that horrible woman could do to hurt me – I had my dad, and he clearly wasn't bothered about her seeing us hugging because he didn't relinquish his hold on me either.

The second knock was much louder, enough to make us both turn our heads towards the door. As we did so, the handle twisted round almost at once and the door burst open. Oliver started to march in but stopped, nearly falling over his feet. His face contorted itself as he looked at us.

'That's disgusting!' He almost spat the words and his dad ... *our* dad and I jumped apart as if we'd been stung. I hadn't expected a reaction like that and he didn't even know yet, unless he'd been listening at the keyhole.

'Oliver!' Dad exclaimed. 'What on earth ...'

'You should be ashamed of yourselves!' He glared at us then his eyes rested on his father. 'I can't believe you'd do something so sordid! And with Mum here, too! And as for you ...' He gave me the kind of look I'd been experiencing from Miranda only worse, because his disgust was based on something tangible.

'Oliver!' Dad shouted.

'She's only twenty-seven, Dad!' Oliver turned to leave before snarling over his shoulder, 'Bloody hell! She's young enough to be your daughter!'

# CHAPTER TWENTY-SIX

I didn't know who was more shocked by what Oliver had just said, Charles or me, but I couldn't believe he could have thought something so ridiculous. Charles moved towards the door to go after him. The conversation they would have when he caught up didn't bear thinking of. Oliver had sounded outraged. I couldn't know if he'd blurt out in his anger what had nearly happened between us. Would Charles believe that I really hadn't known Oliver was his son? That I'd thought red-haired Will was? It wasn't a chance I wanted to take.

'No!' I nipped in front of my father. 'I'll go and talk to him.'

Oliver wasn't in the restaurant or the kitchen. The ballroom was locked and there was no sign of him in Reception, just my wicked step mother giving some poor soul a hard time on the phone. Torn between running to the staff block in case he'd gone there to shred my clothes – I really do watch too much television – and trying his own room in the family wing, common sense sent me up the stairs, back to the scene of the almost crime. This was the last place on earth I wanted to be.

I didn't need to worry if I'd got the right door – he hadn't closed it. It was as if he'd been expecting me.

'Oliver!' My voice sounded shaky as he stood there glaring at me. 'I really didn't know who you were. You never told me your surname. I thought Will was Charles' son – he looks so much like Jemima. The moment I saw that photo of you both and realised you were brother and sister …'

'So you have got some kind of moral code then,' he snarled, 'some things you draw the line at?'

'What do you …?'

'Shagging the boss to keep your job after you did a runner and he went to find you – that's acceptable in Polly-world? Even if he is old enough to be your father …'

'Oliver! That's …'

'Cheating on him with random members of his staff – apparently that's acceptable in Polly-world too. Just how many of us are there? Have you worked your way round the whole kitchen? Do you just leave your bedroom door open at night and let them wander in or do you give them appointment times like the dentist?'

'How dare …'

'Don't leave the gardening staff out, will you? Those fit men, muscled and tanned from working outdoors all day – you'll have a great time with them.'

'Oliver! If you …'

'But you draw the line at shagging his son? What – a bit too close to home? A bit too incestuous for you?'

I winced at the word he'd inadvertently hit a very uncomfortable nail on the head with. 'You couldn't be more wrong about me,' I said with as much dignity as I could muster whilst fighting back the tears prickling my eyes. 'And about your father. When he tells you his news you'll understand just how wrong you are.'

'I'm not listening to another word from either of you …'

'Yes, you damn well will.' Charles' steely voice behind me made me jump. 'Polly, go and fetch Jemima and bring her to my office. Whatever she's doing right now will have to wait.'

I left the two of them alone, Oliver glaring out of the window like a sulky teenager, Charles clenching his jaw. I could imagine how the businessman in him wouldn't need to yell and shout to get his point across. I almost felt sorry for Oliver – almost, but not quite. The things he'd said to me had shocked me. I had to remind myself that he didn't know the truth, that he'd be mortified when he did.

Charles could have phoned Jemima and told her to come, but I guessed he wanted me out of the way so he could say whatever it was he wanted to say to Oliver without an audience. When I got outside, I was glad of the fresh air on my face. I wanted it to blow away all the hurtful things I'd just heard.

The overwhelming urge to say 'Hi, sis!' to someone I knew would be genuinely pleased to see me had to be stamped on with a very firm foot. She was on the phone with someone who was changing their booking when I got there, and she rolled her eyes as she doodled what looked like a fluffy, high heeled shoe on the appointments book with a Hetherin Hall pen. My little sister – and she really was my little sister. We had so much catching up to do. I felt a huge rush of affection and thought of some of the sisterly things we'd be able to do together. It felt like a balm, trying to soothe away the worst of Oliver's words – I was going to need a lot more of it.

'Charles,' I just managed to stop myself calling him Dad, 'wants an immediate conference in his office.'

'Ooh, no Ollie?' She looked at me with wide eyes. 'Has he run off with his pretty photographer friend and left the restaurant in the lurch?'

'Er, no, I think he's already on his way. Come on.' I ushered her out of her own spa and steered her round via the back of the kitchen where we wouldn't be visible from Reception – now was not the time for a confrontation with the wicked stepmother. That would come later, whether I liked it or not. I shuddered at the thought.

'Are you OK?' My little sister put her arm through mine and it gave me such a warm feeling.

'I'm fine, thanks.' I put on my best smile. 'Those were very fancy shoes you were drawing.'

'Mmm, I saw them in a shop in town. Do you fancy coming with me?'

'Yes, I'd like that.' I couldn't help smiling. 'Just not today.'

'Why? What's going on?'

The kitchen door opened, and Will came out so I was saved from having to think of a reply.

'There you are.' He looked quizzically at me. 'Mrs H has got her knickers in a right old twist about you. What have you been up to? She wanted me to tell Mr H to sack you!'

'What! Why?' Jemima looked horrified, which made me even fonder of her.

'Who knows,' I shrugged. 'Anyway, we have to go. Jemima and I have a very important meeting in Charles's office.'

Will laughed and shook his head. 'Oh, *Charles,* is it? Do you know, I think you're the cheekiest sous chef I've ever worked with.'

'No, but you hum it and I'll try and sing along.' I noticed them both looking blankly at me. 'It was something my mum used to say. I think it came from a tea advert with chimps dressed as removal men and one of them dropped a piano on the other one's foot.' They both still looked blank so I stopped talking. It suddenly felt a ridiculous conversation to be having under the circumstances anyway.

As Jemima and I approached the French windows, a shadow of apprehension flitted across me. I knew I'd be accepted with open arms by Jemima, just like I had been with Charles, but Oliver and his mother were going to gang up on me, I was sure of it. He was still looking like a sulky teenager who'd had his games consoles and secret stash of lads' mags confiscated when we trooped in.

'Jemima, darling, come and sit down,' Charles nodded at her.

'What about Polly?' Jemima asked, moving up to make room for me.

'Polly's fine where she is.'

Was I? I looked at him. Maybe he could inform my knees of that and they'd stop the annoying feeling that they were about to start shaking.

'There's something you two need to be told,' he started, looking Jemima and Oliver full in the face. 'It's to do with something that happened before you were born, before I even got together with your mother.' He gave me a comforting smile.

'What's this got to do with Polly?' Oliver challenged. Jemima looked at him as if to say *just shut up and listen* and he sunk further into his chair.

'Before I started going out with your mother, I was going out with a lovely girl from Wintertown called Rosie. We met when we were doing holiday jobs at Netley Magna Country Club. Rosie was my first love.'

'What happened?' Jemima asked.

'Things didn't work out, sweetheart – sometimes they don't.'

I thanked him in my head for giving the edited version of their relationship and leaving sleazy Martin on the cutting room floor where he belonged.

'Then she left the country club and I never saw her again.'

'Seems a bit of a pointless story,' Oliver mumbled.

'Her name,' Charles studiously ignored Oliver, 'was Rosie Hanson.' He paused, either for dramatic effect or because he'd run out of steam, and all eyes turned towards me.

'That was your mum?' Jemima's voice was full of surprise and I nodded.

'Do you want to tell them the next bit, Polly?' Charles asked me. I didn't, but felt I probably should. I took a deep breath.

'Not long before my mum died, she wrote me a letter.' I realised that might be the wrong place to start and so back tracked a little. 'My mum brought me up single-handed. She'd always told me that my father had died just before I was born and I never questioned what she told me.' I could see something change in Oliver's eyes, as if he was looking at me with a different type of suspicion to the one he'd felt earlier. 'As I said, when she knew she was dying, she wrote me a letter, telling me who my real father was and why she'd kept it a secret all those years. You see, he came from an influential local family, and when she found out she was pregnant, she was afraid his family might try and make her get rid of me.'

'That's awful,' Jemima sighed.

'Sounds like something out of a soap opera,' Oliver sneered, and I wanted to slap him.

'This was the eighties, Oliver,' I snapped. 'Even that short a time ago things were very different to how they are now.' I accepted the glass of water Charles held out to me and took a sip.

'Once I was born, she knew there was nothing they could do and she came back to Netley Magna to try and find him and tell him, but he wasn't there anymore. She was told he'd gone to Switzerland so she had no choice but to wait until he came back. By then, he was engaged to someone else.'

'Dad?' Jemima looked thoughtful. 'Didn't you do your Hotel Management training in Montreux?'

'Yes, darling, I did, and that was where I got engaged to your mother.' Charles looked at them and then at me. I didn't know about him, but I could almost hear the pennies dropping.

'You mean you're Polly's father?' she gasped, looking back and forth between us. 'Polly's my sister?' She jumped out of her seat and hugged me. 'We're sisters!' she practically squealed.

'I know!' I practically squealed back.

'And that's that is it?' Oliver's voice cut into the jollity. 'Polly turns up here with a letter she says is from her dying mother and we all just say, *Oh how lovely! Welcome to the family!* I think you should at the very least do a DNA test, Dad. She could be anybody. She could be ...'

'We've already done one, Oliver.' Charles looked disappointed in his son. Frankly, I was furious with him – he was behaving like a spoiled brat. What was his problem? Did he think I was after a share of his inheritance? How could I ever have thought there was anything attractive about this self-centred idiot? 'And the results came back today. We had just read them when you so rudely burst in on us. They were conclusive.'

'Test results can be fixed.' Oliver glowered at me.

'I can assure you, these haven't been,' Charles was gritting his teeth.

'You can assure me all the hell you want.' Oliver leapt up out of his chair and strode for the door. 'That girl is *not* my sister and there is nothing you can say or do that'll ever make me believe she is.' He was still shouting as he slammed the door behind him, but I could no longer make out his words.

# CHAPTER TWENTY-SEVEN

'Morning, *Miss Hetherin, ma'am,*' Will grinned, standing to attention and giving me a salute before flicking a tea towel at my legs in a manner hardly becoming a head chef. This sort of behaviour had been going on for almost a week.

'Good morning, *mere employee.*' I side-stepped the tea towel then swiped it out of his hand. 'You'd discipline a commis chef for doing that.' I wagged my index finger at him, trying not to laugh. 'And lecture him about having someone's eye out. Any idea when you might get bored with calling me ma'am?'

'Er … Yes to the first, yes to the second, and probably not for ages yet to the third,' he chuckled. 'Just think of all the shifts you've worked under false pretences. You've been a very naughty sous chef!' He had the cheek to wink at me before disappearing into his office. I shook my head and got back to showing the newest commis chef how to devein and butterfly prawns properly, a basic skill he'd arrived sadly lacking.

So much seemed to have happened since we'd found out I was definitely Charles's daughter. I'd been moved out of the staff accommodation block, getting a few staff tongues wagging in the process, and into the family's wing of the main building. Charles, or rather Dad as I would have to get used to calling him, had told me I could have my new room – with en-suite bathroom, no less, redecorated however I wanted it. Personally, I thought it was lovely the way it was. He'd also presented me with a fancy credit card which I'd tried to refuse, accepted with embarrassment, then tucked away at the back of a drawer in my new room.

Jemima had been beside herself with joy at finding out I was her big sister. Miranda too had been beside herself, but in a less joyful, more lip curling, teeth baring, venom-spitting kind of way, which really was as scary and unattractive as it sounds. She had insisted I was a gold-digging little tramp who would bleed the family dry. Ever the gentleman, Charles had bitten his tongue so hard he'd looked in danger of biting right through it. When Grandma Hetherin heard what Miranda had said, she'd told her in no uncertain terms to go and look in the mirror if she wanted to see a pot calling a kettle black. I'd always thought it was the kettle calling the pot black, but whichever it was supposed to be, it was lovely to have Grandma and Grandpa on my side. I don't know if Grandpa knew he was on a side, or that there was even a side to be on, but he was so lovely it didn't matter.

She tried briefly to play the wounded wife who'd been last to know. I wasn't privy to what had gone wrong in their marriage or why they were to all intents and purposes living apart, but the wounded wife act had received such a poor review even from her own daughter that she'd given up after the first scene. Then, before taking herself off in a flurry of huffiness, Miranda's show-stopping pièce de résistance had been to warn them theatrically that I would probably murder them one by one until I was the sole inheritor of the Hetherin estate. I had to give it to the woman, she knew how to make an exit.

Her departure left the sky a little bluer, the grass a little greener, and Oliver the only fly dipping its toes in

the infinity pool of ointment. I could understand him
being uncomfortable with the knowledge that he'd almost
bedded his own half-sister. I could understand him being
disgusted by the thought – I had, after all, been through
these emotions myself. But it hadn't actually happened.
Thanks to my seeing that photograph and realising in time
what it meant, we hadn't actually crossed that line.

I'd been profoundly hurt by the disgusting things he'd
said about me. Deep down, he didn't mean them, he
didn't believe what he'd said, I was sure – it had been
anger and confusion talking. I hoped that when he'd had a
chance to calm down he might apologise and maybe we
could put the embarrassment behind us and have some
kind of half-brother – half-sister relationship.

I certainly didn't hate him. Why he was quite so
vehemently against me I could only put down to him
agreeing with his monstrous mother and thinking I was
after a third of Dad's money. Could he possibly believe he
was in danger of my cooking him a toadstool omelette? If
this was the case, he couldn't be further from the truth but
somehow I didn't think telling him that would do much
good. Anyway, if Jemima wasn't bothered about a
potential lessening of her future nest egg, I didn't see why
he should be; I hadn't had him down as the mercenary
kind – but then he clearly thought I was mercenary and/or
murderous when I wasn't, so we'd made a pretty good job
of misunderstanding each other.

If Oliver had been able to put himself in my shoes for
a moment, he might have had an inkling of what
becoming part of a family meant to me. I couldn't have
cared less about the Hetherin money. Charles could have
been an out of work homing pigeon fancier and as long as
he was my dad, then my dad is what I'd want him to be.
The whole family could be in minimum wage jobs or on

benefits and living on the type of estate policemen aren't too keen on visiting and if they were my family, then I'd want to be with them. To have a father, grandparents, a sister, and a brother – even if one of them was horrible and an idiot – these were things I used to imagine when I was growing up, although of course I always imagined Mum being there at the centre of it. But Mum had given me this family. She'd made sure I wouldn't be alone. As far as I was concerned, and I was pretty sure Charles felt the same way, she would always be at the centre of it. But Oliver had grown up with this lovely family. This was all he'd ever known. Of course he had taken it for granted. He would never understand.

He had barely shown his face since revelation day, sending the snooty boy waiters into the kitchen with any food orders or to ask about the specials. They treated me with as little interest as they'd ever shown me, which was how I liked it. Mel and Lulu and the other waitresses, however, were giving their tongues so much exercise it was a wonder they didn't get cramp. Funnily enough, they all fell silent whenever I happened to come anywhere near them. Desperate to know what was going on, the only thing they had felt able to ask was why Oliver was being such a pain, or as Mel so quaintly put it, 'like a bear with a sore arse' – she's got a lovely way with words. She did tell me he was taking a week's leave which I hadn't known about, so her gossip did have its uses. Apparently he was going on some photography trip with that gorgeous girl from the photographic society. I hoped they'd both have such a lovely time playing with shutter speeds and developing things in cosy dark rooms that they'd forget to come back. Mind you, he'd really have to drop the sore-arsed bear routine if he wanted to keep on the right side of a girl like that. I couldn't imagine her being short of male attention, so she wouldn't need to put up with any of his self-indulgent nonsense.

So when he left for his trip, there would be a week of only Polly-friendly Hetherins. It was a warm and welcome thought. I tried not to be too greedy and wish it was a month.

# CHAPTER TWENTY-EIGHT

'There's something wrong with this parsley, dear.' Grandma waved the small bunch of coriander at me and I put my knife down and out of her reach. 'Are you sure those communists have washed it properly?'

'It's coriander, Grandma,' I smiled, glancing around to make sure none of the commis chefs had noticed, pretty sure that none of them took any notice of anyone over the age of fifty, anyway. I was tickled pink at being able to call her Grandma. I couldn't really remember my maternal grandmother as she had died when I was about three and so I had no memory of ever calling her Grandma or Gran or whatever she would have wanted to be called. 'And they're *commis chefs*. You mustn't call them communists, you might offend them.' I knew my words were falling on deaf ears – I'd heard Will correct her enough times. She and Grandpa lived quite happily in their own pre-politically correct world most of the time, popping into the century the rest of us inhabited whenever they wanted company or fancied something to eat. I wished I'd been there the day she'd taken Will's mobile phone to their bungalow and tried to change the channels on their television with it. Or even better, the day Grandpa had used Oliver's brand spanking new iPad as a table mat and put a bowl of hot soup on it. The look on Oliver's face must have been priceless. I wondered if I could get him to do that again.

'No, dear, it can't be coriander.' She picked up a coffee spoon with her free hand. I knew it would end up in her cornflower blue cardigan pocket any minute. 'I don't like coriander – nasty, hard seeds, you can break your teeth on them if you're not careful. You need to grind them up in a pestle and mortar before you use them – that's the best way.'

'Thanks, I'll remember that.' I gently took the slightly wilting herbs from her hand, wondering when she'd managed to pinch them, and went through the motions of giving them a good wash. I'd take a bunch of parsley over to her later if that was what she really wanted. 'Would you like a nice cup of tea?' I always wondered why we say a *nice* cup of tea, as if we'd offer somebody a horrible one. Mind you, I could think of a few people.

'Thank you, dear.' The spoon arrived in her pocket, making a muffled clink against something she must have slipped in earlier without me noticing – was she going for the full set? 'I was just going to make a pot for George and myself. Don't forget the cake, dear, will you – I rather fancy seed cake.' With that, she wandered out through the restaurant. How many more coffee spoons would she manage to collect by the time she reached the French windows? She'd soon have more than the restaurant at this rate. How often did Dad have to mount a surreptitious raid on their bungalow to retrieve the hotel's silverware?

I was halfway through putting together a tea tray for the three of us when Jemima wandered into the kitchen through the back door. How did she do it? It was as if she had an inner bloodhound who could sniff out a snacking opportunity, except she would want me to put something healthy and boring like carrot sticks on the tray.

'If you want carrot sticks, you'll have to chop them yourself,' I pre-empted her.

'I'm perfectly capable of chopping carrot sticks.' She tried to look indignant then pouted prettily instead. 'Why do I need carrot sticks now, anyway?'

'I'm making up a tea tray for Grandma and Grandpa and I assumed you'd want to join us but with something other than cake.'

'Ooh, can I have lemon and ginger tea?'

'You can, as long as you make it yourself.' I ignored the fluttering eyelashes but gave her full marks for trying. She had the fresh version on the go all the time in the spa – they got through more ginger than we did in the kitchen most weeks, so I was pretty certain she wouldn't be happy with me chucking a teabag in a mug – even a fancy posh teabag, which to her was just a regular, common, or garden teabag anyway.

'I'll just cut some lemon slices and have lemon tea then.' She made her way to the walk-in fridge and came back with a lemon and a couple of carrots. We grinned at each other as she picked up a peeler and started attacking her carrots. 'Is that seed cake?'

'It is.' I wrinkled my nose at the smell of caraway as I eased a couple of slices of my least favourite cake onto a large tea plate. I had wondered at first why the pastry kitchen kept making such an old-fashioned and not particularly popular cake, not realising it was mainly for the senior Hetherins' benefit.

'Yuck!' Jemima passed sentence on the cake, but would have said the same of most patisserie items.

'Yuck indeed,' I agreed, adding a couple of slices of farmhouse fruit cake and four fingers of the pastry chef's delicious shortbread and putting the plate on a tray. I added a fourth cup, saucer, and side plate and got on with tea making.

'Do you think Grandma and Grandpa really understand

who you are?' She was now chopping the kind of dainty little carrot sticks that wouldn't look out of place at a doll's tea party. I was itching to take the serrated knife out of her hand and give her a straight edged one, but didn't want to be bossy.

'I'm not sure about Grandma.' I put the teapot and the hot water pot on the tray. 'Sometimes I think she does and other times I'm not sure.'

'Grandpa doesn't have a clue, does he?' Jemima added her carrot matchsticks.

'I doubt it, but he seems happy enough for me to be around.'

'You keep feeding him – what's there for him to be unhappy about?'

'I keep finding myself feeding you too.' I treated her to my best Hetherin eyebrow raise and she giggled.

'And look how happy I am!' She picked up a carrot stick and went to nibble the end of it. 'It's such a shame Ollie's being such a pig. I can't think what's got into him lately.'

'Well, we don't have to worry about him this week.' I shuffled things around on the tray to make room for the lemon slices.

'Maybe he'll have such a nice time playing photographers in Eastbourne or Hastings or wherever it is he's gone that he'll come back in a better mood.' She looked at me hopefully. She really was a glass half full kind of girl.

'Yes, maybe.' I tried to sound convinced. I wouldn't be holding my breath.

We took the tea things – or rather, I carried the tray while Jemima accompanied me – to the cottage. A black and white film was playing to itself on the television screen –

Grandpa, mouth open, was gently snoring in front of it. Grandma was reading a large print *Dick Francis,* holding her reading glasses in front of her eyes rather than wearing them.

'Tea time!' Jemima trilled, stooping to kiss them both. 'We've brought your favourite, Grandma – seed cake.' I liked this *we* business. Cheeky minx hadn't even carried her own carrot sticks.

'How lovely, dear, do come and sit down.' Grandma patted the seat next to her. 'George!' She sounded like a posh hospital matron. 'George! Tea and cake dear!'

'Mmm, lovely,' he mumbled, opening his eyes.

I placed the tray on the coffee table and set out the cups and saucers. 'Would you like me to pour?' I looked at Grandma.

'Thank you, dear,' she said, putting her book down and her glasses on top of it.

\* \* \*

While Grandpa wolfed down his cake and Grandma and Jemima sipped their tea, I couldn't help looking at the photographs that covered the walls and almost every available surface. My dad – it gave me a little rush of excitement every time I called him that – featured at various stages of his life in a lot of them. So too, did Jemima, who'd looked like a little angel as a small child, and Oliver, who hadn't. The wicked step-mother only appeared in a few family groups, where she hadn't been on the end of the line and easily chopped off. It was the oldest pictures I was most interested in, seeing my father as a young man and hopefully as he'd been when he met my mother. It felt kind of like a new link to her. Jemima caught my eye.

'Grandma, could I show Polly your old photo albums? You know, the ones from when Dad was little?' My clever sister grinned at me. Was she a mind reader, or just very perceptive when she chose to be?

'Of course, dear.' Grandma put her cup on its saucer. 'If you know where to put your hands on them. I can't think where I last saw them, in the attic, possibly.'

Jemima jumped up, went to the old-fashioned sideboard, and opened one of the cupboards. It was jam-packed full of battered board games, ancient-looking Monopoly, Risk, and Cluedo crammed in with games I hadn't heard of like Flutter and Cop-It. An image of them sitting round a table at Christmas, rolling dice, laughing, and probably cheating a little bit, flashed through my mind as she closed that door and tried the other.

'Here we are!' she said with a flourish. 'The Hetherin family history in photographs.' A cupboard full of leather-bound, red, brown, and blue albums met my gaze. How many pictures of my dad growing up would be in there? Would there be pictures from the summer he worked at Netley Magna Country Club?

'Oh, well done, dear.' Grandma peered over at the open door. 'I wonder who put them in there.'

Jemima's dainty fingers manipulated the first album out from between the tightly packed pile and the top of the cupboard and put it on the small dining table by the window. I joined her. Feeling like a child on Christmas morning faced with a beautifully wrapped parcel, I stroked the supple, dark red cover, eager to see what was inside but not wanting to rush this moment. Inhaling the scent of old expensive leather, I slowly opened it.

'Oh, you don't want to see those!' Jemima grimaced at a couple of pictures of herself, aged about six or seven, in what looked like a posh school uniform complete with straw boater and pig tails.

'Oh yes, I really, really do,' I teased, scrutinising them

before turning the page and coming face to face with Oliver, a couple of years older, sporting short grey trousers and a heavy-looking leather satchel and looking like he'd just stepped out of Greyfriars. A snort of laughter escaped me.

'I know! Just look at those knees,' Jemima exclaimed. I kept my eyes firmly on the satchel.

The whole album was full of photos of my sister and brother, at school events, on outings with the Brownies or Scouts, attending birthday parties. There seemed to have been a lot of friends' birthday parties. I hadn't been to many growing up, not understanding until years later that I hadn't gone because we hadn't been able to afford the presents for me to take.

The next album was older – Grandma and Grandpa on a cruise. I made polite noises and said how lovely everything looked. On another day I would love to look at them properly, but what I really wanted to see was my dad the year *Dirty Dancing* came out. I'd have to get back to the kitchen soon – just because I was now a Hetherin didn't mean I could start slacking. Jemima pulled out another album and I promised myself this would be the last for today – it would probably be baby pictures or family weddings or something, anyway.

The clothes were the first thing that leapt off the page – they were so late eighties, early nineties, I'd seen enough of Mum's photos to know. I held my breath as I studied the first picture.

'Look at those shoulder pads!' Jemima squeaked in my ear. 'What did they look like? Look, there's Dad. What a hideous jumper!'

'Where?' I homed in on where she was pointing. He did indeed look like a Noel Edmunds wannabe, but he was with a group of other lads. And their clothes looked too warm to have been worn in the summer. I turned the pages, scanning their contents as I went. Dad had a lot of friends, male and female, but I couldn't see my mum in any of the pictures.

Itching to open just one more album but knowing I had to get back to the kitchen, I swallowed my disappointment – of course there wouldn't be a photograph of my mum and dad together, waiting to leap out at me the very first time I looked at a family album.

'I need to head back.' I closed the album and handed it to Jemima. 'Thanks for showing me. I'd love to see the rest when there's more time to look properly.'

'No problem. Just no laughing when you get to the ones of my first school nativity,' Jemima grimaced. 'I was the angel Gabriel and one of my front teeth had come out the morning of the show. I looked a fright!'

\* \* \*

As I made my way back to the main building, my own primary school nativity – or it might have been junior school, I couldn't remember – flashed into my mind. I'd sung *Little Donkey* with the choir. Mum had helped me practice so much I'd known the words off by heart. Somehow I couldn't imagine Miranda doing that with a five-year-old Jemima. My sister and brother might have had a privileged up-bringing, but Dad would have been busy building his hotel empire so he wouldn't have been around all the time. And I couldn't imagine Miranda tickling her children, helping them with homework, or tip-toeing into their bedrooms at night with a coin from the tooth fairy.

The thought made me a little sad for the children they'd been. Yes, even Oliver.

# CHAPTER TWENTY-NINE

Isn't it amazing how a week can either drag on and feel like an eternity, or whizz by and be over practically as soon as it's started? The last week of school before breaking up for summer holidays always dragged, whereas the last week of those holidays always seemed to disappear with indecent haste, leaving you wondering where it had gone. This was how the week of Oliver's absence felt – one moment I had the luxury of seven days without his sneering, snarling presence and then, before I knew it, he was due back the next day. That felt like a very short week. I wanted to report that week to the Trades Descriptions people because it certainly didn't feel like seven days to me. If I'd paid good money for that week, I'd want a refund.

And as if it wasn't enough that he was due back practically before he'd even gone away, he was due back just in time for the biggest wedding of the season. We weren't just doing the reception for this one; we were doing the whole damn thing. The families of the bride and groom were even staying in the hotel the night before and the night of the big event.

*Please don't make me work this function, please don't make me work this function, please don't make me work this function!* My new mantra whirred on a loop inside my head. I'd tried to make every hint I could think of to get myself out of having anything to do with this wedding, except actually telling Dad I couldn't work – because then of course I would have to explain why, and I didn't want to put my new-found father into therapy. Could I transmit my plea telepathically? I knew we were going to be run off our feet but ... the memory of the last wedding and what happened afterwards sent a hot flush coursing through my body, building up in intensity until my face felt like it had been boiled. Surely that would qualify me for a day off sick. I must look like someone who shouldn't be allowed to handle food. Or be too close to other people.

I felt sick. But that was probably the unwanted images flashing through my mind – Oliver and I kissing, stumbling to his bedroom, tumbling onto his bed, pulling at each other's clothes. I felt really sick. Surely they could manage without me for one day.

'We're only just going to be able to manage, Polly,' Dad sighed. 'The biggest function of the year and we haven't been able to get any temps in thanks to Miranda antagonising our regular agency. If anyone phones in sick we're going to be right up against it. It's all hands on deck for the next forty-eight hours.'

*Crap!* I don't ever want to do a wedding here ever, ever, ever again.

'Anyway, after the way you fixed that damaged wedding cake, I think you should be on duty for every wedding we do.'

*Just kill me now*! Go on – suffocate me in a vat of royal icing and leave it to set hard – it'd be a mercy killing.

'Thank goodness Oliver will be back in the morning. Between the two of you ...'

I didn't hear what Dad thought the two of us would, could, or should be capable of doing between us. I was too busy trying to quell the tidal wave of panic threatening my entire body. I felt hot and cold at the same time. Was I going to throw up or was I going to faint? Or have a heart attack? My blood pressure felt like it was going into orbit. Not just a bloody wedding. Not just bloody, bloody Oliver. But a bloody, bloody, bloody wedding-Oliver-torture combo. How much royal icing would it take to asphyxiate a five foot five and a half – without her clogs on – sous chef?

'I'm sure we'll be snowed under in the kitchen and …' I started to say.

'Don't you worry about the kitchen,' Dad jumped in, thwarting my plan to be as far away from Oliver as possible. 'Will's done enough of these functions, he could keep the kitchen on its toes with a blindfold on and one hand tied behind his back. No, it's co-ordinating the kitchen and ballroom that requires your special skills. You seem to have a great flair for this kind of thing. I need you to be the link between Will and Oliver.'

*Oh, that's just great!* If the universe was so hell bent on torturing me, couldn't it just rip my toenails out, shove me in an Iron Maiden, and be done with it?

'Take these with you and look them over.' Dad handed me a clipboard with an inch thick wodge of A4 pages clipped to it. 'Menus, seating plan, special requirements, schedule, and anything else you'll need.'

*Does that include a one-way ticket to anywhere else?*

'The cake is coming down from London tomorrow afternoon. Reception have been instructed that you'll be in charge of that.'

*Oh good, I'm the cake-sitter as well as everything else – should I stick a broom up …* On second thoughts, maybe I shouldn't ask – I didn't want to give him any more ideas for things to lumber me with.

'Oh, and make sure you pay attention to where the bride's uncle is sitting. He's not to be given alcohol under any circumstances. There's non-alcoholic wine set aside for him and sparkling grape juice for the toasts ...'

'What if he helps himself to somebody else's?' I finally got a word in. 'I'm not going to have to wrestle a glass away from him, am I?' A Mr Bean-type scenario managed, for a moment, to oust Oliver from its centre-stage slot in my brain.

'Don't worry,' Dad chuckled. 'His wife will be keeping a firm eye on him. The groom's family don't know how bad he is, and the wedding isn't the best time for them to find out. We just need you to keep an eye on the waiting staff – make sure no one pours him some of the real stuff by accident ...'

'I'm not being funny,' I butted in, waving my well-stuffed clipboard at him, 'but what's the wedding planner going to be doing while I'm busy doing her job as well as my own?'

'Some B-list celebrity's wedding in a Scottish castle,' my father sighed.

'Run that by me again?'

'Apparently both brides were insistent on the very same date and the very same wedding planner.' He rolled his eyes. 'Unfortunately, that was where their demands parted company, and of course the planner can only be in one place.'

'And the celeb one's going to be more high profile, so of course that's the one the planner has to be at?' Nice work if you can get it.

'In a nutshell.'

'OK, but in the absence of the actual wedding planner, isn't all this checking and keeping an eye on everything really Oliver's job?' Honestly! If I was going to be doing his job for him too, there was no point in him being there at all.

'The poor lad can't be everywhere at once, Polly!'

'Hmph!' A horse-like snort escaped me before I could stop it. *Poor lad, my foot!* And as for being everywhere at once, it certainly felt to me like he was. Everywhere I didn't want him to be.

'He'll come round eventually.' Dad patted my hand, apparently taking my horsey sound effect for concern that Oliver was still miffed at having a long-lost sister appear out of nowhere. 'And you never know, it might be a step in the right direction – the two of you working together. He might appreciate your help. He might start to see things more clearly.'

*Yeah, right.* He might have been initiated into a cult while he'd been away. Or had a personality transplant. Or grown a second head – one with a fully functioning brain in it.

'Let's not hold our breath,' I shrugged with as much nonchalance as I could muster under the circumstances. Although the thought of holding mine until I went blue in the face and passed out sounded much more fun than the next few days were going to be.

# CHAPTER THIRTY

Just how much was being spent on this wedding? And how much was being spent on the wedding the planner was going to be at instead of this one? Were these people very minor royals? Or maybe C-list celebrities I hadn't heard of?

Of course the menus were what I was most interested in, but the other lists of requirements just kept pulling my attention back. The florists were going to have their work cut out for them. It seemed that not just the tables for the sit-down meal, but every other available flat surface in every public area of the hotel was going to have a tall, clear vase of raspberry pink dendrobium orchids and cream calla lilies as a centrepiece, flanked by crystal bowls of raspberry pink and cream roses. And the bannisters of the grand staircase, the backs of chairs, and any other available vertical surfaces were going to be swathed with cascades and garlands of two other kinds of orchids. Also cream and raspberry pink. Personally, I'd always thought an orchid was an orchid, but it seemed I was wrong.

The cake that had apparently become my responsibility was also going to be cream and yes, raspberry pink. Three cheers for the start of the raspberry season. The vintage Rolls-Royce wedding cars – cars? I thought there was usually just one. The vintage Rolls-Royce wedding cars would be cream. Why did they need cars if everything was happening here?. I'd be interested to see if it, or rather they, arrived with seasonal fruit-coloured ribbons attached. It was all starting to sound like some kind of Barbie fantasy and I wondered how much input the groom had been allowed. At least they hadn't forced a colour scheme on the food, although I did notice the champagne was pink. Oh, and one of the desserts.

I chuckled to myself as I sat up in bed with the pages from my clipboard spread around me. It was getting late, but this was just too fascinating.

Plus, this would be my last Oliver free night and I wanted to make the most of it. When I went to bed tomorrow I'd be able to feel the vibes of disgust, suspicion, and hatred wafting along the corridor from his bedroom to mine. *His bedroom.* Why did I have to think about that?

Snatching up the clipboard, I pulled out a random page – *concentrate, Polly, just concentrate on the clipboard* – then I was overwhelmed by a sense of déjà vu. I'd said something very much like that to myself while I'd been working on repairing that wedding cake and trying not to think about Oliver. *Crap!*

I closed my eyes. When I opened them I would forget all about Oliver and what had happened and focus my whole attention on the page in front of me. I would learn, off by heart, whatever instructions lay on that page, and throw myself into working so hard on this wedding that instead of being Polly, I would become just an efficient blur, whirring around the festivities like a twenty-first century Mary Poppins, keeping the vegans happy, the glasses topped up, the small children entertained, the squabbling waiters quiet, and the dipsomaniac uncle sober.

I opened my eyes and looked down. And groaned. A

picture of the bridal suite greeted me, its king-size bed adorned with rose petals, tea lights flickering on the bedside tables and window ledges, champagne nestling in an ice bucket on the dressing table, next to two champagne flutes and a dish of chocolate truffles.

The universe really hated me.

# CHAPTER THIRTY-ONE

The second I stepped out of my room the next morning, I knew Oliver was back. That subtle scent of sandalwood in the corridor told me he must have walked past my door just moments earlier. This was all I needed. I'd hoped to at least get the breakfast shift out of the way before his return, but it seemed luck was not on my side. I tapped gently on Jemima's door – I didn't want to wake her, but if she was already awake I could do with a sisterly hug. No answer.

Forcing my feet to take it in turns to put themselves one in front of the other, I made my way down the stairs, telling myself very firmly that I had nothing to fear from Oliver and his blustering. Technically I hadn't done anything wrong – in fact, it was only down to my unusually quick thinking that neither of us had done anything wrong – so he should be thanking me, really. I wasn't about to suggest it, though.

The kitchen was already in full swing when I walked in. They hardly looked as if they'd miss me if I turned round and walked back out.

'Oh, Polly, there you are,' Will greeted me, coming out of the pastry kitchen. 'Can you come and sort out the pastry kitchen before Steve and Greg start chucking utensils at each other?' OK, so they would miss me.

'Just call me Ban Ki Moon,' I rolled my eyes as I passed him. He had the cheek to laugh.

He hadn't been exaggerating. It was practically dough hooks at dawn in there, the two chefs firmly planted, hands on hips, one on each side of the work bench and in between them, a stack of what looked to be a dozen trays of eggs. I hoped it wasn't going to get messy.

'My Bavarois has to be started now,' Steve was growling at Greg.

'It doesn't take that long to boil up some milk and melt some gelatin,' Greg was scoffing in reply.

'A Bavarois is not just hot milk and gelatin.' Steve's face was already a dangerous shade and getting redder by the second. 'And this one has to be done in two stages to get the colour effect ...'

'Yeah, yeah.' Greg leaned closer, his knuckles now pressed on the bench and I wondered if I was going to have to get in between them to save the eggs. 'Pudding's the most important part of the meal, blah, blah, blah ...'

'Actually,' I threw my oar in as loudly as I could, which surprised them into silence as I don't think they'd even noticed I was there, 'this one is.' I was suddenly very glad I'd done my homework. 'It was the bride's choice and meant to represent the colours of her dress.'

'A pink and white sodding wedding dress?' Greg sneered. 'Now I've bloody well heard it all ...'

'It seems the bride is a huge Gwen Stefani fan,' I explained. 'She's a singer,' I added noticing their faces go even blanker than usual. 'She got married in this really stunning pink and *cream* dress and our bride seems to have had a copy of it made.' I'd thought it was taking it a bit far too, but this probably wasn't the time to mention it. Or the fact that the marriage hadn't lasted.

'Yeah, whatever.' Greg continued his stroppy teenager act. An act he was far too old to think he could carry off. 'The fact still stands that I need these eggs to get on with my canapés and the running buffet for the guests arriving this evening. It's not my fault somebody,' he now looked me up and down, 'forgot to increase the order.'

'The order will be in later this morning at the usual time. Plus the extra, which we did indeed remember to order.' I felt like banging their stupid heads together. And who's stupid idea had the running buffet been? Certainly not mine.

'Yes, but I need to get on *now*,' they both chorused, glaring at each other. Forget teenage strops, it was like dealing with a couple of wilful seven-year-olds. I dreaded to think what would happen if they regressed any further. I did a quick calculation – a dozen trays of thirty eggs, that made three-hundred and sixty.

'How many egg yolks do you need to get started with the Bavarois?' I looked at Steve.

'A hundred and eighty for the raspberry and a hundred and eighty for the vanilla. That's three-hundred and sixty,' he added, looking defiantly at Greg. 'And I'll need the whites for the Pavlovas.

'And how many eggs do you need for your canapés and buffet dishes?' I asked Greg, fully expecting him to also lay claim to three-hundred and sixty of the damn things.

'Well, I need forty whole ones for the bacon and egg tartlets ...'

'You won't be able to fill them until I've done the pastry cases for them.' Steve folded his arms across his chest.

'Forty for the mini toad in the holes' Greg continued, 'forty for the frittata bites, forty for the blinis, forty for the veggie gougères, forty for the crepes, forty for the dill omelettes for the salmon roulades, twenty for the parmesan puffs, and twenty yolks for the aioli dips. I'm no mathematician,' he smirked, as I carried on doing the calculations with my fingers,' but I reckon that makes three hundred and sixty ...'

'Two hundred and ...' Steve jumped in.

'No, it's three hundred and ...'

'That's three hundred and twenty.' Oliver's voice leapfrogged mine, making us all jump and my head spin on my neck like something out of a horror film. How long had he been standing in the doorway? 'Don't think of getting a team together and applying to be on *Eggheads,* any of you. Or if you do, for God's sake, don't tell them you work here.' And with that he turned on his heel and left us to it. It suddenly felt very hot and the ovens hadn't even been switched on yet.

'Right,' someone squeaked. The way the two chefs were looking at me, I guessed it had been me. 'Take a hundred and eighty each and get on with whatever needs to be done first.' I was still squeaking but in a slightly more natural pitch. 'I'll make sure you get the rest as soon as the delivery arrives, and I don't want to hear another word about stupid eggs.'

Without waiting for any arguments, I went straight to the still room and poured myself a tumbler of cold water from the dispenser, half expecting steam to come whistling out of my ears, the way my pulse was pumping. And this was only the first hour of the first day of him being back. I filled the tumbler again and rolled it back and forth against my forehead, slopping some of the refreshing liquid about my temples and letting it run down the sides of my face. If I was in this state now, how was I ever going to get through the rest of this weekend?

# CHAPTER THIRTY-TWO

**The wedding breakfast:**
\* \* \*
**Starters:**
**Lobster, Crayfish & Hamble Crab salad (s)**
**Carpaccio of Hampshire Buffalo**
**Arlesford Watercress soup (v)**
\* \* \*
**Main Course:**
**Roasted Monkfish with Romesco Sauce (s) (n)**
**Roast Hampshire Venison wrapped in Pancetta with**
**Redcurrant Port Jus**
**Tart of New Forest Wild Mushrooms (v)**
**All served with a selection of seasonal vegetables**
\* \* \*
**Dessert:**
**Raspberry and Vanilla Bavarois**
**Chocolate Platter**
**Seasonal Fresh Fruit Pavlovas**
\* \* \*

Every section of the kitchen had a full breakdown of their own components of the wedding breakfast menu. I personally wasn't going to be cooking any of it, but I envied the chefs who would be running around – except they wouldn't, because it wasn't allowed in the kitchen – like cats on a hot tin roof at the very last minute, getting all the elements together at precisely the right time. They thought they knew what stress was, but I'd happily swap places with any one of them.

I felt like a fraud, still wearing my chefs' whites whilst nipping about with my clipboard and checking up on people who really didn't need checking up on. Would anyone actually notice if I skedaddled back to my room and hid for the rest of the day? Of course, if I did, that would be the one time my presence was actually needed.

Jemima's spa was doing a brisk trade, starting with the lunchtime arrival of the very first members of the wedding party who'd travelled down from Cumbria – they should have got themselves invited to the planner's other wedding and saved themselves a journey – and had booked a couple's massage followed by mani-pedis for both of them and a facial for her. They sounded determined to make the most of the weekend. I hoped they weren't the dipsomaniac uncle and his wife, although as far as I knew, my policing of his drinking was only scheduled for the wedding breakfast itself.

The staff at the terrace bar were gearing up for a busy afternoon and evening. They didn't need my interference, so I made my way back to the pastry kitchen to see how Steve was getting on now he had his full complement of eggs. With Oliver having been last sighted in the ballroom, it seemed like as good a place as any to hang around and kid myself I was doing something useful. The vanilla portions of the Bavarois were firming up nicely in the fridge.

'Polly! You seem to have homing pigeon tendencies where this pastry room is concerned.' Apparently I was wrong, as Oliver's voice caught me off guard for the second time that day.

'My instructions were to keep an eye on all departments.' I forced myself to look him in the eye as I spoke. As soon as I did, he looked away.

'Well, Steve's been working for us for more years than I can remember and he's done more weddings than most of the staff here put together, so I think he can manage perfectly well without you getting in his way. In any case, the wedding cake has arrived, so if you could drag yourself out of here and sign for it ...'

I clomped out of there, saved from having to hear the rest of his pompous speech by the sheer volume of noise in the main kitchen. My clogs didn't even make a dent in the din. The reception area was a haven of calm by comparison. Well, it was quiet anyway. A less imposing space would have been swamped by the six overly sturdy-looking cake boxes that ranged from fairly normal wedding cake sized to gargantuan. *Goldilocks and the Three Bears* popped into my mind, only with three visiting relatives on steroids. I hoped the wedding planner hadn't got the cakes mixed up – this looked much bigger than the dimensions on my clipboard.

'Sign here, please.' An equally gargantuan delivery man with a tattoo of a dove on his neck – at least I think it was a dove – shoved his own clipboard at me. *Oh no, you don't, there's no way I'm signing anything until I've inspected the merchandise.*

'We'll just need to open up the boxes first.' I put on my best no-nonsense voice – he was much bigger than your average chef and could probably pick me up with one hand like King Kong, although I don't imagine any wedding cake company would last long if its employees started man-handling the people accepting their deliveries. And he had said please. I stayed with that thought as he produced a Stanley knife and applied it to the sealed flap on the largest box.

The sketch I'd been given of the cake really didn't do

justice to its hideousness. If it had been cream it wouldn't have looked so bad, but the raspberry pink effects, which looked to be much darker than intended, made it look as if it had been decorated in the middle of some terrible massacre. I couldn't imagine any bride who wasn't an extremely extreme Goth being happy with this. What on earth was I going to do? It was too late to send the monstrosity back. Or was it? Could they scrape off the darkest bits and redo them in a lighter shade and then re-deliverer them in time? While I gazed in full awe at the truly awful bottom tier, the delivery man opened up the other five boxes. As the cakes got smaller, so too did the percentage of *Texas Chainsaw Massacre* pink that covered each one.

'Bloody hell!' Oliver's voice snapped me out of my daze. 'That's a bit red, isn't it?'

'You think!' All our awkwardness was temporarily forgotten in the face of this monstrous cake that right now was bigger than both of us – probably literally as well as figuratively.

'Look, is someone gonna sign for this?' The delivery man waved his clipboard at Oliver. 'I've got to get back and pick up the next delivery. All this faffing about's gonna put me behind schedule.'

'Is it meant to be that colour?' Oliver peered further into the biggest box and shuddered.

'Cream and raspberry, it says here.' The delivery man tapped his clipboard with his pen. 'Six tiers, cream and raspberry, to the bride's specifications. So it's not one of our designs. This is what the bride ordered, this is what she paid for, and this is what she's got. Now, will one of you sign so I can get going?'

Oliver and I looked at each other. There was clearly going to be no taking back, re-doing, and returning. I took the pen, started to sign my name, but Oliver pulled the clipboard away. 'You can at least help me take them through to the ballroom.' The man looked like he was going to refuse, but quick as anything Oliver picked up the two smallest boxes and said to him, 'Follow me. We can do this in two trips. She'll have signed by the time you get back and then you can be on your way.'

As I signed the docket, my mind whirred into action. The bottom tier was much too big for the trolley and stand I'd had Mel prepare based on the dimensions provided. I was certain the bride must have got her measurements mixed up – some people did get metric and imperial muddled up. She could have mistaken millimetres for centimetres, or centimetres for inches. Or cubic feet. The largest of the cakes was the worst. If we used the next in size as the bottom tier, I could probably cut away the worst of the icing and re-ice it with a paler shade. If the bride was really set on six tiers, I could cut down the big one to make it the smallest and re-ice it from scratch. It wasn't as if I had much else to do or actually needed to go to bed at a reasonable hour, so I'd be bright-eyed, bushy-tailed, and on the ball the next day.

'I notice you just assumed I could do something to make these hideous cakes look presentable.' I kept my voice as professional as possible as Oliver and I stood in a sea of cake boxes in the ante-room at the back of the ballroom.

'You performed miracles with the last one in a very short amount of time. You've got just under twenty-four hours to sort this one out, you should be able to do it blindfolded.'

'And you don't think the bride is going to want to see her cake at some point today? You don't think there's the tiniest chance she's going to look at this horror film prop her wedding cake has turned into and completely freak out?'

'We'll just have to keep her away from it until you've worked your magic on it.'

'Oh, no pressure then!' This was the man who a little over a week ago had been calling me all the names under the sun, now I was suddenly the cake whisperer.

'What choice do we have, Polly – let her see it like this?'

'Alright, I'll work on it in here with the door locked. Nobody comes in but me. You do whatever you have to, just keep the bride away until I tell you it's done. OK?'

'OK,' he nodded.

'Right. Get me the key for this door and a Do Not Disturb sign, then go and keep a look out for the bride.' I sighed as I watched him go. How had I become the official sorter out of wedding cake catastrophes? And why was it that whenever there was a potential wedding cake catastrophe, it was always Oliver I was lumbered with to help me sort it out? I picked up my clipboard and started to make a list of all the things I'd need from the stores and pastry kitchen. Steve was not going to be happy with me. Not happy at all.

# CHAPTER THIRTY-THREE

It took two trips with a full trolley for me to get everything I thought I would need to make a silk purse out of this particular severed and dripping sow's ear. Then I locked myself in and set about scraping the scarlet icing from the bottom half of cake number five.

Fortunately for me, our bride had gone for sponge cake, rather than traditional wedding cake, where I would have had to hack off royal icing without taking the marzipan with it. Unfortunately, the cake company she'd chosen had used ready-made icing bought by the tub. My butter cream version was going to taste very different – infinitely better, without all the additives – but definitely different. I was starting to feel quite angry on the bride's behalf. She'd obviously had a rough but not very practical idea of what she wanted, and this company had gone ahead and made her a ridiculous cake, far bigger than she needed, and probably charged her an absolute fortune for it. It was like somebody going to a hairdresser they hadn't been to before and asking for a completely unsuitable haircut and the hairdresser just going ahead and doing it without trying to suggest something more appropriate. I'd be recommending that the wedding planner never let her clients use them again. In fact, as the wedding planner, she should bear some of the responsibility. I found myself grinding my teeth as I wondered just how much of her attention our bride had received once the Scottish-castle-minor-celeb-bride had appeared on the scene. It made me even more determined to get this mess sorted out.

I purloined the smallest of the pastry kitchen's mixers after explaining briefly, and quietly, to Steve. If it had been for anything else, he'd have argued about needing it himself, but if anyone understands the importance of cake, it's a pastry chef.

While the mixer's beaters worked overtime to soften the butter enough for me to add the icing sugar, I studied the patterns piped on the remaining cakes. They were just simple flowers and rosettes with the ubiquitous shell border, nothing to overtax anyone who could fill a piping bag. How much prettier it could have been. I wanted to make it look as lovely as possible for the bride, but I didn't want to veer too far from her original ideas.

I was getting the piping bags ready when someone tried to open the door. I held my breath. Nobody other than Oliver and I could know what I was doing. This place was such a goldfish bowl – it would only need someone like Mel or Lulu to find out there was something wrong with the cake and it would be round the hotel in minutes. The wedding guests would know, and the poor bride didn't need the stress. The sound of the mixer was a constant whirring and from outside it might sound like it was coming from further away. The handle rattled up and down a couple of times before whoever was on the other side gave up and went away. I breathed again.

I didn't remember it being this stressful last time. I'd fixed that wedding cake in the amount of time it took for the ceremony to take place. And that had been with Oliver hovering about trying to help, his sandalwood scent sapping my concentration. *Stop it. This is no time to be thinking about Oliver. There will never be a good time to think about Oliver. Not like that! Not ever again!* I shook my head, as if to shake any last, stray thoughts of him out of it.

Now a brief moment of panic gripped me as I was about to add the food colouring. Luckily, the colour prints of the flowers Dad had added to my clipboard gave me the confidence to go for it. I watched as the colours swirled into the pale, creamy mix, disappeared for a while, then slowly blended themselves in. It was trial and error, only hopefully without the error.

I was filling the row of piping bags when my phone bleeped and Oliver's name came up. My stomach turned over as I opened the text with my icing-free thumb nail. *The bride is here. How is it going? Oliver.* Trust Oliver to be one of those people who send grammatically correct texts. *OK, will let u know when done – P* I tapped back with my nail, hoping he would get the subtext and leave me in peace.

It must have been about an hour later when I heard voices coming towards me. The mixer wasn't on and I could clearly hear Oliver's voice. I held my breath.

'As I said, Tiffany, the cake was safely delivered and my co-co-ordinator has locked it away to keep it safe. You wouldn't want anybody accidentally knocking it over, would you? She'll be back soon and you'll be able to see it for yourself ...'

'I won't be able to relax until I've seen it,' came a thinly-disguised Essex accent. 'Give her a ring and get her to come and unlock it. I'm sure she won't mind, I mean, it is *my* cake.' I looked at my phone. Oliver knew I had it with me – he wouldn't risk calling it from right outside the door.

'Well, if I know Polly,' Oliver's voice was getting

louder, 'her phone will be on silent so she doesn't have any distractions ...' *Yeah, except that it isn't because I didn't think of it before.* I put down my piping bag as noiselessly as possible and wiped my hands on my apron.

'But what if there was an emergency and you had to get hold of her? I mean, if two people are co-ordinating a wedding, they should be able to get hold of each other.' I picked up my phone and quickly scrolled to the options – was it options or ringtone I was looking for? I couldn't even remember the last time I'd put my phone on silent. In a panic that I was going to take too long fiddling with it, I just switched it off.

'Well?' The thin veneer over the accent was slipping.

'Hang on a minute ... no, she must have switched it off. I'm getting that "the number you have dialled" message.' Oliver sounded apologetic. I heaved a sigh of relief then clasped my hand to my mouth, in case I'd heaved it loudly enough for her to hear.

'Well, there must be more than one key for that room. I've worked in places like this, there's always a master key.' Her voice was already moving away from the door. 'Let's go to Reception and get it.' *Bugger! She's not going to let this go!*

Should I put the key back in on my side? But then if it was locked from the inside it would be obvious that somebody was in here. This was stupid – all we were doing was trying to fix the damn cake without giving the bride the stress of knowing there had been anything wrong with it. The way we were carrying on, you'd think I was injecting weed killer into it, in some dastardly wedding cake massacre plot – which was ironic considering how it looked when it arrived.

Not knowing what to do for the best, I turned back to the cake and carried on icing it, only more quickly. If she was going to come bursting through that door, I needed this cake to be as close to ready as possible – she sounded like someone who might sue first and ask questions later.

* * *

Even though I was expecting it, the sound of the key in the lock made me jump and I smudged the rosette I was piping. I scraped it gently off and took a deep breath in preparation for the inquisition that was about to follow.

'Good grief, Polly!' My dad slipped through the door and locked it behind him. 'I've heard of Bridezillas but I've never actually met one. She's got Oliver on his hands and knees behind the reception desk looking for this.' He held out the key, with a raised eyebrow. 'It was a good job he'd explained to me about the cake before she arrived.' Dad now took a good look at the offending item. 'Interesting colour scheme,' he grinned.

'If you think the *after* is interesting, take a look at the *before.*' I nodded towards the bowl of scraped off chemical-additive-scented scarlet gunk.

'I won't be asking for a nice rare steak for my dinner!' Dad grimaced. 'I just wish this bride could see and appreciate all the extra work you've put in for her big day.' He must have caught the look of disbelief on my face. 'No,' he sighed. 'I don't suppose she would either.'

# CHAPTER THIRTY-FOUR

It felt like I'd been bent over the cakes for hours by the time I straightened up, after piping the last flower onto the smallest one. My back felt like it was almost locked into position. I reckoned I could have applied for a job as Quasimodo's double but at least I was finally happy with the look of the thing. I'd done some gentle stretches and rubbed my poor back with my fist before tentatively placing each tier on the layered stand then covering the debris on the trolley with my apron and a tablecloth and wheeling it to the kitchen. Then I'd texted Oliver and arranged to meet him and the bride to show her the *lovely* wedding cake.

'It's a bloody disaster,' our pretty Bridezilla scowled, lessening the prettiness somewhat. I had to turn away so she couldn't see me roll my eyes. And to get a lungful of fresh air – had nobody ever told her that less is more when applying perfume? If she only knew what the cake had looked like when it arrived. 'And it's a hell of a lot plainer than I wanted,' she grumbled. 'I knew that stupid cow at the bakery wasn't listening to me. I mean, I've paid a bloody fortune for this cake and it's gonna ruin the whole day.' Now she was pouting. 'You'll have to tart it up with some of the flowers. The florists are bringing extra for emergencies.' She walked round the huge stand, scrutinising the decorations I'd kept simple because I'd thought that was what she must have wanted. 'Yeah,' she continued, 'it looks really boring. And *cheap*!' As that thought hit her she looked even more disgusted with it, and then a glint came into her eyes. 'Some flowers on it'll make it look better. Yeah. Use loads, especially the orchids and lilies, and ...'

'Not the lilies,' I interrupted. 'Unless you want your guests keeling over.'

'I want lilies!' She really wasn't getting it.

'Calla lilies are poisonous,' I said in my firmest, most no-nonsense voice, the one I use on misbehaving commis chefs.

'I'm sure I've seen wedding cakes with them on, and I've never been to a wedding where anyone died.' She looked at me suspiciously.

'You possibly have, but it's a bit like playing Russian Roulette, isn't it? And,' I added when she looked like she was still going to insist, 'I'm sure you don't want to risk spending your wedding night watching your family and friends being driven away in ambulances.' I let that thought sink in.

'Alright,' she grumbled, glaring at me as if I were going out of my way to deliberately spoil her big day. 'Just the orchids and roses. But make sure you make a note of what you use. I'm gonna demand a refund from the bakery for how many flowers it needs to make it look like a bloody wedding cake. Hopefully they'll take it out of that cow's wages – I mean, that'll teach her to pay more attention when somebody's ordering a cake for the most important day of their lives.'

Blimey! If she'd been here when it arrived her head would have spun round like the girl in *The Exorcist* – not very bride-like.

Oliver and I glanced at each other. He looked like he'd rather be anywhere in the world than in this room right now. I wouldn't be averse to a little teleportation myself, but there's never a charming time lord around when you need one.

'The florists will be here first thing in the morning,' Bridezilla continued. 'Seven o' clock sharp. You'll have to get what you need from them straight away. Or get one of them to come and help you if you can't do it yourself.' She gave me one of those cold smiles that didn't reach as far as her impossibly blue eyes, then went back to looking in disgust at her wedding cake. The warm, full-faced, look-how-lovely-I-am smiles would be reserved for men. Or anyone she needed to charm into doing what she wanted. I didn't fall into either category, being merely a female member of staff. I briefly wondered whether, if she knew I was a Hetherin, I would be eligible for a smile upgrade. 'Text me as soon as it's ready and I'll come down and have a look.' She flounced towards the door, tossing both her unfeasibly long blonde hair extensions and the words, 'Oliver has my number,' over her shoulder as she passed through it.

I closed my eyes as I rubbed my forearm wearily across my forehead and waited for the vapour trail of perfume to follow her. Don't you worry, I silently told her. I'm pretty sure we've all got *your* number.

# CHAPTER THIRTY-FIVE

'You poor thing!' Jemima's voice was as soothing as the peppermint foot balm she was rubbing into my aching feet.

'And if that wasn't a boob-job under all that fake tan, I'm Darcey Bussell,' I let my inner bitch snipe. I let out a long sigh while my sister gave a gentle chuckle. 'How long have you got her for tomorrow?' I asked, wishing I could just go to sleep now in this peppermint and clary sage-scented haven and wake up after the bride and groom had departed for their Caribbean honeymoon. I'd happily do all the clearing up.

'Just an aromatherapy massage and a mani-pedi,' Jemima said, clearly assuming I knew how long those things took. 'She's got *her own people* coming to do her hair and makeup,' she giggled.

'*Her own people* indeed,' I sniffed. 'Who on earth does she think she is?'

'Well, according to Oliver she's new money – very new money!'

Normally I'd tease Jemima about her gentle snobbery, but we were talking about a complete Bridezilla and I'm only human. 'How do you mean, new money?'

Well, it seems her parents won quite a lot on the lottery a year or two ago. She's an only child, so it sounds like she was already a bit spoiled, but once their win came in she started planning this wedding. Her fiancé's from

Hampshire. He'd brought her here on a date once and she must have decided it would look good in the wedding photos.'

'Yeah, that sounds about right.' I opened one eye. 'What was that old saying about all fur coat and no knickers?'

'No idea! Anyway, Oliver reckons she's had her parents throw a fortune at this wedding, thinking expensive means classy, but he says she doesn't have a clue. And if anyone disagrees with what she wants, she throws a hissy fit until she gets her own way.'

'That explains the hideous cake.' I was starting to feel sorry for the poor girl who had taken her order. I'd have to get in touch with the company myself – it wouldn't be fair for some probably-not-very-well-paid bakery assistant to have to lose any of her wages to contribute to Bridezilla's power trip.

'There you go – good as new.' Jemima lifted my feet from her lap and placed them on the little towel on the floor. 'I'll get you a clean pair of socks.'

I sat up, knowing better than to argue about putting back on the ones I'd been wearing all day. Jemima kept a drawer stocked with fresh white cotton socks. Nobody was allowed to put their used socks back on after one of her treatments, not even her sister.

* * *

We walked arm in arm back to the main building, the music getting louder and louder. The terrace bar was still doing a roaring and raucous trade and I wondered how many hangovers there would be in the morning. Still, that wouldn't be my problem – I'd be busy re-re-decorating the blasted cake. At this rate I'd be having nightmares – if I got any sleep at all with that racket going on – about being chased and swallowed whole by it.

# CHAPTER THIRTY-SIX

A bright and sunny morning dawned – the exact opposite of how I felt. The music had gone on, thumping away until at least three and finished with an ill-conceived conga around the grounds, which seemed to leave a lot of the party disorientated. There was a lot of stumbling about and shouting to each other before collapsing in fits of laughter. No amount of clutching the pillows as tightly to my ears as possible could muffle out the commotion and so, by the time all was eventually quiet, I was having quite murderous thoughts of indeed finding some weed killer and injecting it into the cake. Or giving the stroppy madam her way and covering the damn thing with lilies. I'd like to think it wasn't only the thought of all the negative publicity for Hetherin Hall and my family that stopped me.

At five minutes to seven, bleary-eyed and trying not to yawn while I gulped down a mug of strong, fragrant coffee, I was downstairs, awaiting the arrival of the florist's van so I could grab whatever they'd let me and get on as quickly as possible. Figuring Bridezilla would find something to grumble about however long I spent titivating the stupid cake, I had a wildly optimistic plan to quickly attach whatever blooms they gave me and then disappear and grab an hour's sleep so I'd be alert enough to keep a watchful eye on the dipsomaniac uncle.

Seven o'clock came and went but that was alright –

I'm not the most punctual person in the world myself. At ten past, I went round to the kitchen in case they'd mistakenly arrived at the tradesmen's entrance instead of coming to the front of the hotel, where they were supposed to park so that everyone could see the big van and know what an expensive and exclusive florist the bride was using. They weren't there, so I wandered back to the front office. At twenty past, I checked my clipboard for a mobile number as well as the shop number. I'd give it another couple of minutes; it was easy to get lost around these country lanes if you didn't know the area.

Cleaners were milling around, getting a start on the day before the guests started coming down for breakfast. I'd never noticed how quickly and quietly they worked before. At twenty-five past, I phoned the mobile number. It was engaged so I tried the shop number. Also engaged. I wondered if the driver was lost and ringing the shop to check their directions. Oliver walked past the door and saw me dithering with the phone.

'Aren't you supposed to be planting flowers in that cake mountain?' He was tapping the end of his pen down his own particular To do list and only half paying attention to me. His hair was wet from the shower and he smelled of some fancy, masculine soap I couldn't name, and sandalwood. If I hadn't recently found out I was his half-sister, my pulse would have been picking up last night's conga beat. Which it actually was, but that was down to the wave of caffeine surging through me on an empty stomach.

'I will be. Just as soon as the flowers get here.' I peered down the driveway again. When I turned back he'd gone, so I went back to phoning, first the mobile then the shop – both were still engaged and they were the only numbers I had. My hour's power nap was starting to look less likely – I'd be lucky if I managed a quick cat nap and, as my stomach was rumbling, I headed back to the kitchen to grab a piece of toast or whatever else I could shovel down before the van finally got here. I'd just buttered a crusty, golden, toasty bit from the end of a loaf and was raising it to my mouth when my mobile rang. Dad.

'Polly.' He didn't wait for my greeting, which told me something was up. 'There's a situation with the flowers. I need you in my office now.' And he hung up.

Great. Brilliant. Just what I needed. I wrenched a corner from my toast with my teeth and chewed as quickly as I could whilst zipping back through Reception to Dad's office. Oliver and Jemima were already there and Will followed me in a few seconds later, cannoning into the back of me by the door. We must have looked like the Keystone Kops, but nobody was laughing.

'This stays between the five of us for now.' Dad looked seriously at us. 'The florist's van is stuck in a ditch near the pond outside Netley Parva.' We all quietly groaned, but I think my heart plummeted the fastest. 'We have to drive to the van and pick up the flowers and the flower arrangers and bring them here. Sorry, Will,' he nodded at him, 'I know you're up to your eyes in it in the kitchen, but the florist can only send a smaller replacement van and so I'm hoping with five cars we can do it in one trip each.'

'It's alright,' Will nodded back. 'Everyone knows what they're supposed to be doing'

'Polly.' Dad put his hand on my shoulder. 'I know this is going to put you way behind with this infernal cake …'

'It can't be helped,' I shrugged, silently wishing Tiffany whatever-her-name-was had chosen just about anywhere else to have her sodding wedding.

We all went and got our cars and drove, probably a

little faster than we normally would, in a convoy towards Netley Parva and the pond. This was getting a bit surreal – it was as if this wedding was cursed; first the cake, and now the flowers. If this went in threes, as these things are supposed to, I wondered what would be next.

One of the front wheels of the florist's van was well and truly stuck in the ditch and it looked like a tow truck would be needed to pull it out. The driver must have come down this lane, realised it was wrong, and tried to do a three point turn and misjudged the verges. Talk about more haste, less speed. I wondered how many times he'd kicked himself since.

The driver turned out to be a woman, which I was sure Oliver and Will would have lots of chauvinistic fun reminding Jemima and I about later. She and two other women, all in green polo shirts and big green aprons, were standing by the van looking stressed. They were probably running to a tight schedule as well, and were soon busy sorting out what could go in which of our cars and what was too big – or too delicate for our amateur handling – and needed to wait for the smaller van, which would hopefully be there soon. Jemima's MG was only deemed suitable for the boxes of buttonholes and corsages, with one of the flower arrangers sitting in the front with her. The little boot and front passenger seat foot-well of my Jazz were carefully packed with as many well-protected table centres as they could fit in. After Dad explained about needing the extra flowers for the cake, several boxes of spare roses – I'd only be allowed orchids later, once they knew how many they could spare – were stacked with great care on my back seat. I didn't know what breakneck speed they thought I might be driving at, but I was wondering at one point if they were going to insist on me strapping them into their seatbelts and singing them a nice, soothing song while I drove. I didn't see how Dad, Oliver, or Will fared. As soon as my car was loaded, I followed Jemima back to the hall. At least the flower women hadn't winced as I did my three point turn, like they had when Jemima did hers.

Now all I had to do was get back to the Hall and shove as many roses as I could into that cake before something else went wrong.

* * *

I parked behind the ballroom, as Jemima had, and the three of us carefully unloaded our delicate cargo. Then I took the boxes of roses into the ante-room and left them to it. I wasn't a fan of fresh flowers on wedding cakes, it always seemed the lazy option rather than creating something unique out of sugar-paste or whatever. At least Bridezilla hadn't ordered any of those hideous little figures of a bride and groom to stand on the top tier – maybe even she had limits.

I set about cutting the stems down – at least they weren't thorny. Then I began the laborious job of wrapping each little stem in cling-film without damaging the blooms before they could be stuck into the cake. I arranged pink ones gently on the bottom tier first to see how they looked and then held my breath before sticking in the first one. When I'd gone all round it, I placed it on the lowest level of the stand and examined it from all sides. Then I put the next on the next level to see what the eventual effect would be. It actually looked surprisingly pretty for something thrown together at the eleventh hour.

I repeated the process with the remaining tiers, adding more cream roses with each tier and placing each finished one on the stand to check how it looked before starting on the next. Once I'd got into a little routine, I found I was actually quite enjoying myself. I barely even registered

219

Dad, letting himself in to see how I was getting on.

'That looks beautiful, Polly.' I looked up to see him smiling. 'I think we should advertise that we do our own wedding cakes – cut out the middle man. What do you think?'

'I think if too many of the brides are like this one, it would cost you too much in insurance, Dad.'

'What do you mean?'

'You'd have to insure against me making a cosh out of sugar-paste and bashing one of them over the head with it.'

'Well, let's hope our current bride appreciates all the work you've put in,' he chuckled. 'Or I've got a feeling we might be getting a demonstration of that!'

# CHAPTER THIRTY-SEVEN

As it turned out, the bride was feeling too fragile to come down and see what I'd done with her cake, so her mum came instead. It was hard to imagine this gentle, smiling woman was the mother of the Bridezilla. I lost count of how many times she thanked me. It made me wonder if her daughter was adopted.

Once the cake was finished, I could lock the door on it and go and have a shower and change out of my whites before anybody found something else for me to do. My bed looked so inviting when I walked into my room. Surely I could just have twenty minutes – I'd made up good time with the cake and if I didn't get my hair wet in the shower, I wouldn't have to mess around drying it. I set the alarm on my mobile for twenty minutes, took my jacket and trousers off, and lay down and closed my eyes.

\* \* \*

Pharrell Williams started singing *Happy*. I didn't know he was here. I love that song. My hips started to move – I can't hear that song without wanting to dance.

'Polly! Polly!' Someone was calling me from a long way away. Oliver? Did he want to come and dance too? Then the music stopped and Pharrell stopped singing and there was a banging sound. Where was that coming from? The sound system must be broken. What a shame. 'Polly! Are you in there?' He sounded cross. Was I in where? The music started up again and I started to clap along.

Somebody was poking me in the shoulder with something cold. I turned and found I was on my bed, and Oliver was looking out of the window with a pained expression on his face and his phone in his hand. The *Happy* ringtone on my own phone was playing to itself.

'What the hell do you think you're doing, Polly? Are you ill or something?'

I grabbed my phone as Oliver disconnected his call to me and the ringtone stopped. What time was it? What time had I come up here? *No, no, no, no, no!* Why hadn't my alarm gone off? I'd set it for twenty minutes, I knew I had.

'Polly! Are you ill?' He was looking over my head while he spoke.

'No! I just wanted to lie down for twenty minutes.' I was cringing inside. He'd think I was skiving while everyone else was downstairs working hard. 'I got so little sleep last night,' I started to explain, 'with the loud music and people doing the conga under my window. I set the alarm to wake me, I really did, but I think I must have forgotten to switch it on. I'm really sorry.'

'Well, the wedding's about to start, so if you've caught up on your beauty sleep, we need you downstairs. The cake has to be in position for when they go through to the ballroom.' He turned away and started towards the door.

'Yes, of course. I'm sorry. I'll be right down.' I was mortified I'd let everyone down like this.

'Oh, and Polly.' He stopped just by the door but didn't turn back round.

'Yes?'

'You should probably put some clothes on first.'

# CHAPTER THIRTY-EIGHT

It was like finding myself in some parallel universe where everything was the same yet different. I ran down the stairs, doing up the buttons on my suit jacket and wishing I'd had time for that shower instead of having to make do with a liberal spraying of Ted Baker's Mint body spray. Of course I'd known there were going to be flowers everywhere, my brain just probably hadn't computed how huge a transformation would have taken place in the time between me going upstairs and coming back down. I didn't have time to stop and look at how beautiful everything was, but I could see it peripherally and the whole place really did look gorgeous.

There were waiting staff doing last minute things in the ballroom under Oliver's watchful eye. Neither of us acknowledged the other as I slipped past him and into the ante-room, where I picked up the cake stand and carried it towards the corner of the ballroom where the cake table had been set up. Then, one by one, I brought each tier out, checking how it looked from all angles and tweaking the odd bloom before adding each one. I could hear whispered comments among the staff. I hoped they were saying nice things about the cake. If there was anything wrong with it, it was too late now – I had to leave it alone and get ready to do whatever was needed of me for the wedding breakfast whilst keeping a watchful eye on the dipso-uncle. I couldn't afford to mess that up – I'd blotted my copy book enough for one day.

'That looks bloody amazing,' Mel grinned at me, walking past.

'Thanks, Mel. Let's hope the bride thinks so too.'

'I wouldn't worry too much about her. State she was in last night, I'm surprised she can even stand up.'

'Are you finished with that?' Oliver said, roughly in our direction.

Mel and I looked at each other before both replying 'Yes.'

'I meant the cake.' He sounded weary and I felt guilty for adding to his workload by going missing for a couple of hours.

'What do you need me to do now?' I asked him, hoping there was something that would take me away from the disapproval oozing out of him whenever he had to speak to me.

'They'll be out soon.' He still hadn't actually looked at me. 'Just keep an eye out for anyone who looks like they need anything. Jemima will be here too, so if you need any help just ask her.' Then he walked away, leaving me feeling well and truly told.

'Good,' Mel stage-whispered, suddenly by my elbow. 'Jemima's much more fun at functions than him. He always gets so uptight. Mind you,' she added quietly, 'he does seem even more like a bear with a sore arse than usual today. Maybe he's missing his little photographer girlfriend.' She nudged me in the ribs, and I half expected her to nudge me again and wink twice. 'Or maybe,' she started to giggle, 'maybe they just didn't *click!*' She wandered off, giggling at her own joke and leaving me feeling ... I didn't know how exactly, and I didn't have time to work it out as Dad and Jemima hurried into the room.

'They're going through to the terrace,' he announced, and the waiting staff immediately rushed off towards the bar to pick up their trays of champagne cocktails, Bucks Fizz, and soft drinks. 'Are you feeling better, Polly?' Dad patted my shoulder. 'Oliver said you had a bad head earlier?'

'No, I'm fine, honestly,' I smiled. So Oliver had made up an excuse for me. The more I knew, the less I understood where my brother was concerned.

'Let me know if it comes back,' Jemima said. 'I've got some lavender oil at the spa that works wonders. Just like you've done with that cake – it looks fabulous. You're so clever.'

'She certainly is,' Dad agreed, making me feel warm and fuzzy inside. 'But right now, we have to keep our eyes very firmly on a short, grey-haired gentleman wearing a pink and purple, diagonally striped tie.' As if choreographed, the three of us raised our eyebrows, smiled, then made our way through to the terrace bar.

'Over there,' Oliver mouthed, sidling up and indicating our target with an almost imperceptible nod of his head. 'Standing by the white-haired lady in the flowery dress.'

'With the purple pashmina?' Jemima asked.

'No, his hair's white.' Dad did a quick scan of the crowd. 'There are too many people to see from here. We'll split up and walk round and meet up at the end of the bar.'

I wandered to the furthest end of the terrace, feeling as if I'd stumbled into an episode of *Spooks*. If only. If it was an old episode I could have accidentally spilled a drink down Richard Armitage and he'd have to take his shirt off...*No! Concentrate. Grey hair, pink and purple stripy tie. Grey hair, pink and purple stripy tie* ... I spotted him – the dipsomaniac uncle, that is, not Richard Armitage –

talking to the mother of the bride. One of the waiters was about to reach them with a tray of champagne cocktails. I quickened my step.

'Polly, could you ...' Lulu tried to attract my attention.

'I'll just be a minute.' I side-stepped her and tried to walk faster, but the waiter was already there. The mother and uncle were helping themselves to the strong cocktails. *Great. Polly cocks it up again.* The man we were supposed to be keeping away from the alcohol was about to get a brandy and champagne hit right in front of me. There was nothing else for it – I carried on towards them and tried to look like I wasn't deliberately bumping into his elbow just as he was raising his glass. 'Oh gosh! I'm so sorry,' I wittered as he winced in horror at the cold liquid splashing down him. I took his glass and dumped it back on the tray, grabbing the waiter's white cloth from his arm and dabbing at the man's front. His lovely pink shirt was splattered on either side of his pink and purple tie which had taken most of the deluge – his pink and purple *paisley* patterned tie.

*No, no, no, no, no!* How had I thought that was a stripe? It had looked like a diagonal stripe from where I was. It had. I looked at him, opening my mouth but with nothing coming out.

'Come with me, sir.' Lulu appeared by my side, gently taking his arm. 'A bit of soda and a hairdryer will sort that out in no time. I watched, still doing my guppy impression while he allowed her to lead him away, still not having uttered a single word.

'I'm so sorry,' I repeated to the mother of the bride. 'I'm not normally so clumsy. Of course I'll pay for it to be cleaned properly, after the wedding ...'

'Don't be silly, dear,' she patted my hand, 'accidents happen. I take it,' she added confidentially, 'you mistook the man I was talking to for my brother-in-law?'

*She didn't miss a trick, did she?* 'Er, I …' I could feel the blush creeping over my face.

'He's the grey-haired man over there, in the grey suit with his back to us.' She pointed her glass towards a shortish man being clapped on the back by a much taller, broader one who was roaring with laughter. 'And he's quite safe at the moment – my husband is making sure he doesn't stray from the orange juice in his hand. Although, try not to spill anything down my husband – he's the tall chap. He's from the temperamental side of the family.'

'Thanks.' I looked at her kindly face. 'I'll definitely be careful around him.' Like father, like daughter, I thought, as I made my way back to the bar to tell the others. They were already there, and they already knew what I'd done.

'For God's sake …' Oliver was muttering under his breath.

'Never mind, Polly.' Jemima was glaring at him. 'At least it wasn't red wine.'

'Thank God she wasn't around for the flaming Sambucas last night,' Oliver persisted.

'If you've quite finished,' I glared at Oliver, 'he's the man over there,' I indicated with a nod, 'talking to the bride's father and drinking orange juice. And if anybody needs me,' I turned to walk away with as much dignity as I could muster, 'I'll be in the kitchen.'

\* \* \*

The rest of the afternoon went by without incident. Every course of the wedding breakfast looked fabulous and nothing was spilled down anyone. The dipso-uncle, once identified, was kept away from the real wine and champagne. The speeches were mostly very funny and the cake received a lot of admiration. Even Oliver managed to pull the poker out of his backside and was starting to relax.

The guests had more drinks in the garden and on the terrace while some of the tables were moved out of the ballroom to open up the dance floor for the evening party. Then the DJ and band took it in turns to keep everyone on their feet until the buffet supper was served.

'So,' Emboldened by a glass or two of fizz, I turned to Oliver as we lurked on the outskirts of the festivities. 'It hasn't been so bad, has it?'

'We should have that printed on our advertising.' He carried on looking straight ahead. 'Come! Celebrate your nuptials at Hetherin Hall. It isn't so bad!'

'That wasn't what I meant, and you know it.' I tried to catch his eye, but as I couldn't do that cartoon thing where they come out on stalks, I couldn't quite manage it.

'So, what did you mean? The fact that you managed to get through the rest of the reception, *so far*, without throwing another drink over one of the guests? Are you expecting a round of applause?'

I opened my mouth but nothing came out. Whoever said that men couldn't do sarcasm had clearly never met Oliver Hetherin. Although, if they did, they would probably just claim he was the exception that proved the rule. A huge sigh escaped my lips. 'What I actually meant,' I said slowly, 'was that we managed to co-coordinate, or whatever it was you called it, and work together for a whole day without ... well ... I was going to say without any awkwardness, but let's just say without *too much* awkwardness.' My words ground to a halt as he turned and stared at me. What was that look that passed across his face? 'I ... I mean ...' I stammered, suddenly aware of sounding like the awful Tiffany, 'doesn't ... doesn't that prove that we can work together? I ...' I just stopped myself from saying *I mean* again, 'I ... I just think that ... well ... it's a start, isn't it?'

'A start?' His voice was barely a whisper. If I hadn't seen his lips move, I wouldn't have known he'd even spoken.

'Alright ... so there'll probably be a few awkward moments for a while ...' I cringed inside as I heard the words tumbling from my mouth. They sounded foolish and inadequate and I wished they'd stop, but they kept on tumbling out. 'But ... one day ... eventually ... we'll find that we can work together normally. Hopefully even have some kind of ... half ... brother and sister relationship ...' The words finally stopped and we both just stood there looking at each other, like two people who'd just witnessed an accident.

Suddenly he grabbed me by the arm and yanked me out of there. The shock was diluted by the force of his fingers digging through my jacket as he pulled me along the corridor. When we reached the little room where the spare tables and chairs were kept, he manhandled me inside. Then he closed the door behind us.

# CHAPTER THIRTY-NINE

'You haven't got a clue, have you?' Oliver growled, the amber flecks in his eyes sparking dangerously. 'How can that be, Polly?' He finally loosened his grip on my arm. 'The one person in the whole damn world who should have some idea of the torment I've been going through and you really don't understand. How is that possible?'

'Of course I understand.' I wanted to rub the circulation back into my arm, but didn't want him to think he didn't have my full attention. 'Don't you think I was horrified too? To think how close we got to ...'

'Horrified?' Another look I couldn't interpret flitted across his face.

'But we didn't, did we? We didn't actually cross that line ...'

'We were on my bed, kissing, touching, undressing each other ...'

'Alright!' My hand went up as if to stop him putting that nightmare image back into my mind – as if it wasn't capable of slipping into it unbidden and freaking me out whenever it wanted to, anyway. 'You don't need to draw me a picture – I was there ...'

'And if you hadn't seen that photo of Jemima and me ...'

'But I did!' I couldn't help it, I had to rub my arm.

'But what if you hadn't?' That look passed across his face again.

'Then we'd be having a much more embarrassing conversation. Or we wouldn't be able to bring ourselves to speak to each other at all.'

'So you're alright with this – with how far things went between us?'

'No, of course not! Oliver, I'm coping with it the best way I know how, but I'm a long way from being *alright* with it. We're brother and sister ...'

'*Half* brother and sister,' he corrected me.

'We're still related by blood, even if only half ...'

'Tell me, Polly. Can you still look yourself in the eye when you look in the mirror?'

'Yes ...'

'Well, I can't.' That look reappeared on his face and this time it stayed put. 'I can't look myself in the face. I'm struggling to look you in the face. I feel sick every time I think about what happened. I feel disgusted with myself.'

My heart went out to him. He must be far more sensitive than I had given him credit for. 'You've no real reason to feel disgusted with yourself,Oliver. It was a mistake. Neither of us knew that the other was ...'

'What do you feel, Polly? What do you feel when you think about us lying on my bed together?'

'Embarrassed that anything happened at all but relieved it didn't go any further.'

'Do you want to know what I feel?' He didn't wait for a reply. 'Half of me feels like you, relieved that it didn't go further. But do you know what?' His hands curled into fists by his sides, his knuckles white. 'The other half of me, the half that makes me feel disgusted with myself ... that half of me wishes you hadn't seen that photo!' He broke off as if stunned to have heard it out loud.

I opened my mouth, but once again nothing came out. We both just stood there, stock still – it could have been a second, it could have been an hour – time seemed to stand still as well. Then somebody in the corridor turned and rattled the door handle, breaking our trance.

'I … I …' Oliver stammered, before flinging himself round towards the door and wrenching it open. He was through it and gone, almost knocking over the member of the wedding party on the other side, before I knew what was happening.

'Sorry,' the man ever so slightly slurred, oblivious to having been almost steamrollered by the hotel's restaurant manager. 'I was looking for the Gents.'

'Er …' I had to come back to the real world so I could get my bearings – this must have been how Alice felt when she climbed back out of the rabbit hole. 'Er, that way.' I pointed to the left. 'Straight on, second door along.' I closed the door and stood with my back against it. Had that really just happened? Or was I asleep and having some weird, Freudian nightmare where my half-brother had just told me he wished we had … I couldn't breathe.

I opened the door, almost tumbling out as if I had taken myself by surprise. I didn't know how to react, what to do, or where to go, but I had to get out of that tiny, stuffy room. The noise from the party rolled down the corridor in a tidal wave. The band were playing *Lady in Red*. I walked towards the terrace, desperate for some fresh air on my hot face and for some semblance of normality. Fat chance. I didn't think I even knew what normal was anymore.

# CHAPTER FORTY

Had he really said that? Had Oliver truly just admitted he wished we'd slept together? He couldn't have meant that. I left the terrace and kept walking – past the rose garden, past the spa, past the staff block.

How many times had I relived that night in my head, wanting to rewrite the scene, desperate to change the outcome? How many times had I wished this or that? That Oliver and I hadn't been attracted to each other or that I'd been right and Will was my brother? Never once had I wished I'd found out too late! I must have misunderstood him.

I stumbled and slowed my step but kept on walking. It would be dark soon but I didn't care. Distance – I had to get some distance between me and Hetherin Hall. There was nothing else for it; I'd have to leave. Oliver and I couldn't work together. We couldn't live under the same roof. How had I ever thought that was going to work? How naive and stupid can one person be?

*Take your blinkers off! Remember how you felt when you saw him with that photography girl? When you heard him with her?* That week they'd been away – I'd been so glad to not have to face him. But I hadn't let that girl enter my thoughts, had I? And when she had sneaked her way in, I'd quickly sent her packing, hadn't I? Why?

# CHAPTER FORTY-ONE

'Hair of the dog?' Will chuckled at me as I edged my way into the kitchen towards the end of the breakfast shift. Just how rough did I look? Like I'd spent one half of the night aimlessly walking the grounds and the woods beyond, and the other half tossing and turning on my suddenly uncomfortable bed? Like I'd found something warm and wonderful, but now I had to walk away from it because I'd done something monumentally foolish and capable of causing heartache to the family I now knew and loved?

'How about a bacon sandwich and less of the cheek?' I was trying for mild but dignified indignation. By the look on his face I achieved 'guilty and not hiding it very well'. I downed a glass of juice without even looking to see what it was, poured another, and helped myself to some coffee. Waiters and chefs were milling around, but I let them get on with it. They'd gone off duty a lot earlier than I had last night. Or rather, this morning.

'At least you've made it in. You've beaten Jem and Ollie – I thought *she'd* be the first in.' The sound of their names in the same sentence caused a ripple of pain to snake its way through me. Jemima, my lovely little sister – we'd missed out on the first twenty-odd years of each other's lives, and now we'd have to make do with a long-distance relationship. Oliver – I couldn't bring myself to think about him now, having done little else all night. The *what ifs* and *what if nots* made my heart ache too much. And then there was Dad. How could I ever make him understand why I was leaving when I couldn't tell him the real reason? And Grandma and Grandpa – would I ever see them again? '... I said, if you don't want this sandwich, I can give it a very good home. Polly?' I suddenly realised Will was talking to me.

'Sorry, I was miles away.' I took the sandwich and wandered to the restaurant door, peering through the little round window to see who was in there before going through.

I had the place more or less to myself. Most of the wedding guests would have ordered room service so they wouldn't have to get up and get dressed too early. The long weekend couple from Cumbria were just finishing up the last of their toast before going out for the day. They were still bickering over where to go as they got up from their table – he wanted the motor museum at Beaulieu, she wanted Exbury gardens. I wished I had so little to worry about.

'Is there something wrong with that sandwich?' Will plonked the inevitable mug of builders' tea and a sausage sandwich the size of a paving slab on the table and sat down in front of them. 'That's pedigree bloody bacon, that. Grilled to perfection, if I do say so myself. At least eat that part of it, even if you have taken a violent dislike to the bread.' I followed his eyes down to my plate and the mess of torn and scrunched bits of bread I must have been pulling apart without realising. 'Are you alright, Polly?' The concern in his voice made me snap out of it.

'Yeah, thanks, just tired,' I lied. Although it wasn't a proper lie. Well, the *just* part was, but I really was very tired. And I didn't think it was the kind of tired that even a good night's sleep would get rid of. I pushed my plate towards him.

'Are you sure?' he asked, pulling the bacon out with his fingers and stuffing it into his mouth. He needed to do some serious work on his table manners. I watched his face, mesmerised, while he chewed. He had kind eyes. He'd be really handsome if he brushed out his grungy hair. Why couldn't he have been the one to flirt with me over a wedding cake? Why couldn't he have been the one who made my heart race? Why couldn't I have fallen for him instead of Oliver?

*What!* My breath caught in my chest. It felt like someone had thrown a bucket of ice over me. After all the walking last night, all the tossing and turning, it suddenly hit me in the face and I knew for sure what I had to do, and that I had to do it now. I swallowed the last of my coffee – the last of my last breakfast at Hetherin Hall. It was time to go and tell Dad I was leaving.

# CHAPTER FORTY-TWO

'He's gone!' Dad looked up at me from the letter he was reading, confusion and hurt etched on his face. 'Oliver's packed his bags and gone. I don't understand.' He held the letter out to me.

I could hardly read the words for the guilt swimming around like a shark in my head. This was my fault. They'd been happy until I turned up. They'd been a happy family, living and working together, and then I'd come along and messed it up for them.

'Dad, I …' What could I say? 'I'm so sorry …'

'It's not your fault, Polly.' He hugged me to him while the voice in my head yelled, *Yes, it is your fault! You did this! If you'd told them who you were when you first got here, none of this would have happened!*

\* \* \*

Oliver's phone was switched off when I rang it. It was switched off when Dad rang and when Jemima tried. Even Will had a go and got the same 'The number you are dialling is unavailable' message. God bless Will – the most incurious person I had ever met in my life. Happy to do anything to help out in a Hetherin family crisis without wanting to know a thing over and above what he was told. It flashed across my mind that this blind loyalty to the Hetherins might be something to do with Jemima, but I'd taken a disastrous wrong turn down that track before and I was never going there again, no matter what my internal sat-nav tried to tell me. Why was I even thinking about that now?

'What about Mum?' Jemima looked at Dad. 'He might have gone there.'

'I'll be in the kitchen if you need me.' Will slipped out of the office, probably relieved not to have to stay.

'I'm pretty sure if he'd turned up there, she'd have been straight on the phone to give me a hard time about why he felt he needed to do this.' Poor Dad was looking anywhere but at me.

'Do you want me to call her?' Jemima didn't even wait for his nod before picking up the phone. We both watched while she waited for her mother to answer. 'Her mobile's switched off.' She hung up with a sigh and looked at us as if we would know what to do next.

My conscience was prickling me. Should I tell Dad why Oliver was gone? He needed to make some sense of his son leaving, but once he knew what had very nearly happened between us he could never un-know it. *Why couldn't Oliver have waited just one day? I should have been the one to go, not him – if I hadn't been in denial so long, I'd have seen that. None of this was his fault!*

Jemima was busy tapping out texts to Oliver and Miranda when Dad stopped pacing round the office and asked, 'What about that girl he was friendly with – the one from the photographic society? Do either of you know …'

'He won't have gone to her, Dad,' Jemima shook her head. 'Her boyfriend went on that trip too. Ollie told me yesterday,' she added to me – I must have looked surprised. 'I'd been teasing him about her.' She looked tearful and I put my arms around her and gave her a hug. It wasn't much to make up for the heartache I'd caused.

'Shall I have a look round his room – see if he left

anything that might give us a clue where he's gone?' I forced myself to ask. I felt helpless just standing about in the office. The scene of the crime was the last place I wanted to be, but I needed to be on my own for a few minutes to try and think of some way I could explain to Dad why Oliver had felt so desperate to get away that he'd packed his bags in the night and disappeared. Dad nodded and I left the room to get the master key.

It took all my willpower to open the door to his bedroom. The memories of the night we'd tumbled through that door were flashing through my mind like one of those old-fashioned cine-camera films, the images flickering on and on as if the reel just kept playing over and over without having to be rewound. I had to do this. There might just be some little clue, some hint.

The scent of sandalwood slapped me round the face as soon as I opened the door, taking me somewhere I didn't want to be and starting to open up an empty space inside me. The curtains were still drawn, the room in darkness. Feeling like an intruder I crossed the room to open them, the emptiness growing. Sunlight flooded the neat, uncluttered room – it just looked like a posh hotel room now rather than somebody's own bedroom. How many people would tidy up after themselves as they walked out on their lives? I ran to the wardrobe and opened the door to find empty wooden hangers, evenly spaced. There was nothing else, not even a bit of fluff. I pulled open the drawers in the tallboy, nothing but the same clean drawer liners as I'd found in mine when I'd moved in. Ditto the bedside cabinet. His desk drawers held pristine packs of A4 paper, photographic paper and manila envelopes, a roll of bubble-wrap, a box of blue pens and another of black, but nothing personal.

I lurched towards the en-suite. The sandalwood scent

was stronger in there, but the only other thing he'd left behind was the used bar of soap in the soap dish. There wasn't even a stray cotton bud in the rubbish bin. It was as empty as I felt.

As sobs took hold of me, I crumpled onto the edge of the bath, my head in my hands, my forehead propped against the cool porcelain of the sink. 'Oh, Mum,' I sobbed. 'What have I done?'

# CHAPTER FORTY-THREE

As we were being denied the chance to speak to Oliver, Dad and Jemima were bombarding him with emails, pleading with him to come home. In desperation, I composed one. It was long and wordy and took me most of the day – how do you say the things I needed to say to him in an email? But then I didn't know how I'd have said them face to face either. I was about to press *Send* when my finger froze. I couldn't send this – what the hell was I thinking? What if he had lost his mobile or it had been stolen, or he was staying with Miranda? What if she, or anybody else who wasn't him, read it? That wouldn't just be letting the cat out of the bag. That would be throwing the cat on stage, choreographing it a dance routine, and making the damn bag into a costume for it. No. I pressed *Delete* and waited for it to disappear from the screen before starting again.

\* \* \*

Dear Oliver,
Please don't delete this.

I have tried to write this message many times but none of the words I wrote ended up sounding like what I was trying to say, so I'm going to give this one last try.

I should have been the one to leave, not you. None of this was your fault. It was mine, for not telling you who I was when I first arrived. If I had done that, none of this would have happened.

I spent all last night going over and over in my head what you told me. At first I thought I must have misunderstood. It wasn't until this morning that I realised I had been in denial.

You probably won't believe this, but I was about to tell Dad I was leaving when he told me you had gone. Please come back. He is so upset and of course he doesn't understand why you disappeared like this. I will make sure I am gone before you get back, but I can't leave until I know you are coming back. I don't think Dad could cope with two of us leaving without any explanation.

Please let me know you have received this and that you will come back to Dad and Jemima. Once I have heard from you I can make arrangements to be gone. I will do my best to keep things as normal as possible with them and hopefully you and I can get away with a minimal amount of contact in the future.

Please forgive me. I only ever wanted to find my family. I never wanted to hurt anyone.

Find someone wonderful and have a happy life.

Your half-sister, Polly.

\* \* \*

I read this one through. It was a bit drippy and inadequate – like putting one of those tiny round plasters that don't stick to anything on a big, gaping wound – but the words sounded innocuous enough to not raise anybody else's eyebrows, while hopefully making him see I hadn't come to Hetherin Hall with the express intention of tearing a family apart. Would he read it, though? Or would he delete it as soon as he saw it had come from my email address? I offered up a little prayer as I pressed *Send*. That was all I could think to do for now, other than start getting my things ready for a quick getaway when he did decide to come back.

# CHAPTER FORTY-FOUR

It felt as if we were sleep-walking through the rest of that day and the next, constantly checking our phones whilst putting on our brightest smiles for the guests. The atmosphere outdoors did nothing to help the atmosphere indoors. While the sky worked its way from dove to battleship to gunmetal grey, electrical tension crackled in the air. Will kept bringing us tea and sandwiches, most of which ended up in the bin. I couldn't have swallowed a thing. Jemima hid the bin under Dad's desk so Will wouldn't be offended that we hadn't been able to bring ourselves to eat them.

Dad was supposed to be on his way to Vienna for a series of meetings about the proposed new hotel there. He didn't even change any of those meetings into conference calls, just postponed them outright until further notice. The longer this went on, the harder it was to not tell him what I'd done and how I was responsible for Oliver's disappearance. My mind swung back and forth like a pendulum – I have to tell him, I can't tell him, I have to tell him, I can't tell him.

The first low rumble of thunder was almost a relief. Then came a few fat drops of rain, splashing like giants' tears against the window before the heavens opened. It was like some great big washer on some great big tap in the sky had come loose and there wasn't a giant plumber available to fix it. I hoped wherever Oliver was, he was indoors.

When we eventually went to our rooms to try and get some sleep, I didn't even bother getting undressed. I made myself a mug of coffee with the posh kettle I'd bought Mum a couple of Christmases ago and sat at the desk with my tablet, trying to formulate a plan from an idea that had started buzzing around in my head. If I left, Oliver would come back, but Dad would still be upset at one of us leaving. But what if I persuaded Dad to let me work in one of his other hotels? I'd still be part of the family business, and things could get back to normal around here. I might as well be as miserable abroad as I would be here.

I went onto the Hetherin International website. When I'd last looked at it, it had been out of curiosity over what my father had achieved – now I was looking for somewhere to move on to, and these other hotels took on a whole new significance.

Hetherin House in Harrogate looked lovely but I happened to know they had a full complement of kitchen staff there and a waiting list of hopeful applicants for the next position that became available. Harrogate was a bustling spa town; hotels there didn't suffer the staffing problems that a hotel in the middle of the Netley villages, out here in the sticks, did. So that meant going abroad.

I clicked on La Petite Maison Hetherin, Paris. The city of romance. Probably not the best place for me right now. La Petite Maison, a charming, nineteenth century building situated in Porte Maillot, just five minutes from the Champs-Élysées – as the online brochure stated. And it was charming – the word *chic* had leapt to mind the moment I'd first seen pictures of it, with its quaint courtyard garden with little stone fountain and orange trees in tubs. It also claimed it to be perfect for those

Parisian long weekend shopping trips. I could imagine those Parisian long weekend shoppers wanting croissants from the local boulangerie and bowls of hot chocolate or café au lait for their breakfasts before hitting the shops. I could imagine them grabbing a quick bistro lunch while they were out. And then in the evening, I could imagine them sharing big bowls of moules-frites washed down with large glasses of Sauvignon Blanc, bottles of icy Belgian beer, or whatever the cocktail of the day was. That would explain why the *bijou* restaurant in the hotel was quite so bijou. There would be nothing for me to do there to take my mind of my own life.

Next I looked at La Grande Maison Hetherin, Saint-Émilion. Oh, this was more like it – the chef in me fell in love all over again with this place every time I looked at it. La Grande Maison – two adjoining magnificent eighteenth century townhouses situated on the beautiful river Dordogne. A haven of gastronomy, specialising in the freshest local ingredients and the best wines from the local vineyards. That sounded like my kind of place! I was about to scroll down when there was a light tap at my door.

'Polly?' Jemima's voice was just audible through the door as I padded over to open it.

'Are you OK?' I asked, ushering her inside.

'I couldn't sleep. I was going to go down to the kitchen and make some hot milk, then I saw the light under your door. You couldn't sleep either?'

'No – I didn't really try, to be honest. Would you like some camomile tea? I've got a few decaf sachets if you'd prefer a coffee.'

'Camomile tea, please. You're so organised, Polly.' Jemima paused as she noticed what was on my tablet screen. 'What were you doing?'

'Well,' I started slowly, switching the kettle on, digging out a second mug from the box under the table of things I'd brought with me from my flat but hadn't sorted out yet, and putting a camomile teabag into it, all the while trying not to look as if I was buying myself some time. This was going to be difficult. I hadn't even thought about what I might say to Jemima. 'The thing is ... you see, I thought that it might be a good idea ...'

'You're not leaving too, are you?' Jemima jumped in, panic scrawled across her face. 'Polly, you can't. You've seen what Oliver going like that has done to Dad.'

'That's why,' I tried to explain. 'Oliver's only gone because of me. If I went away, he'd come back and everything could go back to normal, to how it was before I came along.'

'So you think if you went off and worked in one of the other hotels, Oliver would come back here?'

'Yes, I do.'

'That's crazy.'

'Is it?'

'Yes! And in any case, if Oliver is so selfish that he'd run away like a spoiled brat just because you've taken his place as the Hetherin firstborn ... I think Dad would rather have you here than him. I know I would,' she added, looking at me with eyes full of fierce loyalty. Of course, she didn't know that Oliver wasn't being selfish. Or that it was nothing to do with sibling jealousy. How could I make her understand without telling her the truth?

I poured the boiling water over her teabag while I tried to think. It wasn't fair on Oliver that everyone thought he was the bad guy. But if I told her what had happened between me and our brother ... as close as Jemima and I had become, I didn't think she'd ever be able to look at Oliver or myself in the same way.

'Look, Jemima,' I said gently, handing her the mug. 'Oliver is going through some kind of turmoil at the moment; his head must be all over the place.' I put my hands up to stop her interrupting again. 'He obviously feels the need to be somewhere I'm not right now. I think we should respect that and give him some space and I believe that if he knows I'm going to be working at one of the other hotels, he'll feel able to come back sooner.'

'But Dad's still going to be upset because one of his children has gone away!'

'He'll be less upset this way,' I tried to assure her. 'Look, Jemima, you're twenty-three, Oliver's twenty-five, and I'm twenty-seven. Do you really think Dad believes we're all going to be living and working here under the same roof forever? What about when one of us wants to get married? Are our future spouses going to move in and live and work here too? Haven't you ever thought about spreading your wings a bit? Even as far as Harrogate? Hetherin House has a spa too ...'

'I know. I set it up.'

'And you didn't fancy staying up there for a while? Enjoying a bit of independence?'

'What – live up North?' She looked as if I'd suggested she run a reindeer farm in the North Pole.

'Flat caps, whippets, and cycling up a hill accompanied by a brass band to buy a loaf of Hovis aren't compulsory up there, you know. There's some beautiful countryside in Yorkshire. And Harrogate's a spa town – think of the effects of that lovely water on your skin.'

'What's wrong with my skin?' She wandered over to the dressing table and looked in the mirror, and I couldn't help thinking we'd gone off track a bit – but if the idea of the spa water didn't do it for her, I certainly wouldn't waste my breath mentioning the famous Betty's Tea

Rooms where I would be every day if I were in Harrogate, pigging out on Fat Rascal buns – Jemima would be horrified.

'I just think I should run the idea past Dad,' I said, when she turned back round. 'He might agree it's worth a try.'

'He won't. And anyway,' she pouted, 'what about you and me? We've only just found each other. If you go off to France, you'll meet some French chef and fall in love and you won't want to come back at all.'

'That's not going to happen,' I promised, knowing for certain that was a promise I'd have no trouble keeping. *Fall in love?* I thought, staring out of the window into the sopping wet summer night, after she'd gone back to her room. That was the cruellest joke of all. How could I ever fall in love when my heart had been turned so completely inside out by someone it could never have?

# CHAPTER FORTY-FIVE

It was Jemima who saw Oliver's car first. Dad was driving round the block in the drizzle, trying to find a parking space when she squealed, 'He's here, he's here. Look!' And there it was, just round the corner, apparently, from Miranda's Belsize Park flat. Dad let us both out and went to try and park. I was already on the pavement by the time Jemima had opened her door, unfurled her umbrella, and only then, stepped out of the car.

'Come on,' she nagged and then raced, as much as anyone can race in high-heeled boots, across the shiny wet pavement and up the wide front steps of the big white house. We'd discussed with Dad my idea about going to one of the Hetherin International hotels this morning, which had precipitated our drive to London. Dad had decided Oliver must have gone to Miranda's, as they seemed to have become incommunicado simultaneously, and Jemima had made it clear she was determined to persuade Oliver to come home without me leaving the country. I kept catching her looking at me in the car as if she wanted to say something, but maybe Dad's presence was stopping her – she probably wanted to make me promise I wouldn't leave. I couldn't do that.

I followed her up the steps more slowly – now we were here my legs felt like they were encased in concrete – just like my heart. How was he going to react to my being here? I shouldn't have come – I was the one he wanted to get away from. I should have stayed back in Hampshire. Yet again I'd done the wrong thing.

Jemima had pressed the bell and the door had been buzzed open by the time I caught up with her. 'Come on,' she nagged again. I wasn't so keen on this bossy side of my sister. She must get it from her mother.

'They just let you in?' I couldn't believe after successfully evading us for the last few days that either of them would just open the door to us.

'Don't be silly, I didn't ring Mum's bell.' Jemima raised her eyebrow. 'He'd be down the fire escape before we could get up the stairs. No, I rang a few bells at once ...'

'Very impressive.' Maybe I should have stayed in the car.

'And some man with a nice voice buzzed me in.'

'Well, let's hope he isn't a psychopath who collects young women under his floorboards then,' I muttered, peering behind me for Dad while following her through the heavy old door but not closing it. Was it too late for me to go back to the car?

'In Belsize Park?' she scoffed. I turned and looked at her. She didn't appear to be joking, but I didn't have the energy.

Luckily, Dad came striding up the steps. 'They let you in?' He looked surprised.

'No. They don't know we're here,' I sighed, 'thanks to double-o six and a half over there.' I nodded at Jemima, who had already crossed the enormous black and white tiled entrance hall and was halfway up the first flight of stairs.

This beeswax furniture polish-scented place was a very far cry from the building my old flat was in. The hall table, with its lush green potted plant and neat little stacks of uncollected post, looked sturdy, old, and well cared for. Its wood matched the bannister, which had one of those big old acorn-shaped ball things at the bottom. How many little boys' bottoms had bumped into that as they slid down that bannister over the years, I wondered as I reluctantly plodded up after Dad and Jemima. I didn't belong here. Everything in me screamed to be allowed to turn round and go far, far away – France, Italy, Outer Mongolia.

Miranda's flat was on the top floor. Correction – Miranda's flat *was* the top floor. Of course she would have the best apartment in the place. She'd also staked her claim on the whole of the top floor landing with a collection of plants that wouldn't look out of place at Kew Gardens, and an enormous front door mat that didn't say 'Welcome'.

'Look, Dad,' I jumped in with one last try as Jemima was about to ring the doorbell. 'I really think it would be better if it was just you and Jemima here when they open the door. I'm sure ...'

'No, Polly.' Dad caught hold of my arm as if he thought I might be about to go running down the stairs. 'It's better if we're all here. We're a family. Oliver is part of that and so are you. We need to present a united front.'

Poor Dad. He had no idea just how united Oliver and I had nearly become. And now Jemima had her finger on the bell, so there was no more time to argue myself out of this. I could hear the click-clack of footsteps and imagined a pair of hideous, high-heeled slippers with feathery bits at the front crossing a parquet-floored hallway. There was a tall figure, slightly distorted by the leaded strips separating the pieces in the stained glass panel in the door, getting bigger as it got closer. If this was an episode of *Dr Who*, the door would swing open and a half-converted

Cyberwoman would be standing there.

The door opened a few inches, held back by its security chain, and I took the opportunity to shuffle to the side so I couldn't be seen. Perhaps if I shuffled far enough Dad and Jemima would forget I was here, too.

'Charles,' came Miranda's voice. I hadn't been completely wrong.

'Miranda,' Dad replied.

'Hello, Mum.' Jemima stepped forward and at the sight of her daughter, Miranda pushed the door almost closed and slipped the chain off.

'Darling,' she air-kissed Jemima, welcoming her in. 'What are you doing in town? You should have told me you were coming.' Jemima disappeared down the hallway, but then she had mentioned needing the loo while we were looking for somewhere to park. I was still hiding in the shadows and hoping to stay there.

'We've come to talk to Oliver.' Dad took my elbow and ushered me through the door, earning me a filthy look from my step-monster.

'What makes you think Oliver is here?' She carried on glaring at me as if I'd walked some stinky dog mess into her house and was about to run about wiping it all over her soft furnishings.

'I believe those are his shoes,' Dad calmly nodded towards a pair of men's loafers under the coat rack to the side of the door.

'Well, somebody had to look after the poor boy.' She gave Dad a defiant toss of the head. 'You don't seem to give a damn about him anymore, not since *she* came along!'

'Maybe I should ...' I edged back towards the door.

'No, you don't.' Dad caught hold of my arm as if I were a naughty toddler about to run into the road. 'Polly, you have exactly the same right as Oliver to be part of this family. *Doesn't she, Miranda?*' Now he was giving her the sort of look that dared her to disagree. 'Doesn't Polly have *exactly* the same right as Oliver?'

They glared at each other as some kind of battle of wills took place. I just stood there, wanting to be somewhere else, anywhere else. Seventeenth century Salem would do.

'His aftershave's in the guest bathroom.' Jemima came wandering up the hallway looking pleased with herself.

Miranda shot her a disapproving look. 'I see you're taking your father's side on this.'

'Why do there have to be sides, Mum?' Jemima sighed. 'OK, Dad had another child. But that was before he and you got together. You can't blame him or say he lied to you, because he didn't even know Polly existed. So he hasn't done anything wrong. And Polly hasn't done anything wrong either. She didn't know he was her dad until her mum died. You shouldn't be angry with her. You shouldn't be angry with either of them.'

Dad and Miranda kept glaring at each other through Jemima's little speech. It was as if they'd been frozen in that position. Jemima and I looked at each other. I was touched by what she'd said but didn't think now was the time to say anything.

'Where is Oliver?' Jemima finally asked when the laser-like silence became too uncomfortable.

'He's out.' Miranda's eyes gleamed at the small triumph of inconveniencing our plans. 'He'll be out all day so there's no point in you waiting. He's enrolled in a photography course here,' she crowed. 'He'll be staying with me while he studies. He never wanted to go into the hotel business but because he was your eldest child … well … because he *thought* he was, he didn't want to let

257

you down. But you have a new eldest child now, so there's no reason for Oliver to carry on doing something he doesn't enjoy.'

'You've talked him into this,' Dad hissed. 'He was perfectly happy at the Hall, doing his photography as a hobby.'

'He was suffocating in the middle of nowhere, surrounded by cow dung and horse –'

'Rubbish! He's got friends there, a job he's good at …'

'A job he hates! London will make a man of him.'

'If he stays here, you'll make an old woman out of him …'

'That's rich, coming from you.'

Jemima edged past her snarling parents and we slipped out of the flat, unnoticed, leaving them to it. 'Come on,' she said, and trotted down the stairs. I didn't need to be told twice.

'Where are we going?'

'Oxford Street.'

I slowed my steps a bit. Was she for real? 'I don't think this is a good time to go shopping, Jem.'

'We're not. We're going to the London School of Photography.' She reached the bottom of the stairs and turned round. 'That's where he'll be. He's had brochures for that place for yonks, he used to bore me to death with them. I know exactly where it is. It's just round the corner from Soho Square.'

'OK, which way is the nearest tube station?' I looked around, trying to get my bearings – NW3 being completely the opposite side of the city from SE15.

'Tube station?' Jemima laughed, putting her umbrella back up against the drizzle and making me wish I'd remembered to bring mine out of the car. 'Come on,' she ordered, marching towards the main road.

I had a brief moment of panic that she might be thinking of walking there until I realised she was trying to hail a cab in the rain. Oh well, at least contracting pneumonia would be better than being back at Miranda's flat right now.

# CHAPTER FORTY-SIX

It was twenty minutes later when we eventually managed to get a cab to stop for us. We'd shared Jemima's umbrella, but my third of it had only kept about a quarter of me from getting drenched.

'Oxford Street, please, the Tottenham Court Road end,' she instructed the driver, and then she sat back in her seat while I just sat still and tried not to squelch too much.

After another twenty minutes, we'd only just crawled past Euston Square. 'We'd have been much quicker on the tube,' I mumbled out of the side of my mouth in case the driver could lip read and thought I was criticising his driving. 'He'll be on his way back to your Mum's by the time we get there.'

'Well, we'll just have to play it by ear.' She stared out of the window. 'It's not like we can phone him and ask him to wait for us, is it?' It was true. While none of us had given up on trying his mobile – although slightly less frequently now than the day he left – he still hadn't given up on ignoring our calls.

'Where d'you want dropping, then?' The taxi driver had started to slow down and was looking at Jemima in the little mirror. I looked at her too, as this had been her bright idea and I hadn't a clue where this studio or school or whatever it was was supposed to be.

'Well?' I asked.

'Um ...' She was twisting her head back and forth, looking out of both sides of the cab as if trying to recognise something. I joined in, although I had no idea what sort of building I was looking for. We'd just drawn level with a small Pizza Hut when she grabbed my arm and cried out, 'There he is!'

'Where?' I scanned the direction she was pointing in, panic making me wish both that it was him and that it wasn't.

'He's just turned the corner into that road.'

'That's Dean Street,' the taxi driver called back to us. 'It's a pig to get down at the moment 'cause they've dug some of it up. D'you want to get out here?'

'Yes please!' Jemima barely waited for him to stop before she jumped out and headed off after Oliver. At least it had stopped raining.

'Excitable, your friend,' the driver grinned, as I emptied out my purse and gave him the entire contents, which didn't allow for much of a tip.

'Sorry,' I grimaced at him. 'I didn't come prepared ...'

'No problem.' He nodded towards Dean Street. 'You'd better get after her. Good luck – you might need it,' he added with a wink and pulled back out into the traffic as soon as I shut the door.

By the time I caught up with Jemima, she was standing outside Pizza Express, looking very pleased with herself.

'Look!' She grabbed me and pointed through the window to a table of eight people on the far side of the restaurant. Oliver must have been the last to arrive – everyone else already had a menu in front of them, but the girl he'd sat down next to was sharing hers with him. I was torn between wondering how he could be so heartless as to go out for pizza when we were all frantically looking for him, and trying not to wonder who the girl was. She was pretty, though, with lots of artistically dishevelled hair, and I took an instant and totally unreasonable dislike to her. In a parallel universe, that could have been me sitting there with Oliver and a group of friends. That could have been me smiling at him, pointing out the specials, suggesting we share some dough balls, or whatever it was she was doing. 'Come on.' Jemima pulled me towards the door.

'We can't go in,' I spluttered. 'He's with a group, he'd be embarrassed.' Plus, I really didn't want to meet his new friend.

'It'll be fine,' Jemima said, adding, 'come on, Polly,' loudly enough as she pushed through the door for him to hear my name and look up. He didn't look as if it was fine at all as he stood up and strode towards us.

'What the hell are you doing here?' Oliver growled at us, startling a couple of young women at the table nearest the door who quickly looked down to study their menus with the deepest concentration.

'Mum said you'd enrolled in a photography course and I remembered the place you used to keep going on about,' Jemima gloated. 'Mind you, I didn't think it would be this easy to find you.'

'A regular pair of Charlie's Angels, aren't you,' he scowled, then homed in on me. 'I suppose you thought this was a good idea? Following me here when you must have known how much I wanted to get away from ...'

'I didn't,' I snapped. 'As far as I knew, Jemima and I were just escaping becoming witnesses for the prosecution at your mother's flat. I hadn't even known where we were going until Jemima hailed a cab ...'

'What's going on at Mum's?'

'She and Dad are fighting over who's going to get the blame when you start wearing tin foil on your head or move into a bungalow with twenty-seven cats and a python or whatever it is they think you're going to do because having me as a sister has completely ruined your life.'

'I'm so glad you can find something to laugh about in all this.'

'Believe me, Oliver, no one's laughing. Jemima and I have seen the effect your leaving has had on Dad. He's been distraught – you must have seen how many times we've tried to phone or text you.' I suddenly remembered the email I'd sent him. 'Did you even read my email?'

'What email?' Jemima looked puzzled.

'Go and order yourself a coffee, Jem.' Oliver gave her a look I wouldn't have argued with, then pulled me out of the door and round the corner. I almost had to run to keep up with his stride. He didn't say a word until we reached a square with a little park in the middle of it and he sat us down on the nearest soggy bench at least a foot apart from each other.

'Oliver?'

'Of course I got your email,' he sighed. 'That's why I had to stay away.'

'I don't understand.'

'You'd have gone, wouldn't you? If I'd said I would come back, you'd have gone.'

'Of course I would.'

'How could I do that to you? Haven't you lost enough?' His voice was gentle now, so was the look on his face. I so wanted to touch his face – it hurt my heart that I never could again.

'I …'

'I grew up with two parents, Polly. They may not have loved each other in the end but they always loved Jemima and me. You grew up not knowing Dad. You lost your

264

mum recently and now you've only just started to get to know Dad. How could I be responsible for taking that away from you?'

'It wouldn't have been your fault ...' My voice was suddenly croaky, my eyes prickling.

'And it wouldn't have been yours either. Don't think it was easy for me to leave – it was the hardest thing I've ever had to do. But I had to. The only thing that could have been harder would have been to stay and see you every day, knowing we can never be anything more than half-brother and sister.'

I felt a tear escape and slide down my cheek. I rubbed it away with the back of my hand.

'You see,' he handed me a clean handkerchief, 'I can't even wipe your tears away because I'm scared to touch you. I'm scared of the memories, the feel of your skin under my fingers, the taste of your lips ...'

'Oh my God!' came a voice from behind us. We both froze. Neither of us needed to turn round. We both recognised the voice – Jemima's.

# CHAPTER FORTY-SEVEN

'Jemima!' I heard someone gasp. It might have been me. It might have been Oliver.

She didn't move, she just stood there like an ice sculpture, a perfect depiction of shock expertly carved into her face.

'Jem.' Oliver stood up slowly, as if she were a timid foal and he didn't want to frighten her away.

'Jemima.' I found myself doing exactly the same thing. 'Nothing happened,' I pleaded, 'not really. Neither of us knew we were brother and sister, but we found out in time.' Her eyes flicked back and forth between Oliver and myself. She was probably trying to decide which of us was the more disgusting. 'I thought Will was your brother – the two of you are so much alike. But when I saw the photo of you and Oliver, I realised ...'

'That's right, Jem,' Oliver tried to reassure her. 'The moment Polly realised I was your brother, she stopped ...'

'It was all a stupid misunderstanding,' I jumped in, inwardly frowning at Oliver but not able to actually look at him. The last thing Jemima needed was either of us adding to the unwanted images that must already be flocking into her head. 'I should have told you who I was when I first arrived at the Hall, then none of this would have happened.'

'Stop! Just stop.' Jemima put up her hands as if to stem the flow of words pouring towards her. 'You two need to go and talk to Mum and Dad.'

Oliver and I looked at each other and then back at her. She didn't sound as repulsed as I would have expected – that must be the shock.

'Jemima,' I pleaded again. 'They can't find out about this.'

'Jem, please,' Oliver looked at her, horrified.

'Trust me,' she said gently, suddenly the adult out of the three of us. 'It'll be for the best, I promise. Come on.' Then she shepherded us back out onto the street and started marching back towards Oxford Street to hail a taxi.

Oliver and I looked at each other. I didn't know which of us was the more scared.

\* \* \*

None of us said a word on the drive back to Miranda's, each of us looking out of a different window. I wondered if Oliver, like me, was wishing the journey could take forever so we didn't have to see the look on Dad's face when he found out what we'd so very nearly done. When we got there, Oliver paid the driver while Jemima took my arm, walked me up those white front steps, and rang her mother's bell. We waited for him and the three of us went up together.

'I see you managed to catch up with each other,' Dad looked relieved, while Miranda looked like a bad-tempered headmistress. Dad gave Oliver a big hug, clapping him on the back. 'I'm so glad to see you, son.'

Jemima cleared her throat and marched into the centre of the living room. 'Right,' she said, turning round to face us. 'We are going to sit down and have a family powwow. There have been too many secrets. That stops now.'

'What on earth are you talking about?' Miranda's voice was like nails down a blackboard as she stood up to leave the room. Oliver and I looked nervously at each other. I tried to swallow the fear that was growing inside me. This was going to be the moment I forever disappointed the father I'd just met. This was going to be the moment Oliver and I were condemned for a mistake that would make the rest of the family look at us differently for the rest of our lives. Nothing was ever going to be the same again.

'Sit down, Mum,' Jemima commanded. 'I have something to say, and you all need to hear it.' She waited for her mother to take her seat again. 'Dad, do you remember when Will first started working at the Hall?'

*What? Where was she going with this?* Oliver and I caught each other's eye again. He looked as bewildered as I felt.

'Yes, of course I do, darling,' Dad smiled indulgently, clearly expecting a trip down memory lane, albeit with a rather dramatic command to join in.

'Do you remember how people kept mistaking him for a Hetherin because of his hair and ...'

'I can't imagine how anybody could mistake that scarecrow-headed boy for one of us,' Miranda exclaimed. 'I still don't understand why you haven't made him cut it. It looks –'

'He's the best damn head chef we've had at the Hall,' Dad snapped. 'Sorry, darling,' he looked at Jemima. 'You were saying?'

'Do you remember how I got interested in family trees and seeing if we were distantly related?'

My mouth went dry and my heartbeat started doing a fast rhythm that didn't feel safe. I could sense Oliver's eyes on me. This was how she was going to lead up to it, with some rambling story about how easily people make that kind of mistake. It was a brave effort, but I couldn't see it deflecting from our situation.

'Do you remember I wanted to have a look through the family papers and junk we've always kept locked up in the attics and you tried to convince me it was a silly waste of time and talked me out of it?'

'Y ... yes.' Dad suddenly didn't look quite so comfortable.

'Well, the next business trip you went on, you were away for two weeks. I'm sorry, Dad, I went up there while you were gone.'

'Jemima!' Dad had gone pale.

'It was only when I went through one of the boxes of letters that I understood why you hadn't wanted me to.'

'Charles!' Miranda had gone a funny colour too. 'Charles, what is she talking about?'

'I made a decision to never tell anyone what I found out.' Jemima looked back and forth between her parents. 'I thought that would be the best for everyone. But today I found out something else.' Now she looked at Oliver and myself. 'And if I keep quiet, two lives are going to be ruined. Mum.' She looked at Miranda. 'Dad.' She looked at Charles. 'It's time you told Oliver the truth.'

# CHAPTER FORTY-EIGHT

We must have looked like a roomful of startled rabbits. Dad's eyes were flickering between Jemima and Miranda. Miranda's were doing the same between Jemima and Dad. Neither of them were looking at Oliver. Nobody spoke. I might have thought I'd suddenly gone deaf if it hadn't been for the surprisingly loud ticking of the big, posh-looking carriage clock on the mantelpiece.

'Well, somebody say something!' Oliver was the first to regain the power of speech. 'Jem?' His eyes settled on her. 'You can't make a statement like that and just leave it hanging. Is this anything to do with what Polly and I were talking about?'

Jemima looked from one to the other of her silent parents then said, 'Yes.'

'Are you saying Dad really did know about Polly being his daughter?'

'No!' Jemima and Dad chorused. 'This isn't about Polly's relationship with Dad,' Jemima carried on, 'it's about yours.'

'Jemima, that's enough!' Miranda snapped, jumping out of her armchair. 'It's time your father took you and Polly home. You've got a long drive and he's going to be tired.'

'Mum, if you or Dad don't tell him now, I'm going to have to.'

'There's nothing to tell. You're just confused. Tell her,

271

Charles!' Miranda spun round to face Dad, the pitch of her voice getting higher and higher. 'Tell her to stop this nonsense at once!'

Dad stood up slowly from his chair at the dining table. He looked defeated, but determined. 'It's time, Miranda.'

'No!' she cried, stepping ahead of him, pulling him round to face her. 'We agreed!'

'Well, something's clearly happened to change things.' He looked at Jemima, who nodded.

'I'll never forgive you for this, Jemima!' Miranda gasped.

'I think the issue of whether Oliver will forgive us is more important.' Dad pulled his chair closer to the sofa where Oliver and I were seated. He sat down on the edge of the chair and sighed deeply. 'Oliver.' Dad leaned forwards. His fingers looked loosely entwined in his lap, but I could see his knuckles getting white. 'You have to believe that the decision not to tell you what I'm about to tell you was taken with your best interests at heart. If Jemima hadn't found out and, for whatever reason, become convinced that you need to learn about this now, we'd never have told you.' Dad paused a moment, as if collecting his thoughts and putting them in order. 'You have to understand, the actual physical reality of the situation is not what matters. What matters is that I, your mother, and your sister have always loved you very much and nothing is ever going to change that.

'Am I adopted?' Oliver's voice was calm and quiet. 'I did sometimes wonder ... when I was a teenager ... people used to comment on how different I looked from the rest of you ...'

'Yes,' Miranda knelt down by Dad's chair and took Oliver's hands in hers. 'You're adopted. And as your father says, we love you and that's never going to change.

So, that's nothing bad is it?'

'Mum!' Jemima cried at the same time as Dad shouted, 'Miranda!' One look at their faces told us this wasn't true, this wasn't the big secret that Miranda was obviously still desperate to keep hidden.

'That's not it, is it?' I had a feeling I knew what it was and why Miranda was the one who had the most to lose by it coming out.

'You keep out of this,' Miranda snarled at me. 'You're at the bottom of this. I knew you were trouble from the first time I set eyes on you. What, a third of the Hetherin money not enough, you want to get your hands on half? What, then? What are you planning to do about Jemima? Well you won't get your greedy hands on her money. She's the only legitimate Hetherin out of the lot of you ...' Miranda froze, her mouth still framing the word *you* as she realised what she'd said.

'Dad?' The strangulated sound came from Oliver's lips. My heart ached for him, for the shutter that was crashing down on his life until then, forever distorting the way he'd look back on his childhood. 'Is that true?'

'Yes, son.' Dad wiped his eyes. 'And that's what you'll always be. I might not be your biological father – we might not share the same DNA – but you always have been, and always will be, my son.'

'I need some air.' Oliver stood up.

'Oliver, darling.' Miranda scrambled up from the floor. 'Let me explain.'

'Jemima? Polly?' Oliver nodded towards the door, ignoring his mother's plea. I stood up and the three of us went to Miranda's front door. The last thing we heard before we shut it behind us was Dad telling Miranda to be quiet and stay where she was, and to give Oliver some space.

Then the three of us walked down the stairs and out of the building.

# CHAPTER FORTY-NINE

We walked to a wine bar round the corner from Miranda's flat. Or rather, Oliver walked there, marched inside, ordered a bottle of Sauvignon Blanc and three glasses, and took himself to a corner table. Jemima and I followed and waited, ready to talk or listen or whatever it was he wanted us to do. None of us said a word as a waitress appeared with our wine, showing Oliver the bottle before opening it and pouring a thimbleful into his glass. These few actions seemed to take on such a slow motion quality that I felt like screaming at her to hurry up. God only knew what Oliver felt. He gestured to the girl to just pour it. As soon as she left, he downed half his glass in one.

'I want to know everything,' he said to Jemima. 'I want to know exactly what you know. Everything. Even if you think it's something I won't like.'

'Well,' Jemima took a dainty sip of her wine, 'like I said, I'd wanted to go through the papers and things in the attics and Dad had been a bit funny about it. Maybe if he hadn't, I wouldn't have been so curious.' She took another sip before carrying on. 'You know how anally retentive he is about filing and storing things. He's even got locks of our baby hair in little plastic boxes, and my old ballet certificates and yours for swimming. There were boxes and boxes of letters and cards, all sorts; letters he wrote to Grandma and Grandpa when he was studying in Switzerland, postcards from holidays, letters to and

275

from Mum when he was away on business. And diaries. I knew I shouldn't look at those especially – but I couldn't help myself. Most of my childhood memories of Mum and Dad together are of them bickering, or of one of them not speaking to the other. I wanted to see what it had been like from Dad's point of view. Some of the early stuff was a bit soppy – he'd really been in love with her – so I skipped on a few years and suddenly there was talk about them splitting up; Dad was working all hours, Mum was bored and feeling neglected. I looked at the date and saw it was a year before you were born.' She put her slender hand on top of Oliver's for a moment before picking up her glass again. 'I knew things must have worked out for them because otherwise we wouldn't have come along, so I kept reading. But things got worse and worse and then Mum walked out on him.'

'A year before I was born?' Oliver downed the rest of his wine, poured himself another, and topped up our glasses even though I hadn't touched a drop yet. My hand kept playing with the stem of my glass. I felt for Oliver, having the story of his birth completely rewritten. And I felt for Jemima, finding this out and having to keep it to herself. She was made of sterner stuff than I'd realised. 'What happened after that?'

Jemima looked like she'd rather pull her own fingernails out than tell him. 'She came back a few months later. Dad was sure there'd been someone else, but when she swore there hadn't, he chose to believe her.'

'And then one day, what, seven … eight months later, this dark-haired baby turned up under the gooseberry bush and he knew he'd been right,' Oliver sighed. 'Most men would have sent us both packing.'

'Dad's … well … he's not most men, is he? It's in his diary, in black and white, Ollie. He fell in love with you the moment he set eyes on you. He vowed you'd never know he wasn't your biological father, that he'd never treat you any differently from any other children he might have, and that he'd forgive Mum for cheating because she'd given him such a perfect, wonderful gift.'

'He wrote that?' Oliver sounded surprised.

'Those words exactly.' Jemima put her hand on his again. 'I can show you when we get back if you don't believe me.'

'I believe you.' And for the first time in what felt like ages, Oliver smiled.

# CHAPTER FIFTY

'I know this is a really, really stupid question, but how are you feeling?'

Oliver and I were still sitting at our quiet corner table at the wine bar. Jemima had tactfully gone back to Miranda's. It felt surreal, after everything that had happened over the last few weeks, and especially the last few hours, to be doing anything quite so normal.

'You know what, Polly? If anyone had told me everything Jem told us, but about somebody else, I'd have said "Poor sod. He must feel like his whole world's been torn apart." But I don't. I feel ... It explains so much ... I always felt a there was something different between me and the rest of the family ... not in a bad way ... just ... different.'

'I see.' I wasn't sure what else to say.

'I really did wonder, when I was a teenager, if I'd been adopted.'

'How would you have felt about that?'

'Back then, I don't know. Now ... Now I know I'd feel lucky to have been chosen by Charles Hetherin.'

'And what about... what your mother did?'

'I don't know. But she is my mother. And by going back to Dad, at least she gave me the best father I could have had.'

'And your biological father?' My curiosity got the better of me. 'Do you think you might ever want to find out about him?'

'No. I don't think so. I can't imagine what would be the point after all these years.' He looked me in the eye, properly, for the first time since we'd sat down. 'It's not the same as you, looking for your father after your mother died. You were looking for a parent you missed out on. And with your mother's blessing. My looking would be like I was trying to replace the one who'd already given me everything I could ever need. Even if I wanted to, I'd never do that to Dad – he'd be so hurt.'

I understood exactly what he meant.

'And talking of hurt ... I owe you a huge apology, I'm so, so sorry for the horrible, hateful things I said.'

'You don't have anything to apologise for.'

'You're kidding!' He looked like he thought I'd gone insane. The little amber flecks that had lost their sparkle were starting to come back to life in his eyes.

Before he could carry on, the waitress reappeared with another bottle of wine. She started showing Oliver the label, but this time he just smiled, gently took it from her, and poured generously into our glasses. He'd seriously dropped out of restaurant manager mode. Had he already, in his mind, moved on from life at Hetherin Hall? The thought made my heart hurt.

'Oliver ...'

'All those awful things I said to you, the appalling things I accused you of. You must have hated me.'

'No!' I put my hand out towards his but stopped myself and had a swig from my glass instead, then left my fingers playing with the long, slender stem of it. 'It wasn't you talking, Oliver. It was the shock. It was the realisation of what we'd almost done. I'd been through that too remember, but I'd had longer to process it than you ...'

'No amount of shock could excuse the disgusting

things I said.' He too, started fiddling with his glass. 'I behaved like an animal, I'm so sorry.'

I could feel tears prickling the backs of my eyes. Unable to speak, I picked up my glass again and drank the rest of its contents.

'Are you really going to Italy?' He was pouring more wine into my glass now. *Why couldn't he look at me when he asked that? Why couldn't things be alright between us now?*

'Are you really staying in London?' *Please say no. Please come back with us.*

'It's something I've always wanted to do,' he murmured. 'I only went into the family business to please ... *Dad* ...' The pain in his voice was palpable. How self-centred was I, focusing on the fact that Charles not being his father meant that we weren't brother and sister, when the biggest, the most important issue was that the man he'd grown up calling Dad, suddenly wasn't. How painful that must be for him.

'He's always loved you as if you were his biological son and that's not going to change, now or ever.' I let go of my glass and moved my hand closer to his. He looked down at it.

'How many secrets can one family cope with?' he asked, still looking at our hands just inches apart. 'Your mum kept one from you, my whole family kept one from me ...'

'And when I arrived, I kept one from all of you.'

'It's a pity neither of us confided in Jemima.' He lifted his glass and looked into it. 'I still can't believe she knew about me and managed to keep quiet. If one of us had just told her how we felt ...'

'I nearly did, a few times, but I was frightened of her reaction. I didn't want her to think badly of us.'

A couple came dashing in to escape the rain that had started up again. They sat by the window, holding hands across the table, engrossed in each other, oblivious to the weather, to the staff, to us. How wonderful to be so carefree in love that nothing else mattered.

'New relationship?' Oliver nodded towards them.

'Very new, I'd guess.'

'I hope they stay that happy,' he sighed. 'I hope the first time something goes wrong he doesn't act like … like some …'

'Spoilt brat?' I grinned at him.

'I was going to say selfish bastard, but I like yours better.' He grinned back. 'How long were you thinking of going to Italy for?'

'I don't know,' I shrugged. *Why doesn't he care more that I might be going away? Why can't he ask me not to go?* 'It was just an idea I ran past Jemima and … Dad. We haven't made any actual plans. How long is your course?' *Please say it's just a week or ten days.*

'Depends on how hard I want to work on it.' He tilted his head a little. 'It's a flexible, full time course, where you tailor which workshops and things you do to suit what you want out of it. If you do the minimum amount, it takes about seven weeks. If you choose to do everything on offer it takes longer, but it has to be completed within six months.'

'Six months!' I cried, making the couple by the window look up from their whispered contemplation of each other's hands, and our waitress glance over in case another bottle was needed.

'But I haven't decided what I'm doing yet. All I've done so far is enrol and start going through the options. I met some of the students,' the corner of his mouth twisted in a grin, 'as you and Jem saw earlier …'

I couldn't help myself. 'The girl you were sitting next to was pretty.'

'Was she?' he shrugged, 'I hadn't noticed.'

'When does it start?'

'In a week or so. When were you thinking of going to Italy?'

'I hadn't thought that far ahead.' *Does he really not care if I go?*

'Rome's my favourite of the Hetherin hotels. I always imagine Audrey Hepburn there.'

'Oh.' I emptied my glass, wishing it was something stronger than wine. 'I was thinking of Viareggio.' I made a grab for the bottle at the same time as he did. Our fingers touched, the way they had back at Hetherin Hall, the night of the first wedding, the night we'd ended up in his room. It felt like sparks were travelling up my arm. Wasn't that one of the things that happened when you were having a heart attack?

'Polly?' His voice sounded breathless and I wondered if he was having one too.

'Yes?' It came out as a whisper. I leaned closer to him.

'Do you think …'

'Yes!' There was that whisper again.

'You don't know what I was going to say,' he breathed, his fingers slotting between mine, just the same as they had before.

I looked into his eyes, the amber flecks dancing like little flames, inviting me in, pulling me towards him. 'You were going to ask if you could kiss me.'

'And what was your answer going to be?'

I leaned into him with a soft, gentle kiss on the lips. 'Was that the right answer?'

'That was the right *short* answer.' He pulled my chair closer with his free hand. 'But I was really looking for a

283

longer one.' And he kissed me, gently at first, then his hands were in my hair and all the pent-up passion of our enforced separation was sparking through us like lightning. Until we knocked our half full wine bottle over and the slosh of chilled wine across our laps brought us back to earth.

# CHAPTER FIFTY-ONE

We were still giggling when we reached his car, parked round the corner from Miranda's.

'Let's go for a drive.' Oliver pulled me against the passenger door and kissed me. This walk from the wine bar had already taken twice as long as the walk there, with all the stopping and kissing in dark doorways. The truly frustrating thing was that after all the turmoil we'd been through, now we could actually be together we had to go back to his mother's flat, where the three of them would be waiting and we wouldn't have a chance to be alone. It was like being given exactly what you wanted for Christmas after having expected nothing at all and being told you couldn't open it until some unspecified date over the New Year. We both wanted very, very much, to unwrap our presents.

'Don't be silly,' I nibbled his ear, 'We're both over the limit.'

'The Heath's only a couple of minutes' drive ...'

'Oliver Hetherin!' I gasped. 'What sort of girl do you take me for?'

'The girl who's been driving me crazy ever since she walked into my restaurant and turned out not to be a waitress called Sally.' He kissed the tip of my nose.

'Really?' I ran my finger along his jaw. 'You hid that well. I thought I was the most irritating member of staff you'd ever employed?'

'You were.' He nipped at my fingertip. 'Irritatingly gorgeous, irritatingly sexy ...'

'And there was me thinking that every time I saw you, you looked like you wanted to sack me.'

'No, I wanted to spank you! I wanted to put you over my knee and spank you 'til you begged me for mercy!' His hands travelled south and he pulled me closer. I wondered if he could feel the fireworks going off in my stomach.

'Well, you're not doing that al fresco on Hampstead Heath on a rainy night!'

'Spoilsport!' He kissed me hard on the lips. 'You realise that once we get to Mum's we'll have to behave and keep our hands to ourselves?'

'I know,' I groaned. 'But you could come back to the Hall with us tonight. Your course doesn't start until next week. We could go back to your room and take up where we left off ...'

'Or you could stay here with me.'

'And your mother?'

'OK, I'll come back with you.' He smiled and my heart did a kind of Mexican wave thing. Maybe we wouldn't have to wait until the New Year to open our presents after all.

# CHAPTER FIFTY-TWO

The hall lights were on at Miranda's, but when we got inside we found that no one was home.

'Polly, look at this.' Oliver held up a note as we kicked off our shoes by the coat rack. 'It's Jem's handwriting. *We've all gone to the Hall to give you some time to yourselves. Have fun! Love Jemima and the oldies xxx P.S Don't do anything I wouldn't!*'

We looked at each other. It hardly seemed possible that every obstacle to our being together had been torn down in such a short space of time. I suddenly felt the tiniest bit shy.

'Shall I make some coffee?' I heard myself ask. *Coffee? What's wrong with you? You're not in a stupid Gold Blend advert!*

'I'll do it,' Oliver offered, and went to the kitchen. I could hear him switching on the kettle. *Get a grip, Polly. This is the man you've wanted from the day you set eyes on him.*

I followed the coffee-making sounds and stood in the kitchen doorway, watching him spoon coffee into a cafetière. He'd rolled his sleeves up. 'Need a hand?'

'The mugs are in that cupboard.' He nodded towards a cupboard door that was nearer him than me. My heart started hammering in my chest as I went to open it. How I didn't drop them was a minor miracle. He reached for the kettle as I put them on the counter and his thigh brushed against my hip, sparking up the electricity between us again. We both stopped what we were doing, looked at each other for the tiniest fraction of time, before falling into each other's arms, our mouths hungry for kisses, our hands for the touch of each other's skin.

He was pulling my cardigan and T-shirt together over my head while I undid the buttons on his shirt.

'Oh God, Polly!' he was murmuring as he kissed my throat. Every inch of me was on fire. My insides felt like molten lava. I'd never wanted anything more than I wanted this man, right here, right now. I undid the buckle on his belt, thankful he wasn't wearing the same one as last time, thankful that nothing about this was going to be the same as last time.

As I undid his jeans, we edged back against a table. I hadn't even noticed it, hadn't noticed that it was just the right height. My back arched in anticipation as he slid the rest of my clothes off, Catherine wheels spinning round in my stomach. My legs drew him to me, wrapping themselves around him.

'You know what?' Oliver mouthed into my hair once we'd got our breath back.

'What?' Whatever it was, I didn't care. I just wanted to stay there forever, holding him in my arms, feeling his skin against mine.

'I'm never going to be able to eat breakfast with my mother at this table again.'

I disentangled myself just enough to see his face and we both burst out laughing.

'How about we forget the coffee,' I drew my finger in a line down his chest, 'and go to bed?'

With a silent smile, he hoisted me up and carried me through to his bedroom. We fell onto the bed together.

'You're so beautiful.' He pulled me even closer, nuzzling my breasts while his strong, capable hands stroked my skin, teasing their way down my body. 'I've never wanted anyone the way I want you.'

I could feel myself melting with desire. 'You know what?' I breathed.

'What?'

'I think, instead of telling me, you should show me again.'

'My pleasure,' he chuckled, kissing my throat.

'Mine too.'

# CHAPTER FIFTY-THREE

*Two months later*

I leant over the beautiful stone and wrought iron balcony of our elegantly furnished suite at Villa Hetherin Rome, scanning the Spanish Steps for a glimpse of Oliver. We'd been so right about this place – I could see Audrey Hepburn wherever I looked.

My train from Viareggio via Pisa had arrived at Roma Termini late last night. Oliver's Leonardo Express from Rome's Fiumicino airport had got in half an hour earlier and there he was, waiting for me. He couldn't wait to show me the delights of his favourite Hetherin hotel.

* * *

Dad had been wonderful, sending me on a tour of the Hetherin Empire while Oliver completed his course. Jemima came with me to Switzerland. She was a whizz with the skis. I was not. She was still laughing at the memory of my going round and round on the ski-lift because I was too scared to get off when she checked in for her flight home a week later.

Paris was lovely, but the first five days were wasted on me without Oliver. I found a defunct hors d'oeuvres trolley in La Petite Maison's basement, which made me think of Mel and Lulu. Perhaps we should send them there on secondment to clean it up and get it ready for use again. Anyway, I tried out a lot of bistros and filled a notebook with ideas for La Petite Maison's bijou restaurant. And I knew exactly where I wanted to take Oliver when he joined me for my last couple of days there – at least the assignment he had to complete while he was there meant we had to leave our bedroom sometimes!

Saint-Émilion offered me everything I'd expected and more, only without an hors d'oeuvres trolley. I couldn't think of a thing to improve upon. It was hard to tear myself away from the scenery, the people, the wine, and the food – oh my goodness, the food. If I lived there all the time, I'd be the size of two adjoining magnificent eighteenth century townhouses myself.

Viareggio was a lot older than I'd realised. I spent most of my week wandering the seaside town, immersing myself in its history as there was nothing for me to do at La Villa except marvel at the wonderful Tuscan dishes the kitchen was so rightly proud of. Oh, and try not to eat everything in sight, because Rome was next and my whole week in Rome would be spent with Oliver.

*  *  *

And there he was, bounding up the Spanish Steps two at a time, with the most outrageously colourful bouquet of flowers I'd ever seen. So that was what he'd needed to pop out for after breakfast.

I stepped back into the coolness of our sitting room, with its tasteful vase of symmetrically arranged, delicately scented, exquisite white flowers on the marble side table, and smiled. *What's he up to?* I quickly checked myself in the mirror, pulling my fingers through my hair, trying to tidy the effects left by Oliver running his fingers through it. The door opened behind me and the smell of an English country garden wafted into the room.

'They smell gorgeous!' I turned to Oliver and he put them in my arms. They were even more colourful close up. 'Do you think the others'll get jealous?'

'What, these stuffy old things?' Oliver walked over to the table, picked up the vase, put it in the corridor, and shut the door on it. 'Those flowers were like my life was before you came along. They looked the part – very appropriate, very proper, very tasteful, not a leaf out of place. But colourless. And so very, very boring.'

'And these?' I smiled at my beautiful bouquet.

'These are what you've brought to my life.' He gently fingered a bright purple flower I didn't know the name of. 'A riot of colour, beauty, fun. And you smell really,' his kissed the tip of my nose, 'really nice.'

'Well,' I looked around us. 'We'd better get another vase for these.'

'No need.' He went to the coffee table and took the upside-down, empty champagne bottle out of the stylish, Art Deco bucket of last night's melted ice, took the bouquet from me, and stood it in its place. It was a perfect fit. 'I think that looks much better, don't you?'

'Housekeeping might disagree,' I giggled, as he wrapped his arms around my waist and pulled me to him.

'What makes you think Housekeeping are coming anywhere near this room?' he whispered, sending a tingle of anticipation down my spine.

'Why?' I whispered back. 'Have you left the Do Not Disturb sign on the door again?'

'I never took it off.' He lifted me off my feet and carried me through to the bedroom. 'You know something, Polly Hetherin? I love you.'

'I love you, too.' I tumbled gently onto the big, four-poster bed, pulling him with me.

'So,' he stroked the side of my face with his thumb, 'what are we going to do about it?'

'Well, we could throw coins in the Trevi Fountain and

make a wish?'

'Not today,' he whispered, kissing my ear, sending a delicious tickle through me.

'We could put our hands in the Mouth of Truth?'

He kissed my neck, turning the tickle into a fizz. 'Maybe tomorrow.'

'Or we could always stay here and make up for lost time?'

'That sounds perfect,' he whispered, starting with a gentle kiss on my lips.

And it was.

\* \* \*

# ABOUT THE AUTHOR

April Hardy grew up on the outskirts of the New Forest. After leaving drama school, her varied career has included touring pantomimes, children's theatre and a summer season in Llandudno as a Butlins red coat. All interspersed with much waitressing and working in hotel kitchens!

After moving to Greece, she spent many years as a dancer, then choreographer, and did a 7-month stint on a Greek cruise ship before working for a cake designer and then training as a pastry chef in a Swiss hotel school in Athens. Whilst living there, she also helped out at a local animal sanctuary.

Relocating to the UAE with her husband and their deaf, arthritic cat, she has lived in both Abu Dhabi and Dubai, where she's delighted to have found herself so unemployable that she has had plenty of time to devote to writing!

A member of the Romantic Novelists' Association and a long-time supporter of Emirates Airline Festival of Literature and the Dubai International Writers' Centre, April is currently Writer in Residence a couple of afternoons a week at the Dubai World Trade Centre Club.

Kind Hearts & Coriander is the second of her New Forest novels.

# Hazard at the Nineteenth

**A stunning romantic comedy**

When the Hazards' only son Jonathon proposes to working-class librarian, Stella, his mother, Joyce, seems adamant he'd be happier with Cordelia, the more suitable girl next door.

Stella's always believed Joyce doesn't like her. Joyce has always tried to put quiet, bookish Stella at ease, but everything she does backfires.

When accident after accident occurs, Stella wonders just how far Joyce will go to get rid of her.

As the nervous bride's dress size diminishes, Stella finds herself asking what else could go wrong?!

# Sitting Pretty

Professional pet-sitter Beth believes her boyfriend, Alex is the one. So when he's offered a job in Dubai, he and Beth marry so they can move there together. But on the day they're due to fly out, Alex says their marriage was a mistake and ends it.

When her old boss asks a favour she agrees on autopilot, and goes to feed Talisker the cat, whose handsome but dour owner Henry travels one week in three. Finding herself in luxury surroundings, with nowhere to go and determined not to hear her mother's "I told you so", she sleeps on Henry's sofa. Next day, Beth has her job back and a plan. For the time being, she'll quietly stay in her clients' homes until she can convince Alex that this is all a big mistake... but the mysterious Henry comes home unexpectedly.

For more information about **April Hardy**

and other **Accent Press** titles

please visit

www.accentpress.co.uk